UNDER THE TREE

UNDER THE TREE

GREG STONE

PINK UNICORN PUBLISHING

LOS ANGELES

Under the Tree, Copyright © 2004 by Greg Stone

Pink Unicorn Publishing
4607 Lakeview Canyon Road #230
Westlake Village, California 91361

pinkunicornpublishing.com

Visit the website:
visitunderthetree.com

ISBN 0-9754397-0-7

Cover design by Tracy Stone

Manufactured in the United States of America

1

The Explorer's tires found the ice hidden beneath the fresh dusting of snow and lost traction, sending the SUV into a skid; nose right, ass left. The driver, accustomed to wintry driving conditions, corrected. The SUV came around, then kept on going; nose left, ass right. The driver corrected again, but it was no use, physics had taken over: momentum and ice conspired to send the vehicle hurtling off the mountain. Gravity pitched in and did its part, accelerating the descent of the doomed Explorer. For the driver, that would have been the end of the story—if not for a lone pine.

The impact shattered the tree's trunk, but the pine remained standing; though bent and certain to perish, its sacrifice halted the Explorer's descent. A moment later, the engine cut out. The driver, blood streaming down his forehead, moaned one last time. Then, once again, tranquillity blanketed the snow-covered mountain pass.

Inside the SUV, dangling from the mirror, a doll, a plump miniature monk, rocked back and forth, as though praying.

Two hours later, a team from Rocky Mountain Rescue, outfitted in orange and yellow parkas, their walkie-talkies crackling commands, râppelled down the slope. Wielding power saws and crow bars, they pried the driver's limp body from the wreckage.

"Get him out of here. Let's move it," the rescue leader exhorted his climbers. They scrambled up the rocky incline and hoisted the driver's body into a waiting Bell Jet Ranger for the flight to intensive care where he would join the barely alive, or, as a pessimist might say, the nearly dead.

At the nurse's station in the Intensive Care Unit, a cop, his cheeks red and his hands chapped from the cold, hefted a plastic evidence bag onto the counter. It held the driver's personal belongings recovered from the crash scene.

"Looks like someone could use a hot cup of coffee," quipped a nurse.

"Or a warm bed," the cop mumbled, blowing on his ice-numbed fingers, flashing a wink, flirting.

She shook her head and shot him a wry smile. "No vacancies. You'll have to settle for the java tonight."

"How's the driver?" the cop asked. "You don't suppose he could answer a few questions?"

"Not unless you're a medium," she joked. "Hot coffee, one floor down. Make yourself at home. If you're waiting for him to talk, you'll be here a while."

And that's a damn shame, she told herself, experiencing a jolt of unexpected sympathy for the patient hooked up to life support in ICU 7, "lights out" in a coma. He must have been a handsome fellow before the wreck left him bruised and swollen. When she had measured his height—or was it his length given he was flat on his back?—she discovered he had stopped growing half an inch short of six feet. She wondered if the near miss bothered him. He weighed one-seventy, his muscle tone was excellent; she knew his fit condition tipped the scales toward a possible recovery, but, she told herself, tongue-in-cheek, there were certain things one was not supposed to do to a body—like driving it off a cliff and slamming it into a tree.

The cop circled behind the counter and stowed his clipboard with the accident report attached, then ambled to the elevator blowing on his hands, trying to shake off the bitter cold.

A tech-savvy candy striper, identified by her name tag as Teri, snooped through the evidence bag, discovered the driver's

Palm Pilot and booted the device; she accessed the stored phone numbers, and started making calls. Two phone calls later she had the crash victim's girlfriend, Chase Callahan, on the line; her next call went out to his mother.

An hour later, Chase sat at the side of her comatose lover and held his hand in hers; for the first time in her life, she wrestled with a hopelessness that negated all options. In the past, when he was troubled, more than likely she was the one that gave birth to a problem- solving insight; now, flashes of intuition no longer mattered—you couldn't share a bright idea with a man in a coma. There was something else she couldn't share: the startling news she had confirmed for the third day in a row—the test strip had turned blue, positive. She was pregnant.

Randi Carte boarded a plane in Los Angeles and, hours later, arrived in the ICU. Before leaving the coast, she had tried to locate her ex-husband, to let him know their son had been in an accident. They hadn't talked for years, and, if truth be known, even now, she didn't want to speak to him, but she felt duty bound to try. He might as well have fallen off the planet; all leads were cold.

The head nurse welcomed Randi with a hug; instantly, without a word, they were on the same page, bonding with the empathy reserved for mothers, linked by an intuitive awareness of a mother's pain. Randi checked the nurse's name tag: Lani, it read. Lani introduced Randi to Chase; they shook hands, their fingers lingering, searching for something familiar. An awkward moment.

Though her son had briefed her—*he was seeing a new girl, she was fantastic*—that had been two years ago and now that they were face to face, Randi, matching her mental picture against the in-the-flesh girlfriend, realized she hadn't pictured Chase accurately. She was taller than expected at five-foot-six. She wore her hair in a simple cut, unpretentious and flattering; her eyes, brown flecked with green, gazed back steadily, unwavering and confident. She was not an extrovert, but neither was she a cowering introvert. Though Randi knew Chase was now "the" woman in her son's life, at this instant, she was little more than a stranger.

Chase, too, had not expected to find herself ill at ease. She presumed she had formed an accurate concept of his Mom based upon his stories; now, she doubted herself. Randi's southern California tan, radiant even in the middle of winter, gave plausibility to the lie that her wrinkles were the result of too much sun rather than aging; Chase imagined Randi running on a SoCal beach, her kick strong and high, an act of defiance shoved in the face of advancing age. Most of all, she did not look like a grandmother.

Chase wondered, and worried, about how Randi would take the news that she was being promoted from mother to grandmother. But this was not the time for discovery—their first encounter, at the bedside of her dying son, was no time to spring startling news on the unwary—so Chase held the secret close, tucking it away in the back of her mind, like a present stuffed under the tree to be opened later.

Most likely, Randi would not have heard Chase's surprising revelation anyway, as her full attention had shifted to her injured son. Finding him entombed in a coma, his bruised and bandaged body sprouting tubes—arterial lines, catheters, endotracheal tubes, and IVs—shocked Randi into raw disbelief.

Lani, the nurse, fearing Randi's stark overwhelm would develop into a full-blown faint, rallied into action with an improvised lecture on the varied purposes of the wave forms dancing on the ICU monitor: graphic displays of blood pressure, intra cranial pressure, and brain waves. Her attempt to use raw data to distract Randi from her fears might as well have been directed at the comatose patient; in the dark recesses of her mind, Randi's intuition unveiled a new fear: she would be called on to make the decision to "pull the plug." Ironic, she mused: she had ushered him into the world without so much as a forethought, his conception and subsequent entrance onto the world's stage the result of an "accident." Now, when it came to his final bow and exit from the stage, she would be called upon to make a conscious decision. It wasn't fair. But there was always hope, wasn't there?

"Perhaps not." Dr. Sloane, the neurosurgeon in charge of her son's care, was not given to inflating false hopes.

Randi hadn't been aware of his entrance. "What did you just say?" Had he read her mind? No, the doctor had seen her before, hundreds of times, mothers filled with unreasonable hope; he did not require a crystal ball to divine her thoughts.

"Your son suffered—severe injuries. We have hemmorraghic contusions in the interior frontal and temporal lobes. We see these often in vehicle accidents."

He pinched his patient above the collarbone; there was no reaction. Randi, however, flinched.

"Our main concern," Sloane continued, "is the swelling. A patient can recover from the original injury, but secondary injury due to swelling can be fatal. The ICP..."

Blank confusion washed over her features.

He started over, "We inserted a tube, into his brain, to monitor pressure, to drain fluid. The intra cranial pressure, ICP, is in the mid-twenties. Not ideal. We'll do everything we can, but I don't want to seem overly optimistic. It's one day at a time."

Randi nodded and inhaled. This ordeal taxed her strength, drained the well of her composure. Before she could exhale, Sloane was gone, a master of the magician's entrance and exit.

Lani followed him out, tossing a frowning apology over her shoulder.

Chase stepped out of the shadows and draped her arm around Randi's shoulder, but, before she could say anything, the cop entered, juggling a generic "grande" in one hand, his clipboard in the other. In contrast to the medical staff, he was upbeat, almost cheerful; he'd seen mayhem in his day...

"And I have a lot of respect for the human spirit," he informed Chase and Randi. "You can't tell by looking. Stuff happens we don't see. If you know what I mean."

Neither Randi nor Chase had the slightest clue what the cop meant, but they nodded anyway, appreciating the kind sentiments. Soon they were answering his questions as he filled out his report.

There was something reassuring about the process, it was as though they were solving a mystery; it was only a game and the minute they uncovered "whodunit," the role-playing victim would no doubt spring back to life—but, in the end, on this day, they failed to solve the mystery.

"Why? What caused the accident?" Chase asked, her plaintive questions directed more to God than to the officer fussing over his report.

The cop sipped his coffee, mumbled something about Mother Nature turning nasty, something about ice and how they wouldn't really know until the young man in the bed was able to talk. He promised that when that moment of recovery arrived, he would return. Then, balancing his coffee on his clipboard, he exited, thawed sufficiently to once again brave the cold and patrol the icy streets in anticipation of impending vehicular mishaps.

Chase wondered again, silently this time, what had happened up on the mountain—this wasn't like him; he wasn't accident prone. The cliche "dead men tell no tales" staged an unwanted invasion of her mental space. She corralled her wayward thoughts, and tried to pull herself together with a series of deep breaths.

Later that evening, three young men, tanned and weathered, uniformed in hiking boots, jeans, and Patagonia pullovers, slipped quietly into the room. They nodded a silent greeting to Chase, then fixed their collective gaze on the bruised, immobile figure laid out on the bed.

Chase recognized the men, but couldn't remember names. They were rock climbers—adrenaline freaks who risked their lives crawling up granite walls like spiders armed with pitons. Her boyfriend had joined their climbing team on dozens of ascents.

The climbers eschewed chitchat; stony silence framed their contemplation. The sight of a climbing buddy plugged into life-support packed the wallop of a heavyweight's uppercut; the Mountain had beaten one of their own, even if the battle had not taken place on a climb. With their mortality center stage and suffering stage fright, they shuffled out, having paid their respects.

Minutes later, Chase's sister, Eva, delivered hot coffee and deli sandwiches with her precocious ten-year-old daughter, Bren, in tow. Lani, the head nurse, pretending to be pre-occupied, looked the other way as the contraband and the minor were smuggled past. Rules were broken, not an uncommon occurrence when doctors and administrators were absent from the floor.

Chase briefed her sister on the unsettling medical prognosis, and then introduced Randi. Bren seized the opportunity, slipped free of her mother's iron grip, leaned over the battered patient and, with a kid's frank honesty, offered her appraisal: "He's gone, isn't he?"

Stark reality put in an appearance; Bren's candid comment fixed their focus on the truth. After an uncomfortable moment, Chase, Eva, and Randi, amidst a quick flurry of kisses, good-byes, and well-wishes, recovered their emotional balance and reality once again went soft and fuzzy. Eva, peppering her exit with profuse apologies, departed with the outspoken Bren firmly in custody.

"But, Mom, I can see," Bren protested as she disappeared into the elevator shaking her head at the foibles of adults. After the doors closed, she said, "Aunt CC was crying, wasn't she?" Eva nodded, biting her lip.

At eleven o'clock, the grave yard staff signed on; the halls went quiet except for the constant beeping of electronic monitors. Guard dogs stationed at the portal of death.

Chase, emotionally exhausted, nodded off, her head falling forward then jerking back.

Randi searched a closet, found a pillow, and propped it up behind Chase's head. The touch of mothering bridged the gap; Chase smiled and snuggled her face into the soft linen and dozed off.

Randi wrapped her fingers around her son's cold hand and whispered, "Ray? Can you hear me? Ray?"

2

The path twisted up the slope, crested over a rise, then carved its way through a meadow dappled with vibrant, psychedelic yellow and purple wildflowers.

The hiker's cranium pounded *thump thump* with his pulse, driven by a heart gone mad in its attempt to deliver oxygen to his brain in the thin mountain air. He slowed his pace.

That was when he saw her—sitting cross-legged under a tree, at the far end of the meadow. The sculpted folds of her diaphanous blue dress pooled on the ground. Her hair was pulled back, framing her pale face set off by strikingly intense blue eyes.

For a moment, the hiker imagined he had stumbled upon Alice—Alice in Wonderland.

If she was aware of his presence, she gave no indication. She appeared as unperturbed as the flowers. Her eyes seemed to take in everything and nothing at the same time.

He crossed the meadow, keeping to the trail, which wound past the tree under which the unusual young woman was seated.

An unwritten law dictates a hiker encountering another on the trail shall respect the sanctity of solitude; one nodded a greeting, tossed a knowing glance, and passed on. In spite of the curiosity aroused by his chance encounter with this striking young lady, the hiker adhered to proper mountain etiquette: as he came upon her position, he nodded a greeting and quickened his pace.

"You're not on the path," she said, cordially.

He glanced down, then shot her a challenging look. "I've

not been trampling the flowers, if that's what you mean."

"Not that path, silly," she said, flashing a patronizing smile.

"Ah, *that* path." It was his turn to patronize. *A commune chick*? he wondered.

In the late sixties, communes, populated with hippies, spiritual seekers, and social utopians, flourished in these foothills. Not far from here, a self-styled guru had penned the book "*Be Here Now,*" which seemed to the hiker to be good, though obvious, advice. The commune scene died out years ago, but sporadic attempts to resurrect the era were not uncommon. No doubt the young lady under the tree was part of the latest such effort.

"How do you know I'm not on the path?"

"Not ready. I can see *that*. Sorry, I interrupted your hike. Have a good day."

Her evaluation was insulting and awakened a desire in him to wilt her arrogance with blistering sarcasm, but he held back and responded politely, "I don't mind the interruption. I want to know what you see. *Why* am I not ready? You can be honest."

"Didn't mean to hurt your feelings," she replied. "I just made an observation, that's all."

"You're part of some cult. Meditating and trying to get out of your head, is that it?"

Though the hiker was not one to engage in the ubiquitous flame wars between "believers" and "skeptics" which erupted soon after the Internet shrunk the planet into a global sandbox, Alice's "observation" hit the same raw nerve that sent skeptics spinning into mad rants. *It was the attitude*, he realized. Believers conveyed their observations as though only holy water touched their lips, while you, the heathen non-believer, were a puppy to be rubbed behind the ears when good and swatted on the bum when discovered peeing in forbidden places.

"Now you're angry, and upset. I've ruined your hike. And all you wanted was to get away, away from all those obnoxious people pushing and shoving their way through shallow lives."

The sarcasm stung. He wasn't sure why.

"You didn't ruin anything. And I'm not escaping from anyone. At that moment, in fact, I was amusing myself, imagining you were Alice—"

"Alice?"

"Alice in Wonderland."

"Oh, *that* Alice."

Her smile, was it sarcasm or genuine amusement? He could not tell.

"But when you fired off that wisecrack about the path, you reminded me of the Evil Queen."

"Well, you're *not* ready, are you?"

Ouch. She was direct; she aimed to kill, not wound. He wondered why he found it so hard to disengage from her banter and get on with his hike—and came up empty-handed.

"I've given a fair amount of thought to spiritual matters," he said. "I'm not the Neanderthal you think I am. I know life is more than beer and pretzels. I understand that. I understand compassion: it pays to be nice."

He winked, a poor attempt at conveying warmth, then gave up any pretense of politeness and continued, "But I don't buy the mumbo jumbo. Not into Ouija boards. I don't run up bills phoning the Psychic Hotline. And I don't have a guru to tell me when to breathe and when to fart."

"Then we'll get along. We're both realists. Though reality may not be what you think it is."

"Oh? You know this? You walked the path? And I'm not ready?"

"Yes. I suppose. Good observation." She rose to her feet, preparing to leave. "You've thought about spiritual matters?"

"Right," he replied.

"Then you know you're a spirit, not a body, right?"

"Like I said, I'm not into mumbo jumbo, but I live a spiritual life—"

"I don't get it," she said, as though talking to herself. She gave free rein to an exaggerated look of puzzlement. "How can one live a spiritual life if one is not a spirit?"

"They've shown spirit doesn't exist."

"Who's shown *that*?" She gaped with disbelief, prodding and antagonizing.

"Scientists. You know..."

"No, I don't know. I'm disappointed. I thought you were a realist."

Again, she rubbed that nerve, setting him off. As much as he wanted to, he couldn't let it go. "Science is real, sweetheart. It's what *is* real. Not—"

"Spirit? If so, then you cannot be spiritual. That's only logical." She winked, signaling she was playing with him.

He couldn't find the spirit of play within himself; he was much too serious and he knew it. Was his real concern the young lady who had appeared magically on the trail? Or was the actual problem the persistent and nagging feeling that he'd forgotten something, something important? He vaguely recalled he had an important message to deliver, but he couldn't grasp what that message might have been. It would come to him eventually; it always did.

"If you're not a spirit, you must be a robot. A nice robot, a polite robot, but a robot nonetheless."

"Forget it." *This wasn't going anywhere*, he thought. Alice had taken too many drugs, crawled down too many rabbit holes, and chased too many mad hatters, or whatever they were called. Besides, he was going on thirty-two, she was at least a dozen years younger. He was debating with a child.

She walked away, disappearing behind the trunks of the birch trees, reappearing, then disappearing again.

A voice emerged out of the memory that was failing him: *"Get him out of here. Let's move it."*

Disappointment lashed his emotions. A nebulous fear of impending loss swelled in his chest. He didn't want her to leave, he didn't want to be alone—but he was frozen, unable to act, unable to make a decision. A moment ago, only his memory was failing him; now it seemed the crisis had spread to all his faculties.

She called back over her shoulder, "So the next time we meet we will talk about spirit?"

"Next time?"

"I have to go now."

"What shall I call you?" he shouted.

"Alice is fine."

"I'm Ray. Ray Carte. Wait—"

3

Randi Carte studied her son's face, the portion not hidden by bandages. She studied his arms, his hands. *It was Ray, but then again, it wasn't. His body, lying so still, seemed...no longer...it was strange, there was something different.*

She had been nine when her Aunt Katherine passed. At the wake, she found herself transfixed by Auntie K's body as it lay on display for mourners paying their last respects. Though she knew she was courting trouble, she just *had* to touch the corpse. She was obsessed with finding an answer to a question she could not even articulate. When her little hand, shaking and trembling, made contact with Auntie K's wrist, an epiphany lit up her world: *Something was missing—this was not Auntie K.* Whatever made Auntie K who she was, was gone. It wasn't that her body had run down like an old machine and quit working. No, something was missing. This was not about running out of gas; it was more akin to a disappearance. The revelation delivered an unrehearsed smile. Maybe she couldn't articulate her discovery, but she *knew*.

The sight of her tiny hand on the corpse and a smile on her lips was too ghastly for her parents to grasp. They whisked her out of the funeral home post haste and, on the way home, delivered a scolding lecture on where she should keep her hands—*to herself.*

And now it was Ray. Something was missing. Bren's frank comment—that Uncle Ray was gone—was not unlike her own realization when she was Bren's age. The only difference, she assured herself, was Ray, unlike Auntie K, was coming back.

Her contemplation was interrupted by the arrival of Father

James McCarty, a priest assigned to minister to patients.

"You're the mother?" he asked.

She nodded. She wasn't Catholic, but Father McCarty's affable smile promised comfort no matter what your denomination. His smile could coax a pagan barbarian into his embrace. A decade of selfless service at the hospital had transformed his very presence into a salve for troubled souls.

"I heard Dr. Sloane wasn't overly optimistic," McCarty said.

Randi was surprised and relieved: this priest was a straight shooter who wasn't offering watered-down platitudes.

"He was a bit pessimistic," she said, unable to suppress an ironic smile. "He didn't want to get my hopes up."

"As long as he didn't kill your hopes."

Hope, she reflected, was the glue that kept her life together; kill the hope and you killed her. So, no, she wasn't letting anyone trash her dreams without a fight. When she looked up, she found Father McCarty studying her.

"You're wondering about my faith," she said.

"A little curious. It's my business. I guess I can't help but want to take your spiritual pulse."

"What do you think? Will I live through this?" she asked, a tear welling, then receding.

"The prognosis is good, if you're allowed to confront your doubts."

"Doubts?"

"Do you believe in an afterlife?" he asked.

She looked up at him. Light from the window haloed his silhouette, but it wasn't the light she felt, it was something else, a tangible warmth emanating from Father McClarty that made it safe for her to consider his abrupt and probing question.

"I don't *not* believe. But I don't know."

"I don't either."

She was surprised and pleased with his candor.

"That is I don't know in the sense of possessing physical evidence, I can't take you there—but I know in the way we know inside us. Oh, I know that won't win any debates, but it's what we must turn to...when we make decisions."

"Decisions?" she asked.

"There may come a time when they ask you to make a decision about your son's care."

"You mean the decision—"

"—to terminate life support. When... *If* the time comes, it makes a difference how we see our actions. If we believe in an afterlife, we see it one way. If not, we see it in another light."

"To be honest, I don't know how I see it. In some ways, the decision has already been made. I look at his body. Something's different."

"We call it the empty vessel." He paused, his evaluation was more forthright than he had intended.

With a gesture she signaled for him to continue.

"Clergy, like myself, are entrusted to tend to the spiritual in life, but, when it comes to these situations, unfortunately, we see the same empty vessel you see. We should see more, but we don't. When we approach the door that leads to the Other Side, we find it is closed to us."

"Empty vessel," Randi mused. That was what she had witnessed with Auntie K years ago when she had boldly walked up to that closed door and grabbed the handle.

"If you could open that door and see beyond this life, I guess that would make you a medium," she said, more to herself than to Father McCarty.

He flustered.

"That isn't kosher, is it?" she said, smiling and winking.

McCarty realized he had encountered a woman with a sense of humor, an invaluable possession in difficult times. Take all my earthly possessions, he had always pontificated, and I'll be okay, but take away my sense of humor and I'm finished. He chuckled to himself, then said, "While I was in the seminary I didn't study to become a medium, but sometimes I think I should have."

"You studied exorcism, right?"

"Ironic, isn't it?" he replied. "We have a tradition of chasing out the evil spirits, but we can't track the good guys. It appears we're working in the dark for the most part."

"Don't feel bad. Most of us are working in the dark," she said, turning her gaze to her son's lifeless form.

"That's when we depend on faith," he said.

Hope was one thing, faith quite another, Randi thought, as she recalled the year after her divorce, when she joined a congregation and tried to get with the religious program. Prospecting for a religion she could embrace had turned up a dry hole. She could rely on her own stubborn hope, but when it came to faith in someone or something she couldn't see or touch, a line had to be drawn.

"As you can tell, I'm not strong in the faith department," she said. "If I don't know something, well, then I don't know. It's that simple. I leave it at that."

"You see faith as blind trust? There's a time for that, I suppose, but that isn't the only kind of faith. There's another—"

"Why do you suppose we're kept in the dark?" she interrupted. "If heaven exists, why the big mystery? That doesn't figure. That's when logic sweeps away faith."

"Given I'm hired to vouch for heaven, you'd think I would have been given a tour," he said with a smile. "Hard to sell the cruise when you haven't been on the ship."

She gave his hand a reassuring squeeze. "Maybe we're not supposed to know the destination until we arrive. That's what I tell myself. Just...when it's someone else...it's hard. Guess that's the mother in me talking."

"A lot of us Fathers have said the same thing. We're always wrestling with those questions."

"Any answers pop up?"

"Seems like holding hands helps."

He cradled her hands in his.

"There's another kind of faith," he said, returning to his earlier point. "A more important faith. An affirmative, creative faith. It has to do with the exercise of free will. Though we may not control God's creation, we exercise the free will with which we've been endowed. We're not helpless debris floating on a sea of uncertainty. We decide how to respond to life. Maybe that's why we're here, to learn to exercise that free will. Maybe that is the test of our faith."

"Maybe," she said, unconvinced. She closed her eyes and tried to conjure up an affirmative prayer, but it wasn't there. She opened her eyes, thanked Father McCarty with a look, and released his hands.

"I know you'd prefer a kosher medium, but, if you don't find one, and if you don't mind, I'll look in on you from time to time," McCarty said as he exited, tossing her a departing wink.

Only after he was gone did she realize she had been rude—she had failed to acknowledge the kindness of his parting offer of help. She placed her hand on Ray's wrist, as she had done with Auntie K so many years ago, and searched her heart for Father McCarty's elusive faith.

Though Ray called out, entreating her to wait, Alice disappeared into the stand of trees. The blue of her dress flowed like a master's brush stroke past the white trunks of the birch; the afterglow of sunset added to the pallette. The urge to pursue presented itself, but he hesitated: *was he nuts? Maybe he was,* he thought, as he chased after her.

Beyond the birch grove, he encountered a wall of stately pines; their crowns disappeared into the low clouds blanketing the forest. Marching deeper and deeper into the dense woods, into deepening gloom, he found himself encircled by wispy tendrils of fog that morphed into ghostly apparitions.

He pulled up, caught his breath, and shivered. He wondered—*was it the damp cold or fear that made him shake?* His mind balked, refusing to process and deliver an answer. He pushed on in pursuit of Alice, consumed by a vague and haunting suspicion that she possessed the answer to a question his confused mind was unable to shape.

Picking up his pace, he sprinted between tree trunks moist with dew, hurdled over fallen branches and rotted stumps, and struggled to maintain his footing on the damp pine needles. The forest opened abruptly onto a clearing where, standing in the center, was a rustic cabin. The light spilling from its windows was uncanny, an electric light, cold and harsh, not the warm, inviting glow of the candles or kerosene lamps he would have expected. The electric light didn't make sense: there were no power lines, no generator. He climbed aging wood steps onto the front porch, which stretched the length of the cabin, and knocked lightly, not knowing for sure who or what would greet him.

The door opened slowly, as though under its own power.

"Come in," she said, "I was expecting you."

The furnishings were sparse, in classical frontier motif. On a cast-iron, wood-burning stove, a bright blue porcelain coffee pot, its bottom licked by a flickering circle of orange and blue flame, percolated, promising a Maxwell House® moment. In the corner, a cowhide upholstered couch, black and white and brown, lounged in front of two towering pine wardrobes which he imagined were stocked with denim, sheepskin, and leather garments. It seemed unlikely they were a home to frilly dresses; they weren't that kind. Splitting the room was a ten-foot table, hewn out of pine, its dark knots islands in a sea of honey-colored wood grain. Beyond the length of the table, along the back wall, a stone fireplace framed a crackling fire that promised warmth and tranquility.

On the front wall, centered between wood-frame windows, hung a glossy, eight–by–ten, black-and-white photo of Roy Rogers straddling Trigger. The horse's mane rippled, his hooves pawed the air. Roy waved to the camera, a comforting, reassuring "howdy."

Ray had been eleven when he spent a month on a dude ranch. This cabin reminded him of the head wrangler's bunkhouse: homey, yet bare-bones-pragmatic. A man's abode. Which made Alice's presence all the more curious. Ray had admired the wrangler, emulated him. Buck was his name; a tough-as-nails, no-bullshit cowboy nursing a broken heart; a stoic wrangler serving out his jilted-lover's sentence on the earthly plane, without contest or complaint. Ray, recalling his childhood, blushed as it dawned on him that he had been a shameless romantic.

Then he noticed the quality of the light inside the cabin: it was warm and inviting, not the cold, electronic glow he had glimpsed from outside. It didn't make sense—there was a lot that wasn't making sense.

Alice gestured for him to sit at the table but remained standing, silent, waiting for him to announce his intentions.

"It's nice in here," he said.

"What did you expect?"

"That's just it. I wasn't expecting anything. I followed you. And here I am." He looked around the one-room cabin. "What *are* we doing here?"

"You wanted to learn about the spirit."

"Not exactly. You claimed I wasn't spiritual. I didn't agree. In the middle of our little spat, you skipped out and ran away."

"Spat?" she queried, feigning incredulity. "I'm not here to argue with you."

"No, of course not," he replied with sarcasm. "You were sitting peacefully at the base of tree and I came by and..." He fumbled, searching for the right words, not knowing how to characterize his actions.

"If you're not a spirit, how can you be spiritual? You see the dilemma?" she added.

His real dilemma was his not having a clue why he was there, in the cabin, in these woods. He felt like a man dispatched to the market by his wife who forgets what she requested; a man forced to wander the store, trying desperately to jog his memory, becoming increasingly panicked at the missing gap in reality.

Ray tried to fire his memory and plug the gaps, but the attempt was futile; his mind was sluggish and unresponsive, and he wasn't sure why.

"Some people talk about being spiritual, while, at the same time, they believe they're only a body," she said. "I suppose they mean they're compassionate, or they 'feel the energy,' or they experience altruistic thoughts."

"If the meaning of a word changes, if the meaning evolves, we are not forced to discard the word. After discovering there was no spirit—"

"Discovering there was no spirit? Hardly. They quit looking." She studied him for a minute. "I don't want to argue. Maybe it is best you go on your way."

He nodded, leaving would be the best idea. Besides, there

was something he was supposed to do, someone he was supposed to see. If he could only remember...

"Well, if you're not leaving," she said, pointing out his hesitation, "it's time for a history lesson. In the late 1800s, psychologists experienced dreadful feelings of inferiority. Scientists in the physical sciences were making breakthrough after breakthrough, conquering nature. Desperately desiring to catch up, desiring to be esteemed as legitimate scientists, psychologists abandoned the study of man's spirit and turned their focus to animal physiology: chickens, dogs, rats. Did they discover spirit didn't exist? No, they simply tossed the idea out the window."

"That's not exactly the story," Ray argued. A decade ago, all he wanted was a degree and a job, but, then, three years ago, he experienced a period of unsettling doubt. If he was going to make sense of the world, he had lectured himself, he would need a deeper well of wisdom from which to draw his insights. So he returned to the university. What he had learned in those hallowed halls was not what Alice was preaching; she was strictly from la la land and he would have to educate her.

"With the wealth of modern science at our disposal, we now understand humans evolved from a simple organism to what we are today," he said. "We evolved from a common ancestor. The mystery of how we think and feel, all of our psychology, is locked up in the story of that evolution."

She shot him a look of speechless disdain as he continued, "Evolutionary psychologists and cultural biologists have tracked our emotions, our beliefs, our customs, back to our earliest origins. How we think and feel and what we believe is a product of years of evolution—"

"Evolution?" she challenged, adjusting the flame under the coffee pot. She mocked him and put words in his mouth, "Ohhhh, I get it. What evolves? The *body* evolves."

"Right, I do get it," he fired back, fighting sarcasm with sarcasm, not giving in. "Our brains are highly evolved, more so than those of other creatures. That's why we reason; why we feel complex emotions; why we believe we're special; why we dream up spirits and gods and create myths. Religion, for example, was an evolutionary adaptation that encouraged us to be nice to one another, so we would not kill off the species. Which ain't all that bad of an adaptation."

She eyed him with smirking skepticism.

"I'm not telling you anything new," he continued. "Maybe your teachers were a bit behind the times. This, my young lady, is well- researched science."

"Well-researched?" she asked. "Are you sure?"

"Quite sure," he replied. The leading question, the sarcasm, sent a cautionary memory into replay mode. In high school, a girl named Alexandra had captured his affection. He lusted after her as only a teenage boy could, but he soon found his desire could not be unsheathed carelessly as Alex was a "hottie" suffering a chronic case of put-down syndrome. Armed with a razor-sharp wit, she whittled "uncool" classmates into human kindling. If one was inspired to advance in her direction with amorous intentions, one best approach with caution, one better have a plan; strategy and technique were a must. In the end, Ray never did storm her defenses with his lusty intentions. Long before he perfected his courting techniques, he figured out that, in the fortified castle of the ego where the young lady's psyche resided, "nobody was home." If one pursued her, one accepted an invitation to a perpetual duel. Was that the case with Alice as well? Would he match wits with her, fight battle after battle, only to discover he had gallantly stormed a formless void? It was a risk he would take.

"Our consciousness emerges from the integrated neural activity of the brain," he said. "The 'I' is an illusion, it doesn't exist. The brain creates a mental model—"

Her look warned him he was about to be turned out and set adrift in the wilderness.

"Ah, I see. I'm not ready for the path," he said.

"Not ready at all."

She was gawking with her jaw dropped for emphasis—

shades of Alexandra. She paused, apparently considering whether to continue or bail out. Then she told him, "The Theory of Evolution is incomplete. Scientists don't possess the exact history. There's huge gaping holes in the record—so they are forced to bind together a smattering of pieces with naked conjecture."

"So there's nothing to it?"

"Bio-organisms interact with their environment. They are changed as a result of the symbiotic relationship. Elementary."

"Elementary" was obviously meant to let Ray know this was, in her eyes, strictly remedial.

"There's a lot more involved in the evolution of forms than is understood by science. Scientists give us mostly speculation. I thought you were a realist."

"And what are you? A Creationist?" he asked.

"Not in the sense you mean it," she replied.

"Maybe you're one of those...those people who believe in Intelligent Design," he said. "You're talking about God, aren't you? That's what this is about, isn't it?"

She smiled coyly. "Intelligent Design does make sense."

"Ah, yes, the Big Watchmaker in the Sky."

His sarcastic remark referred to the philosophy of the nineteenth-century Anglican clergyman William Paley. In *Natural Theology*, Paley argued that if someone walking across the heath stumbled upon a stone, they could reasonably assume the stone was a product of nature, but if they stumbled upon a watch, they would, upon inspecting the watch, conclude it had been designed. The reason for such a conclusion, Paley implied, was that the watch components were ordered so as to accomplish an overall function that went beyond the simple function of any of its component parts. The intended function of the watch was to keep time, while none of its components—gears, springs, chains, and the like—were designed with time-keeping in mind. Someone had to design the watch with the purpose of timekeeping and assemble the correct pieces in order to create a watch that would accomplish this purpose.

Ray was surprised his memory remained clear when it came to the philosophy he had studied. He recalled how proponents of Intelligent Design started with Paley's argument, cleaned it up, and put a new face on it.

The Intelligent Design movement argued the case for "irreducible complexity," which was the idea that there were systems, like a watch, composed of interacting parts that contributed to a basic function, and, when one removed any of the parts, the system ceased to function. One would not expect a watch to evolve from a single simple part through gradual mutations, it was made of multiple parts which someone must have assembled into a design that accomplished an intended function.

The Intelligent Design crowd argued that certain biological systems were like the watch, their parts must have been assembled with a purpose, an overall, designed function in mind. The parts could not have slowly evolved into a biological system as a result of gradual mutations; these biological systems could not be reduced to a simpler form and still perform their intended function.

They argued that one could lay out all the parts of a watch in a field and those parts would not spontaneously come together to make a watch without the oversight of a designer. The presence of irreducible complexity in nature, analogous to the watch, had been advanced by the Intelligent Design movement as proof of the need for a designer in nature. There must be a designer with a vision and purpose that guided nature's design. In other words, there must be an Intelligent Designer, a.k.a. God. He assumed Alice was leading him into this argument.

She shook her head, paused, then continued, "I'm not talking about God," she said. "Consider bio-engineers who modify genetic properties of plants and animals, or bio-engineers who clone organisms. What are these bio-engineers, if not intelligent designers?"

"Well..."

"A bio-engineer is an intelligent being, designing and modifying bio-organisms. Thus we have an empirical example that proves intelligent design can play a role in evolution."

"But they're scientists, they're people like us."

"So? They're still intelligent designers."

"So" sounded a lot like "elementary." He was getting nowhere. She had erected defenses that would defeat Attila the Hun. It was his fault: he had followed her; he had engaged her in conversation; he had failed to mind his own business. Recognizing his culpability, however, did not set him free. With a sickening churn of his stomach, he unearthed the truth he had not wished to admit: in a way he did not fully understand, for a reason he did not fully comprehend, he needed her. The thought of walking away brought on a chilling panic, a dread of loneliness so daunting it qualified as a candidate for Dante's Purgatory. What would he do if she decided to abort the conversation and banish him from the cabin? But, no, she wasn't about to do that—she was a die-hard debater with a position to defend and she wasn't giving up until she had scored her points.

He looked up, expecting her to continue.

5

Lani was half way through her second shift, heading into the stretch she called the zombie buzz time, the period when her brain went on cruise control and her body's metabolism went into energy-saver mode. One floated through this period of slow-mo detachment, not quite relaxed and yet not fully alert. It was a time when the mind's defensive perimeter wall, lowered to save on energy, allowed stray thoughts and emotions to enter the psyche, a time when one's imagination might be found dancing with strangers. It was that kind of night, she realized, as she leaned against the counter in the nurses's station and let her gaze wander to ICU 7.

The friend named Hal, the patient's business partner, stood like a tree, facing out the window. Moonlight silhouetted his sturdy frame, casting glints of bluish light off his sandy hair. He shouldn't be there: "close blood relatives only" was the rule. Lani wasn't about to enforce the archaic rule.

The mother's face was lit by the glow of the monitor, a face painted with hurt but also a face chiseled with determination, frozen in the pose of a warrior who will not surrender. Lani liked the mother, they had connected. The girlfriend, maybe she was the fiâncée—she shouldn't be here either, but the rule was silly. Anyone who paid close attention knew blood relatives were not always the patient's closest ties. Blood relatives were chosen by God tossing the dice. Those whom we had chosen on our own, however, like the girlfriend, were often closest to our hearts. So Lani wasn't about to play bouncer. She wondered if the lingering period of uncertainty one faced, when a patient was in a coma, was cruel to those in waiting—or a blessing. Did the hours and days spent waiting provide time for loved ones to adjust, gradually, to the loss of someone dear?

Immersed in the zombie buzz, she imagined a bridge, shrouded in fog, leading to the Other Side. Visitors to ICU were stranded on that bridge, ghosts milling about in slow motion, waiting for a loved one to return. It was a familiar fantasy, one that had played out in her imagination many times before, times like this, in the dead of night, when she was half-asleep with nothing pressing to hold her attention.

Visitors lived on that bridge while they were in ICU and Lani had watched them lingering in limbo so often she sometimes felt her own life was lived in the in-between. Off duty, she might go shopping and yet find herself haunted by the drama she knew continued, unabated, at the hospital. Though she was in the "real world," a part of her awareness remained hostage to the in-between. On nights like this, when she was tired and her defenses were down, the ghosts on the bridge gained access to her inner world. She vowed to refuse any more double shifts. No more zombie buzz.

Doctors, on the other hand, had it figured out, she mused. They were in and out before they could even glimpse the bridge, the passage. Somehow, intuitively perhaps, they knew they must avert their gaze. They kept their feet planted firmly on solid ground and imagined they were the anchor that tethered the patient to the living. They preserved life and had no reason to allow themselves to be dragged by emotion and sentiment onto the bridge where outcomes were in doubt. Doctors knew little about death and they preferred it that way; they were on life's team and had no reason to waver. Nurses were different, Lani realized; they were forced by circumstance to watch as family and friends wandered in circles on that bridge, hoping their loved one would reappear in the fog. It was a ritual performed over and over, night after night.

She, like the visitors, would strain to see through the fog

and would imagine the patient making his way, on unsteady legs, back into the arms of those who loved him or her. Of course, as often as not, no one reappeared, and the waiting ended with the players, heads down, grimly exiting the stage, leaving empty-handed with empty hearts. New actors would appear on the stage a week later, or, perhaps, the next day. ICU was a busy place.

How would the drama in ICU 7 end? she wondered. It was too early to tell. She had not felt the arrival of the unseen force that inevitably appeared—it was something tangible, something she could sense quite clearly—a force that would build to a critical mass before the outcome was decided. *This drama was not ready to end,* she noted silently.

6

Alice met Ray's gaze with a look he found entirely un-nervng. *Did she pity him?* he wondered. It wasn't pity. It was compassion, colored with a beautiful sadness. A look one might bestow upon a cute but helpless and wounded animal. Yet the look marked more than sympathy for an injured creature; it possessed a timeless sadness and expressed a mourning that shed its tears throughout all time. It was an invitation for him to weep for himself—an invitation he declined.

"So," he said, recovering his emotional equilibrium and centering himself in his intellect.

"So you made a mistake," she said. "Mistakes can be cor-rected."

"And the mistake was..."

"You assumed consciousness emerged from the brain. You assumed adding up neuronal activity results in consciousness. You assumed our conscious feelings, thoughts, and beliefs originated in the brain. As they say in science: that's not in evidence." She studied him, a student who had unexpectedly flunked the final. "Your mistake? Believing consciousness emerges from structure. The correct answer is the opposite: structure emerges from con-sciousness."

"But—"

"No 'buts.' If you explore consciousness, you will find a huge gap between brain activity and conscious experience—"

"Most would agree the work is incomplete."

"Incomplete?" Her smirk taunted. "In spite of decades of

conjecture, brain activity and consciousness have not been shown to be equivalent. The gap remains as daunting as ever. There's a reason for the gap. You know that, right?"

He didn't know. He smiled, meaning "go on."

She didn't trust his smile and she didn't continue. The coffee percolated noisily, marking the passing time.

"Dualism," he blurted out. "Body *and* spirit. A grand idea that has been discredited."

She raised a skeptical eyebrow and teased him into continuing his rant.

"Descartes. The idea of the little man in the theater of the mind," he said, referring to the philosopher and mathematician who had struggled with the question "who is the observer?" He continued, "Descartes pondered who or what the 'I' was, who or what was aware of the moment-to-moment stream of consciousness. Ryle later mocked Descartes labeling the 'I' a ghost in the machine. He was being sarcastic, I admit, but, nonetheless, he pointed out Descartes' idea had been discredited. It's outdated. There's no little man inside—"

"Of course there isn't," she replied. "A spirit is not a little man sitting inside your head. A spirit is not a thing. It is immaterial. Consciousness is immaterial."

"It's the sum of brain activity—"

"Nonsense. Your friends, the critics, the skeptics, have invented a false picture of dualism, a straw-man argument. They knock down the flawed straw man they have created. The only dualism they discredit is their own distorted version."

"And the real version is what?"

"The body is a stimulus-response bio-organism, a bio-robot, while you, the conscious you, are spirit. When a spirit joins a body we have the composite we call a human."

She poured two cups of coffee, slowly, deliberately, giving him time to think. Perhaps she was giving him time to reconsider his decision to stay.

Lighten up, he warned himself. "Look, if you want, we can

change the subject," he said, offering a truce.

"That wouldn't make any sense," she replied. "These are the questions on your mind. We must clear up any confusion."

"We don't have to."

She shook her head, the patient teacher on the verge of becoming annoyed. "Yes, we must. You don't understand, do you?"

No, he didn't understand. There was a great deal about this evening, about this girl, that he didn't understand.

"In your classes at the university, you learned to love debate, you learned to wrestle with the intellect. This is who you've become. This is not the only way to pursue knowledge, it is not the only road to discovery, but it is your chosen road at this time, so we must proceed down that road."

"Your urgency is touching," he said, sarcastically. "Why don't we use our time wisely and get to know each other? Maybe we could become friends. Is this your home?"

"A home away from home," she said. "You will come to know me soon enough, so, first, let's concentrate on getting to know you. You've become confused by what you learned."

"I should be getting home. As much as I hate stumbling down the mountain in the dark, I must. Though it escapes me now, I'm certain there was an errand I meant to finish."

He stole a glance out the window: the gloomy weather had not improved; the fog was so thick he couldn't make out the trees bordering the clearing. No way he was going anywhere in these forbidding conditions, and yet, for his sanity, he must depart. There was somewhere he was supposed to be, something he must do.

A log in the fireplace crackled, as though extending an invitation for him to stay and soak up its warmth. Roy Rogers, perched in his saddle on Trigger's back, waving, invited him to stay and travel down "happy trails" into fond memories. Ray battled frustration, conflicting impulses pulled and tugged at him.

Alice's voice, softer than before, reached out and pulled him back from the emotional brink. "Make yourself comfortable. Let's clear up a few things."

He flopped down on the hide couch. A strange and paranoid thought flitted past in his imagination. *Was Alice a former student?* As a teaching assistant, a TA, he had supervised recitations. *Was she an undergraduate he had forgotten?* They were known to harbor grudges against difficult TA's. *Was this a practical joke? Had she turned the tables and lured him into a situation where he was forced to listen to her lecture?* If so, the situation was harmless enough.

"Go on," he said.

"Scientists assume only the material world exists. They fail to understand systems that incorporate both the material and the immaterial. The false assumptions of materialism doom science to failure. Dust to dust."

Ray was not about to let her dismiss the work of hundreds, even thousands, of experts, scholars with credentials. Who was she anyway? Something in his nature would not allow her to have the last word.

"Wrong," he said. "Scientists realize consciousness is non material. They know it's a process, like computer software. It's the process—"

"Process? Process is an abstraction. Only a conscious being creates abstractions. A machine, such as a computer, on the other hand, only performs programmed steps; the machine is capable of mechanical computation, incapable of conscious thought. Matter, not being conscious, is not capable of conscious thought. You do realize there's a difference between mechanical computation and conscious thought, don't you?"

"So a robot cannot become conscious?"

"Exactly. Artificial intelligence is based on fantasy."

"Not if there's enough complexity—"

"Complexity has little to do with it. That's also a fantasy, a fantasy used to disguise the gap that exists between mechanics and consciousness. Strictly a black box solution."

"Black box?" he asked, wondering how or why this young lady was so eager to engage him in debate on these matters. He listened as she continued.

"When something we don't understand happens in a way we can't observe, we call that a 'black box.' We can only guess what takes place inside the black box. Those arguing brain activity is equivalent to consciousness rely on such a black box argument. They have no evidence, they assume what they cannot observe—"

"They deduce the answers," he interrupted.

"Guesses. Conjecture. Hunches. That's what you have."

"We are robots," he said. "Our bodies, our brains, are nothing more than complex machines."

Shaking her head, she pulled a worn and water-damaged cardboard shoe box out of a cupboard and dumped its contents: matchbox cars, plastic robots, a green cat's eye marble, and a "Slinky," a fad toy popular years ago. Ray experienced a wave of nostalgia. The toys were remarkably similar to his childhood possessions.

"Our bodies are machines," she continued. "Any machine, even a bio-machine, will never be truly conscious. It may operate as a stimulus-response machine, but that is not consciousness."

Ray scooped up a miniature robot and marched it from knot to knot on the pine table, manipulating its tiny plastic arms.

"A computer or robot has memory—"

"It records data, but a recording is not consciousness," she said. "Storing or manipulating records is a mechanical action. A machine can store, it can manipulate, it can compute. But that's not consciousness. To have consciousness, one must have an aware being who views the record."

She palmed a rock that was sitting on the fireplace mantel. "A piece of matter, this rock, for example, can sit for a billion billion years and will never become conscious. Consciousness is not a property of matter, nor is it a property of specially configured matter. Only the immaterial—the spirit—is conscious."

Ray set the robot down. Alice was advancing an argument many considered meaningless. If spirit is immaterial, we have no way to empirically prove its existence. "We can't know that which we can't see," he said.

"You suffer from blind materialism," she snorted, crossing to the door, apparently exasperated.

He was reminded of Alex once again. But Alice was no Alex: the intellect she commanded was no empty charade, she knew her stuff. He didn't relish the idea of navigating his way down the mountain in the dark, in the fog, but, as much as he preferred the comfort of the cabin, he wasn't about to concede the argument. If the price he must pay for staying the night was giving her the satisfaction that she'd won the debate, the price was too steep.

"Prove it," he said. "Prove that consciousness even exists."

She paused, hand on the door latch, then turned, "This is going to be more difficult than I imagined. But I'll not turn you out, yet. Give me a minute to consider my words."

He could wait. He was not the least tired; something about this place banished all thought of sleep.

"How about a quiz? You like games, don't you?" she asked. "What is more real than that which you observe?"

He shrugged.

"The observer is more real than that which it observes. The observer is primary."

"Run that past me again," he said, uncertain he followed her logic.

"Materialism takes into account only 'things observed' and forgets the observer, failing to realize the observer is the basis of all reality. The act of observing—consciousness—is the most real and most basic factor of reality."

Classic chicken-and-egg argument, Ray mused. The act of observing, of being conscious, involved both an observer and an observed. Which was primary? Could you have one without the other? Ray was no longer sure.

"The observer, the conscious being, is aware of being aware. It can exist without anything to observe, without the physical. It can simply be aware of being aware. Pure awareness. Pure consciousness. Surely you have not forgotten the mystics who meditate and reach the state of pure awareness, a pure state of being-aware-of-being-aware without objects. Thus, the most basic aspect of reality is consciousness."

"But—"

"Without the observer, there's no observation, there's no observed," Alice said. "Scientists love to claim their knowledge is based on observation. In failing to understand the observer, however, science fails to understand the foundation of any observation. All science thus rests on a mystery; science is built on a foundation of sand."

As he puzzled, she studied him curiously.

"You still believe you're only a body," she said.

He nodded. "Yeah, so."

She eyed him with mild concern and censure. Then, as her eyes darted to the window, her frown deepened. She didn't bother to mask her mounting trepidation.

Was there something sinister out there? he wondered, peering out the window. *Should he be afraid?* "What? What is it? What is wrong?"

7

Chase reached across Ray's body and placed a reassuring hand on Hal Sutherland's forearm. They had been studying Ray from opposite sides of the bed; she sensed Hal was having a difficult time.

Hal was tall at six-foot-four, sandy-haired, and out of place: he belonged in the woods, camping or felling trees, or repelling off granite cliffs—a hospital was too far removed from nature's steady pulse for his woodsy tastes.

He was Ray's partner in a new business venture, a start-up called Changes in Action that had nearly stalled on the financial runway waiting for funding approval.

Chase found it easy to read his mannerisms as he struggled to find an appropriate response. Her sympathetic smile welcomed the emotions he needed to unleash.

"The investors gave us the green light," he said, his voice flat, devoid of the enthusiasm that should have accompanied the good news. "After all these months, the damn committee finally approved our proposal. Ray was on his way into town"—Hal choked on his words—"to bring you the good news. He didn't want to phone. He wanted to see your face when he told you."

That made two important messages that had gone undelivered that day, Chase noted, not without bitterness. Initially, she had balked at disclosing the pregnancy, given the iffy status of the fledgling business venture. After all, timing was everything. For days she had vacillated, days she now regretted. Finally, that morning, moments after the third test strip turned blue, she decided to toss prudence aside and devised a plan—she even rehearsed breaking the news to Ray. If he had made it home, they would now be out celebrating.

The irony was impossible to accept: the moment long-over-due success turned the corner, the moment they were within reach of their goal, reckless Fate knocked Ray out of the game.

He had spent years dreaming of, then painstakingly planning, Changes in Action, a program modeled after Outward Bound, in which teachers recruited from inner-city schools were transported to the mountain wilderness where, under Ray and Hal's guidance, they would undergo old-fashioned survival training. The goal of the program, however, had little to do with acquiring wilderness survival skills, it was intended to immerse teachers in real-life situations in which their survival depended upon team-work.

Ray envisioned the program as a catalyst that would foster an appreciation of teamwork and lessen a teacher's emphasis on competition. Students needed to learn to compete, but even more importantly, in Ray's opinion, they needed to learn to cooperate and collaborate. That would require teachers seasoned with the practical experience Changes in Action would provide.

"I'm not going forward without him. This was his dream. And this—" Hal exhaled a breath that was meant to be a curse, almost spitting, as though expelling a foul-tasting poison.

"Hal, I don't know if he's going to make it."

"I know. I spoke to the doctor. They've done all they can. Now it's up to—it's up to someone. If it's up to Ray, I know he'll pull through. He's not a quitter."

Randi entered. Chase had introduced them earlier, but they had hardly spoken. After an awkward moment, during which nei-ther knew what to say, Randi broke the ice, "My son admired you. He called you 'An amazing force of nature.' He trusted you. Said he would climb any peak, as long as you were in the lead."

"Your son led as much as he followed. There wasn't a challenge that could beat him. And that goes for this challenge, too.

He'll make it. You'll see."

Hal's prophecy was equal parts wishful thinking and bluff; it didn't take a mind-reader to detect his doubt. Randi, however, appreciated the forced optimism. She nodded her thanks; her lip trembled, betraying deep misgivings. She, too, was no stranger to doubt. Hal wrapped her in a hug, his generous strength a surrogate for the stoicism that had so suddenly deserted her.

They were interrupted by the brusque entrance of Dr. Seidman. "You the mother?" he asked.

Randi nodded.

Seidman glanced at Hal and Chase, broadcasting the unspoken message "you've been dismissed." Apparently he had "mothers only" business to conduct.

Hal bristled. He was not someone easily dismissed. More than one bar brawl had been instigated by some unlucky soul showing him disrespect. His philosophy of life was strictly egalitarian: all men deserved respect until and unless they demonstrated otherwise.

Chase, sensing his overheated emotions, interjected, "Good. We need a little time to tend to some personal business. Randi, you can handle whatever it is the doctor needs, right?"

Though Randi nodded "yes," her honest answer was "no." As Chase bolted for the door, Randi flashed her an accusing look, an indictment of malicious abandonment. Chase rolled her eyes—*guilty as charged*—then flashed a supportive wink.

In the hall, Chase's thoughts wandered. She had floated a little white lie, claiming she had business to tend to with Hal, but then again, maybe this was an opportunity to include him in her secret. Maybe she would ask him to be her child's godfather. Upon further reflection, she decided to hold out. She wanted Ray to be the first to hear the news, it would be important to him as well. She didn't particularly like secrets, but, she assured herself, there were times when they were warranted.

In ICU 7, Dr. Seidman pulled up a chair and gestured for

Randi to sit opposite. She obeyed his silent command. Ordinarily, such a gesture would not win her obedience, but, under these trying circumstances, at a time when she was helpless and dependent upon the hospital staff for the life of her son, she acquiesced without protest.

"Dr. Seidman," he said, extending his hand.

"Dr. Sloane's associate?"

"No. I'm a psychologist. A PhD, not an M.D. Different kind of doctor. I work with patients. And their families. We explore coping strategies. Find ways to cope. With unexpected hardship. The hospital considers me an important member of the team. In these circumstances."

"Circumstances?"

He studied Randi, appraising and evaluating. Or was he preparing a diagnosis? The silent inspection went on for an uncomfortably long time.

Randi fidgeted, resentment building. She cast a critical eye on Seidman and logged a few mental notes of her own: he was distant, perhaps being "professional"; he dressed neatly, though without a hint of a personal touch, as though his mother dressed him. That thought gave birth to another: though he was her contemporary, he wasn't someone she would consider dating; there was not the faintest hint of sizzle, or even a touch of empathy, between them. It wasn't that she disliked him, it was the unsettling realization that she couldn't find an emotional string to pull. That's when it dawned on her exactly what was happening: Seidman was the one searching for emotional strings to pull.

"Questions?" he asked. "Anything you would like to share regarding your son?"

He was fishing. *For what?*

"I want Ray to get better," she said, noncommittal. Then, bluntly, "Is there something the doctors want you to tell me?"

For the first time, he smiled. "I'm sorry. I didn't mean to cause alarm. There's nothing new to report from the medical side, good or bad. I'm simply extending an invitation. If you want to discuss anything, I'm here. We're both human. And we both realize it can be difficult to come to grips with uncertainty, with the gnawing doubts."

His probing drove a wedge between her and the present; she slipped into private thoughts, unaware she spoke aloud as she ran her hand down Ray's arm, "I always figured I would be the one hooked up to a machine, the one to make the awkward exit, leaving others to grapple with their loss. Always figured my son would have to deal with my death. So this is a bit unexpected. It wasn't in the original script."

"Life hands us surprises," he said, staring out the window. "It would be nice if we could plan, if life was conducted according to our wishes, but it isn't. We live in a universe of probability. Life is a continual roll of the dice. We can never be certain what fate holds in store for us."

"Fate? You believe we live as pawns?"

Seidman turned his gaze to Ray's bandaged body. The sight of the bruised, swollen, and motionless form caused a discomfort strong enough to motivate him to press for a change of venue. "You must be famished. There's a cafeteria downstairs. Care to join me?"

Randi wasn't hungry, but she grabbed her purse and followed, figuring it would do her good to take a break.

In the elevator, Dr. Seidman, eyes locked on the floor indicator, continued. "Unfortunately, or maybe fortunately, we're a part of nature's grand scheme. Organisms that evolved on the surface of a minor planet, circling a minor star in a perfectly ordinary spiral galaxy. If we stop to think about it, I guess we should consider ourselves quite lucky. Our existence is a bit of improbable luck for which we can be grateful."

Randi found his impromptu lecture odd, disturbing, as though he was consumed with convincing himself his stance was valid, and much less concerned with providing her with comfort. She was in the water, flailing about, drowning, in desperate need of a life raft, and he was standing on the ship's deck trying to read the sun-faded instructions on the life raft. If she ignored his argument, however, she invited his probing stare. It was best, she figured, to engage him with as little resistance as possible.

"I suppose I *am* grateful," she said. "One might even consider our existence a miracle."

"A miracle? Perhaps the real reason is much less glamorous."

"A cosmic accident? A roll of the dice?"

"That's the story we hear from the frontiers of science."

She returned the volley with a touch of sarcasm, "It has occurred to me there might be a bit more to the story."

8

"What's wrong?" Ray repeated.

Alice was out of quick responses, no one-liners remained in her arsenal. "Time to sleep on it," she said, snuggling up on the cowhide-upholstered couch in the corner. Within minutes she drifted off.

Was she really tired? Or had she merely grown weary of his company? he wondered. Feeling a damp chill seeping into the cabin, he crossed to the stone hearth and squatted in front of the fire where he toyed with the matchbox cars and miniature robots. Though worn and insignificant, the toys flooded his memory with robust emotions that had failed to age.

Alice, too, was a memory, not the girl napping on the couch— he didn't really know who she was—but the Alice she resembled, the Alice of Lewis Carroll's imagination.

A line from *Alice's Adventures in Wonderland*, a line which rang true in an odd way, came to him: *"When I used to read fairy tales, I fancied that kind of thing never happened, now I am in the middle of one."* It was Alice speaking, at the end of her adventure, realizing dreams and fairy tales were something to be cherished, a sentiment that Ray, in his present condition, found surprisingly touching.

Reflecting on the storybook Alice's epiphany softened his mood. With a twinge of remorse, he realized nicknaming the young lady Alice had been rude. As soon as she awoke, he would apologize and discover her true identity. He would change his tone. Given she was a woman—a bright young lady—she must prefer the colorful language of metaphor to the hard-edged dialect of scientific debate. Though he had to admit she had held her own when it came to intellectual sparring and had proven far more worthy than he could have imagined. Yet, he suspected there were times when she wanted to shout *"Off with his head."*

Recalling the line promptly cued his imagination to present a seemingly random image: the King of Hearts presiding over the court in Wonderland. The image, subject to the mind's malleable nature, transformed from the King into Ray's philosophy professor and thesis adviser, Dr. Alan Kidner, noted lecturer in epistemology, the study of how we know.

Ray, studying for an advanced degree in the philosophy of science, had figured the combination—philosophy and science— covered all the bases when it came to human knowledge. Kidner had been a good match, a perfect mentor. As an epistemologist, his focus on how we come to possess our knowledge was a plus. The honeymoon, however, was short-lived; Kidner, it turned out, was troubled, disgruntled, and dissatisfied. Increasingly isolated from his colleagues, the professor had turned inward, becoming more and more obsessed with his work. Ray feared he himself would suffer departmental censure as a result of guilt by association. He fantasized being shipped off to an academic Siberia where he would be isolated and imprisoned in a sad-but-beautiful "ice house," reliving Dr. Zhivago's fate: a lovely but lonely and terribly sad ending in which he would receive his degree while an aca- demic outcast. He imagined a burly Russian wearing a fur hat pull- ing up in a horse-drawn sled and delivering Ray's diploma with a curt nod. With a snap of the reins, the messenger would be gone, leaving Ray to his silent, frozen outpost.

Though Ray sympathized with his mentor, being acutely aware that the preponderance of philosophy taught at the univer- sity was as dry as old leaves, the ivory-tower musings of long–dead thinkers, and though he relished Kidner's impassioned arguments, he wondered if he had hitched his future to a rapidly fading star which was about to achieve critical mass and implode.

The professor's obsession focused on the gaps in scientific

knowledge of consciousness. He would frequently lecture, "The portal through which all knowledge flows is consciousness. Remove consciousness and you lose all knowledge. Consciousness is the single variable, the primary constant, that figures into all our equations—and it remains an unknown. Thus, all our equations are incomplete, all knowledge incomplete."

Though understanding consciousness was the professor's Holy Grail, it was also a Damocles' sword hanging over his head. In his mind, if he didn't solve the riddle of consciousness, his work was doomed, destined to end up discarded in the dustbin of irrelevant philosophy. Ray, too, kept his eye on that sword, sensing its latent danger extended to him as well.

He glanced over to see if Alice was still napping—she was. Her criticisms had been on the nose, his days in the philosophy department colored his view of the world: his life had become one prolonged debate, an intellectual wrestling match. That's the way it was in academia. To his amazement, Alice had met him where he stood and accepted him for who he was, in spite of dismissing his ideas. The intensity of the affinity he now felt for her, as a result of her non-judgmental acceptance of him, her ability to overlook their differences and see something of value in him, came as quite a surprise. Her compassion was a haunting reminder of his own failure to show Kidner the kindness he deserved. Ray's emotions swirled in a vortex of guilt and regret and plummeted; he sank under the weight of a vivid memory—a dinner party at the professor's house. Present that evening were a handful of undergraduates and one grad student from "the other camp," a young lady named Hilary, whose surname escaped him.

Vegetables—squash and peppers, potatoes and onions—had been skewered and browned on the grill; homemade bread baked in the oven; exotic pastas—tortellini's, angel hair, the dumpling-like pastas called gnochhi's—were prepared al dente; bottles of wine—Cabernet Sauvignon, Merlot, and Chianti—were uncorked and poured. One by one, the lines that tethered the young philosophers' minds to earth were cut loose, freeing their imaginations to float in rarefied Platonic altitudes.

Ray was unable to pinpoint exactly when the evening took its dark turn. In retrospect, he suspected it was Hilary who first challenged the professor.

"Dualism, the antiquated idea that there's a body *and* a soul," she challenged Kidner, "has gone the way of the witch doctor and exorcism. No longer in fashion."

"So philosophy has become a matter of trends and fashion?" Professor Kidner replied, curtly, lowering his fork, aroused to intellectual combat by the verbal challenge the young lady had fired in his direction. He glanced at Ray, fully expecting his student to take up his defense, expecting Ray to man the front lines, rhetorical sword in hand, ready to slay the intellectual barbarians. Instead, Ray looked down, embarrassed, and twirled angel hair covered with Alfredo sauce onto his fork; his silence was a small betrayal he now regretted with unexpected intensity.

The professor had continued, "In *The Republic*, as you should all remember, Plato concludes with the tale of Er, a soldier who dies on a battlefield, then, days later, comes back to life with a detailed story of the Other Side, having undergone what we now call a near-death experience."

Kidner rose and crossed to the fireplace, where he lit a cigar, inhaling and exhaling with a staccato volley of puffs, releasing fragrant, smoky clouds to float above the dining room table. A female underclassman wrinkled her nose, lodging a silent objection. Her male companion, registering her complaint with a smirk, solicited a cigar from the professor and lit up with defiant pleasure.

"A few things have changed since the days of Plato," Hilary countered with a trace of a sneer.

"Have they?" the professor replied. "We have accounts of near death experiences, much like in Plato's tale. Today we have reports of out-of-body experiences, OBEs, just as we had in ancient times. In those days, they recorded accounts of mystical experiences; we do the same. Perhaps things haven't really changed."

"What has changed," Ray interjected, playing devil's advocate, "is science. We've shown these experiences are a product of brain chemistry. Imagination. Hallucination."

"Ah, but have we?" the professor shot back.

At the time, Ray didn't give much thought to his improvised alliance with Hilary. In retrospect, he was forced to admit to himself there had been something latently erotic in the partnership, unstated promises were traded without so much as a touch. He justified his traitorous actions to his conscience with the argument that the professor was an academic heavyweight. A tag team of two lightweight grad students made for a fair fight.

Kidner's expression told a different story, a story of betrayal and heartbreak, a terrible aloneness. The department had abandoned him, now Ray.

"I'm not a neuroscientist, I'm a philosopher," the Professor continued. "As philosophers, it's our job to keep the scientists honest. In that task, we have failed, we have not performed admirably. We have conformed and strived to become fashionable. We no longer lead bravely, we follow like a pack of cowardly curs."

Ray felt the sting of the professor's words; clearly he no longer regarded Ray as a promising young philosopher. He regarded him as a seeker of conformity, a docile mind. It was too late to turn back, sides had been selected, the battle engaged.

Dr. Kidner waved his cigar, an improvised lecture pointer. "No one has demonstrated NDEs are simply imagination. Many espouse that assumption in order to bolster their weak theories, but they have not provided decent evidence, nor even a decent argument. If one looks at the evidence, one finds the NDE is inconsistent with the it's-only-brain-chemistry model. No one has shown they're hallucinations, whatever it is our colleagues mean by that vague, overused term."

Hilary started to speak; he cut her off.

"The most important evidence comes to us from those who report seeing their own body—from a position outside the body."

Though Ray had heard talk of such accounts, he never

considered they might be real, there hadn't seemed to be much reason to give the claims any thought.

"They see doctors in the operating room; they view relatives grieving; they experience floating above their body."

He flicked the ash from his cigar into the fireplace with a flourish. With an ironic smile, he continued, "As far as I know, their brains and their eyes do not pop out of their skulls and float up to the ceiling. Therefore, the reasonably intelligent person, upon studying the reports, concludes such experiences are not consistent with the theory that near–death experiences are caused solely by brain chemistry run amuck."

"But floating, that's make-believe, right?" Ray asked.

"Apparently not," Kidner said. "Some accounts accurately describe events that transpired while the body was unconscious, events that occurred while the brain was out of commission, barely functioning. In some cases, the person describes events that could only be known if they *were* viewing from a position outside their body."

"Wow, cool," the non-smoker blurted out, her fascination overruling her aversion to carcinogenic cigar smoke. With one short salvo of slang, she replaced Ray as the professor's ally.

Her male companion rubbed out the ember smoldering at the tip of his cigar and cleared his voice. "Uh, I had an experience, but it wasn't during an operation. It wasn't anything like that. I was with—" He blushed, then forged ahead. "With this girl." The dinner guests responded with a round of knowing chuckles, encouraging the student to continue.

"We were at this resort, a YMCA camp in the mountains. During the off-season. We sneaked into a vacant cabin and spent the night. I had fallen asleep and was in a sound slumber for a couple hours. I awoke, standing"—he drew quotation marks in the air — "next to the bed, looking down on my body. My girl was next to me, in the bed. Asleep. I was totally awake, totally aware of what I was thinking, what I was seeing, and how awesomely weird it was—to be looking down at my sleeping body. It wasn't a dream. I was awake like I am now."

"Yuk, that's creepy," his companion said with a hint of campfire-story awe. "What happened next?"

"Nothing really. I had the thought I should see what I could do. You know, if I could move around. And, you know, see things. I decided to go for the door and BAM—I slammed back into my body. It was sooo weird. Like I had fallen from three feet off the bed. My body jerked with the impact, waking—Julie was her name. I didn't know what to say to her. Even now, I don't talk about it much."

His companion nodded, "Yes, yes, go on."

He shrugged. "That's all."

"That's not been replicated in the lab," Hilary argued, as she poured the professor a fresh goblet of Cabernet Sauvignon. Ray could not help but wonder if red wine bore any resemblance to hemlock. As Socrates had defended his philosophy with his life, would Kidner drink Hilary's less obvious poison, the venom in her argument?

"Not all science takes place in the lab, my dear," Kidner replied. "Often we must observe phenomenon in the field until we understand enough to duplicate it in the lab." Once again, his smile turned ironic. "When the experiment involves putting subjects into near-death states, there are a few ethical questions to be considered."

Students clinked glasses in a toast to a point well-made. One young man uncorked a Fetzer Merlot and refilled glasses.

Though the students had turned against Hilary, she wasn't about to surrender. "So the argument that these experiences have not been replicated in the lab doesn't hold water?"

"That's merely an attempt to close the door on the subject before the real investigation even begins. Your objection is premature."

Ray jumped in, "Those who claim they were outside—"

"—merely report what they experience," Kidner fired back.

"But experience is not—"

"Not what? Near death subjects perceive in the present, not in a dream state, not in a daydream. These subjects, like us, know the difference between a dream and a waking moment. They've been awake before, they've had dreams before. They know the difference. You know the difference, don't you?"

Damn, Ray thought—how quickly he had made an enemy of someone he had respected.

"So why don't we listen to them? Hmm, why?" the professor asked.

"Because they're lying?" Hilary replied.

"Lying or deluded," Kidner replied. "That's the skeptic's assumption. So, a priori, without investigation, they arbitrarily discount valid reports."

He was right, Ray mused. Skeptics dismissed reports before they investigated. They were not alone. He, too, was pre-disposed to dismiss that which he found implausible at first glance.

"Considering all subjective reports to be invalid and untrustworthy," the Professor said, looking at Ray, "is a very slippery slope, my friend. The only way we can collect raw data in our study of consciousness is to have the subject report his subjective state. We must ask, what did he experience? This is obvious. If you discount subjective reports, you bar yourself from studying consciousness. You're finished."

He re-lit his cigar, signaling the conclusion of his argument and, most likely, the end of Ray's tenure as his student. Ray would be forced to scramble to secure another thesis advisor, *if* he could even find a professor willing to take him on mid-semester. A new advisor would insist he change his thesis topic to something inane, no doubt, like "the importance of Ludwig Wittgenstein's work for the twenty-first century." Wittgenstein had killed himself; Ray wasn't sure he wanted to immerse himself in the man's philosophy.

Ray had felt the loss of Kidner's mentorship acutely, but felt powerless to change the course of events. Now, studying Alice as she napped, he feared he was headed down that same disastrous path: his intransigence would alienate her, his skepticism would close doors, and, in the end, he would lose the friendship of someone who had shown him kindness.

9

Dr. Seidman, with Randi following in his wake, navigated a sea of nurses, doctors, visitors, and hospital workers flooding the corridor that led from the elevator to the cafeteria. After she had indicated, with a touch of sarcasm, that it occurred to her there was more behind our existence than random chance, he had gone stone silent.

Finally, though his eyes remained focused on the floor tiles, he found his voice. "You're religious?"

"Not particularly. Why? You don't believe religion makes sense?"

They rounded a corner and entered the cafeteria. The walls were pale yellow, the furniture was institutional: chrome, plastic, and Formica. The aroma emanating from the buffet was uninviting, but not repulsive.

As they collected trays and silverware and sidestepped through the line, the psychologist answered her question. "Of course religion makes sense. It's ingrained in us, a part of the package. As our ancestors were evolving, there was a need—belief in the supernatural helped them cope with forces unleashed against their survival. Religious myths prevented men from killing one another, the myths kept our species from becoming extinct before we wandered out of the bush."

"Religion is what keeps us from killing each other?"

"Unfortunately, the myths no longer serve that purpose, they're an adaptive mechanism that has lost its value. Now religious beliefs work against us. Though once they prevented killing, now they motivate wars."

He was right, of course. Many conflicts appeared to have their genesis in warring religious ideologies; there was plenty of "my god is better than your god" insanity to go around. But that wasn't the whole story; such conflicts were anomalies, the result of small-minded men using religious beliefs to accomplish all-too-human political goals. That wasn't true religion. Not wanting to incite an argument in the food line, she let the subject drop.

Chase, seated nearby with Hal, caught Randi's attention with a wave. When Randi responded with a relieved smile, Chase, only half kidding, mouthed a warning: "Don't bring him over here." Randi play-acted teasing disappointment, then turned her attention back to Seidman, who was waxing apologetic, "But it's not all bad news. Myths help us deal with death," he said.

"How?"

"Belief in an afterlife allows us to go on with our lives, to accept death. It creates a future for our loved ones, so we can go forward into *our* future. It's healthy."

"So it's okay to believe in a fantasy that protects our emotions?" she asked.

His response was a reassuring hand placed on her shoulder; the gesture failed to work any magic.

She paid the cashier and located an empty table, confused about the direction the psychologist was taking in his attempts to console her.

"If I know the afterlife is a fantasy, what good could it possibly do to pretend?" she asked.

"We may know, intellectually, the afterlife is a fantasy. We may know that fantasy is hard wired into our genes. That does not mean belief in an afterlife doesn't have value, from an emotional viewpoint. Of course, I'm not saying you must harbor such beliefs."

"You don't, do you?"

"No. I left that behind years ago."

"So when one dies, it's lights out," she said.

"What I believe is not important. What *is* important is that you have the emotional tools you need to deal with—"

"I know that. But what were you getting at? You reject the afterlife on an intellectual basis. I got that. And you believe if I accept death as final, I should be relieved. Why? My responsibilities to my son are over? Is that it?"

The flurry of verbal jabs rocked Seidman, forcing him into a defensive posture.

"Some find comfort in the realization that once the body ceases to function, the person no longer exists. The transition is abrupt, which makes it difficult, emotionally, but when we realize the truth, when we realize each of us is a blip in eternity, we gain perspective, and that perspective can be a comfort."

"So it's a comfort," she said, "to believe nothing in life means anything? To believe life is an accident and death is equally arbitrary? To believe the universe began with one big roll of the dice, and we follow with our meaningless game of chance, rolling the dice with each moment of our lives?"

Realizing she had crossed the line from the conversational to the confrontational, she lowered her gloves and lowered her gaze, and picked at her salad. The dressing was stale, stored too long in some over-sized plastic industrial container stowed in some stainless steel pantry; the mashed potatoes and mixed vegetables suffered from a similar history.

"You ever wonder why hospitals, which are supposed to make you well, serve food that could kill you? You don't suppose it's a conspiracy designed to keep patients longer so the hospital makes more money?" she asked, with a wry grin.

He forced a tight smile, still covering, his defenses on full alert.

"I was kidding," she said. "Don't get serious on me. After all, none of it means anything. It's just a roll of the dice."

"Didn't say there was no meaning," he said, resentment building.

"No, you didn't actually say it. But that's what your argument adds up to: we're the result of some cosmic accident."

She pushed her tray to the side, giving up on the lunch, then asked, "You mind answering a question?"

He leaned back, nodded with a wary grimace.

"How does one hard-wire religion into DNA? Where in those tiny little chemical strands are the ideas hidden? How do ideas pass from one generation to another in the DNA? Has anyone located an idea in DNA?"

"Hard-wired is a metaphor." His answer was terse, edgy.

"A metaphor?" She smiled, challenging. "Look, I appreciate your attempt to help. I appreciate your concern. And I'm certain you are a valuable member of the team here. But, frankly, some of these theories are a little bit 'seat of the pants' for my taste, if you know what I mean. Hard-wiring religion in the DNA? Maybe I just don't get it."

"I'm the one who should apologize," he said. "I didn't mean to tear off on a tangent. Whatever you believe, that's all that's important."

"Don't patronize me, okay? If we don't believe the same things, we're not likely to be much help to one another."

Chase and Hal, on their way out of the cafeteria, stopped by to see how things were going; if a rescue was needed, they could swing into action.

Hal, ill-at-ease, shuffled his feet as he studied Seidman with dawning recognition. "Dr. Seidman. I'm sorry I didn't recognize you," he said. "You're on the EDB advisory board, right? The Education Development Board?"

"Yes, yes I am," Seidman replied, pleasantly surprised to have his status recognized.

"You probably didn't realize who I am. Or who the patient in ICU... The EDB approved funding for Changes in Action. You must have approved our proposal."

"I'm sorry, I didn't put it together. The Ray Carte upstairs is the Ray Carte of Changes?"

"As you can see, we're kinda on hold now."

Randi wished for a little pill that would make her small, a

pill that would shrink her until she could hide in the folds of stale mashed potatoes on her plate. She had managed to insult an important man responsible for green–lighting her son's business. "You helped my son with his funding?" she asked, choking on her words. "That was very kind."

"I didn't know your son personally, but, yes, I was quite impressed with his proposal, as were the others on the advisory board." He noticed her embarrassment. "Don't worry, he wasn't planning to do any work with hard-wiring."

"That's good," she said, smiling an uneasy apology. "That's good." She was delighted Ray had not been present to watch her insert-foot-into-mouth and insult his funding source. It was the kind of thing that gave mothers a bad reputation.

Chase, throwing Randi a life-line, asked, "You want to head upstairs with us?"

"Yes. Good idea. Excellent idea. Thank you, Dr. Seidman, for dining with me. I appreciate your kindness."

She half-floated out of the cafeteria behind Chase and Hal, suffering in a dazed state that went beyond simply mortified. She craved a "time out," but, she noted ironically, a "time out" was not built into the game of life. If, as Seidman believed, life was one never-ending Vegas crap game, it was also a game that forbid you to walk away with your winnings. You were forced to keep on playing. It was a game that didn't allow you to cut your losses. No matter how much in the hole you found yourself, the dice kept on rolling, the game kept on going.

10

Ray glanced over at Alice, asleep on the couch, and, seeing she was outside the circle of warmth radiated by the fireplace,
he rummaged around behind the couch and came up with a wool
blanket, which he gently laid over her. It was a simple act of kindness, which reminded him of other, earlier, missed opportunities.
He had been charging through life, with his eye "on the ball" and
now, for the first time, he doubted the wisdom of that driving
focus. Life presented ample opportunity for one to demonstrate
kindness and love; how one responded, whether or not one heeded
the call, was another matter. The thought brought Ray full circle to
re-visit the memory of Professor Kidner.

The morning after the contentious dinner party, Ray had
turned up at the philosophy department intent on making up for
damages and proffering an apology. He would joke with the professor and blame his lapse on the excellent wine. The back-handed
compliment would smooth troubled waters, the damage would be
repaired and his status would be resurrected.

Once he crossed the threshold to Kidner's office, however,
his good intentions deserted him and he found himself, out of force
of habit, assuming a confrontational posture; his out-of-control
ego was not about to let the professor's flawed logic of the previous night prevail.

"You know, Professor, there are those who disagree with
you," he said, thinking of countless psychology courses he had
taken.

"Who?" Kidner replied tersely, challenging.

"Scientists who study the objective—neurons and synapses

and neurochemicals—rather than studying subjective reports of conscious experience."

"That's where they go wrong," the professor responded, with a weary sigh. Then, patiently, "You are unable to see the paradox?"

"Let me guess. The only way scientists know anything is through their own subjective awareness, so if they cannot trust subjective awareness, they cannot trust their own knowledge."

"Exactly," he responded with an ironic grin. "The claim that subjective experience is not to be trusted destroys their own argument, for, they, too, are subjective beings."

He feigned interest in his elaborate collection of well-used pipes suspended in a decorative rack mounted on the wall next to his desk. His Jack Terrier, Sharma, sneezed. Ray imagined the dog's sneeze was an editorial comment on the professor's smoking habits. Kidner bent over and snapped his fingers, summoning the terrier. The canine didn't budge. His short legs rooted firmly in place, he regarded Ray with a skeptical tilt of the head.

Kidner smiled, as though sharing an inside joke with Sharma, and asked Ray, "So, did you get laid last night?"

Ray flustered, it took a moment for him to center his addled mind. "No, I didn't. In the end, I figured it made no sense for the lamb to lie down with the lioness."

"Ah, wise decision."

Ray now seconded the Professor's comment; a month after the meeting, he had met Chase.

Ray's suspicions at the time had circled a paranoid thought: had the professor invited Hilary to the dinner party for the purpose of testing him? He would never discover if there was truth behind that suspicion, as the professor promptly launched into a rebuttal of Ray's earlier assertion.

"These scientists of which you speak pretend to be objective. Their charade is amusing at best."

"Scientists replicate experiments. Their work undergoes peer review. That makes it objective."

"Ah, but it doesn't," Professor Kidner replied. "Such peer review simply means one subjective observer huddles with another subjective observer and they agree they perceive the same thing. Their observations, nonetheless, remain subjective. You can add one subjective observation to another and another and, when you total them up, you still have the subjective. All you're saying is they agree."

He hoisted Sharma off the floor and held the tiny sentry in his lap. The dog pointed his whiskered snout in Ray's direction and fixed his stare on his master's Judas.

Ray wondered what the dog was like when drunk— *good-natured party animal or vicious beast?* While engaged in a staring contest with the terrier, Ray considered Kidner's ideas.

The professor misread his silence for confusion and continued. "When two or three, or a thousand, individuals agree, we call the result the inter-subjective. Simply adding up observers does not establish that an objective world exists separate from subjective observation."

Ray failed to wrap his mind around the professor's argument; his thoughts wandered. Sharma barked, a mini-proctor demanding the student's full attention. Ray entertained the absurd idea that the dog was a marionette, the professor his ventriloquist operator. As though confirming Ray's playful fantasy, the professor rubbed the dog's ears and Sharma licked his master's beard. Ray witnessed a gentle side to his thesis advisor he had failed to notice before.

With a kindly wink that made Ray wonder if Kidner was reading his mind, the professor continued. "If we remove all subjective awareness from the world, does the proverbial tree in the forest still exist?" He puffed on his pipe, then answered his own question. "We can't know."

It was true, Ray was forced to admit to himself. We have no way of knowing if the objective world exists independent of subjective awareness. It was the first time Ray clearly saw the glitch in the science–is–objective mantra.

Professor Kidner lowered Sharma to the floor, side-stepped to the office blackboard, picked up a nub of chalk, and turned to Ray. "Are you sure you understand? If our only way of knowing is through our consciousness, through our subjective awareness, and we take away all subjective awareness—"

"We have no way of knowing."

"Thus," continued Kidner, "the claim that an objective world exists independent of our awareness cannot be verified. Skeptics who claim the subjective is unreliable and not a valid part of science delude themselves. The shoe is firmly on the other foot. It's the objective we cannot verify."

"So the universe is a shared illusion?"

"That's possible. In science, the most we can even hope to demonstrate is the existence of an inter-subjective universe. The inter-subjective forms the basis of our shared reality. For all we know, we might all be dreaming the same dream. The universe might be a shared illusion."

"So, with near-death experiences—"

"Skeptics who claim such subjective experiences have no valid role in science forget all science rests on the foundation of subjective experience. No scientist has ever conducted an experiment without being subjectively, consciously, involved."

"Skeptics claim that when scientists agree, their conclusions become accepted, factual science."

"Using the same argument, we find there are many who have had the near–death experience, and they, too, agree with one another. Researchers have accumulated a large body of consistent NDE reports. We have much agreement on the reality of these observations."

He tapped his pipe on the wastebasket, deposited the contents, then opened a pouch and stuffed the bowl of the pipe with a fresh blend. "You see how scientists—who are merely agreeing with one another—come up short?"

"What about those who have an NDE and don't see anything? Or those who see only black? Or those who don't know what they see?"

"All the evidence suggests the Afterlife has an ideational component. We hear reports of a world of thought forms," the professor replied. "Thoughts become visible. Many who have the NDE see their own thoughts and the thoughts of others. One common thought form that can take shape is that of a black cloud—which is a mechanism used to cover up or block out unwanted thoughts and perceptions. If you don't wish to see something, you put a black cloud over it."

"Hysterical blindness?"

"That's a good analogy."

A student delivering faculty mail tiptoed into the office, dumped a handful of letters into Kidner's mail slot, then beat a hasty retreat as Sharma bounded after him, snapping at his cuffs. Professor Kidner appeared to find the show amusing, apparently the student and Sharma were locked in a drama that would be repeated, over and over, until the karmic pattern was broken.

Ray, not wanting to lose his train of thought, asked, "So those people who have an NDE see the same physical world we see *and* they see thoughts, mental images?"

"It would appear so. They exist in two worlds at once. The so-called experts are unable to explain how we form and view these mental images. When it comes to understanding consciousness, they are living in the dark ages."

Ray felt a twinge of remorse when he thought about the events of the previous evening. No doubt the professor now saw *him* as "living in the dark ages." As a result of his careless reasoning, he had most likely lost his thesis advisor. "About my dissertation. I know you—"

"Can't really help you," Kidner said. "I've made the decision to leave the University."

Ray, shocked, realized there was no point in arguing or pleading. The professor had made up his mind. Ray's puzzled and hurt expression coaxed an explanation from Kidner.

"I've gleaned all I can from Western philosophy. In the East, there are philosophies which attack these problems head on. If we're to find a solution, it will be found there. I must give it a go before I'm too old to travel."

"Sounds a lot like Buddhism. Don't they believe the physical world is an illusion?"

"The good-natured fellow who sat under the Bodhi tree centuries ago came up with a number of intriguing ideas."

Were congratulations in order, or condolences? Ray was uncertain. Kidner had spent his entire life in the pursuit of philosophical understanding and had come up empty-handed; for that, condolences were owed. He was opening a new chapter in his life, traveling half way around the globe looking for a fresh start; for that daring decision, congratulations were due.

At the time, Ray, stunned by the unexpected announcement, offered neither congratulations nor condolences, he merely shook the professor's hand awkwardly and shuffled out of the office, as Sharma tracked his retreat.

Ray's inability to follow Kidner up the steep trail of epistemology into realms where the secrets of the universe resided no doubt confirmed the soundness of the professor's decision to depart. Ray sensed he had contributed to the professor's decision. The philosopher was in need of colleagues with whom he could forge new ideas. Ray had failed to become that intellectual catalyst for Kidner.

After that meeting, Ray never heard from the professor again. Perhaps Kidner traveled to Dharamsala to seek an audience with the Dalai Lama. Perhaps he ended up happily sequestered in a monastery, surrounded by scholarly monks who gave more serious thought to such questions than had Kidner's former students and colleagues.

Over the past year, Ray had given little additional thought to that final discussion with Kidner and he found the clarity of the current recall strange—it was as though the events had taken place just yesterday. It was clear to him that Kidner had attempted to share something of value and Ray had not fully grasped the kindness. Too often, he thought, experiencing a hollow feeling in his gut, we overlook kindness extended in our direction. He vowed to remedy that shortcoming as he looked up and found Alice wide awake, patiently observing, her lips painted with a wry smile.

"Perhaps you're no longer so certain I'm wrong?" She was not the least groggy and sleepy eyed, she was alert, fully in the present.

Her intensity threw him. "I— I remembered a professor I'd forgotten. It was nothing."

Outside the cabin, a Jack Terrier barked. Ray hurried to the window, but his view was obscured by dense fog. In his lumbar region, at the base of his spine, a vibration took form, then rippled up his spine in ever-larger circles, giving birth to a shiver over which he had no control. Something was odd, terribly odd. Something sinister and menacing that could be felt but not seen was making its presence known. He turned a suspicious gaze on Alice, then hastily dialed back his ugly thoughts—he could not afford to chase her away, as he had done with Professor Kidner.

"I'm sorry," he said. "It was terribly insensitive and rude of me to call you Alice. I know it must seem I was making fun."

"If I remind you of Alice, call me Alice."

"But who are you really?"

She responded with a line from Carroll's book, *"I can't explain myself...because I'm not myself."*

Was she mocking?

"I don't mind at all that you argue and quarrel," she said. "I quite like it, because it helps you. Did you know that is what is most important in life? Did you know that helping others is the single most important thing a person can do?"

"Are you mocking? Is this your way—"

"—you're so easily offended, you know!" Another quote. *"Keep your temper,"* she said as she curtsied.

It occurred to Ray she was engaged in a campaign aimed at driving him mad.

"You ask me who I am?"

He nodded.

"Do you remember when Alice, the girl in the story, tried to fancy what the flame of a candle looked like after the candle is blown out?"

Ray was in no mood for riddles, yet he was unable to dismiss the Zen-like puzzle: what *did* the flame of a candle, after the candle is blown out, have to do with them?

"There's a clue in that for you," she said. "But it's getting late and it may be easier if I illustrate."

She slipped the cover off an LCD screen Ray had failed to notice earlier. Using what Ray assumed was an electronic wand hidden in her palm, she sketched, illustrating a sphere.

The sphere collapsed to a point, then filled the screen. It pulsed, collapsing, then ballooning.

"The sphere represents your conscious awareness. Some might call it your space."

She dug a green cat's-eye marble out of the box of toys and placed it on the stone hearth where flickering flames reflected off its glassy spherical surface.

"Focus," she said. "Narrow your focus. Compress your attention. Fill this marble with your awareness. Hold it. Concentrate. When I say "go," expand your attention, all at once. Place it on the trees outside. GO."

With a rush, his awareness ballooned. He couldn't see the trees from his position—not with his eyes—but he found, all the same, he could put his attention on them. He *knew* where they were.

"You see, you can make a conscious decision to expand or contract your awareness. It responds to your will. That is important to know. Your awareness, where you direct your attention, responds to your will."

Turning back to the screen, she said, "This is a body." She illustrated a crude, proportionally-correct humanoid body. She added the sphere of conscious awareness.

"The conscious being, the spirit, can locate itself—here,

here, or here." The last "here" was superimposed over the body.

"This is the spirit. You. Who you really are."

She moved the "sphere of consciousness" around the screen.

"You can view from any position in space. The amount of space you view varies. You can be very tiny, inside a marble, or stuck in the middle of a head. Or you can be vast and find the body is but a sliver in the sphere of your awareness."

"I'm not able to do that," he countered.

"Because you identify with the body."

Using the animated figure, she illustrated how conscious-ness becomes trapped in the confines of the human form. She showed the sphere of awareness metamorphosing into the shape of the body. "The conscious being can pervade any form, then con-sider it *is* that form. It can play the game of *being a body.*"

Ray wasn't buying it. "We can see the body and we know it is real. We can't see spirit or consciousness."

"That's right, there's a difference between that which is seen and that which sees. The observer is immaterial, the observed is material. Two different classes with different proper-ties."

"A conscious observer is immaterial?" he asked, skeptically.

Even though she had been over this with him earlier, she understood how difficult it was to grasp and remained patient.

"This is where science goes amiss," she said. "They do not understand the observer. They fail to acknowledge the observer's immaterial nature. As all science rests upon the foundation of observation, this lack of understanding ripples through the entirety of science."

"The professor once said something like that."

"Yes, didn't he claim that science, in failing to understand the nature of the observer and the observed, rests on a shaky foun-dation? It would seem science's primary challenge should be to establish a sound foundation."

How did she know about the professor? He left the

question unanswered as he thought about how both the Professor and Alice had launched assaults on his reality, and yet, it now seemed to him their concerns had less to do with attempts to undermine his world than with a genuine attempt to have him see something important—something so elusive it was proving very difficult to grasp.

His attention went to the screen; he was so captivated that it didn't occur to him to ask how she had come to know so much. He was caring less and less about science, and debate and logic, and more and more about how this all applied to him, applied to his situation, on this mountain. *What was she really getting at?* he puzzled. *What was she trying to show him?*

"When we have a spirit, together with a body, in a composite form, the result is a human," she said, pointing to the screen.

"Wait," Ray said. "Go back. You said that as a spirit I'm a nothing?"

"Think of it as a No Thing. Not matter. Not energy, either."

Thinking such a thought was not easy; in fact, it was the most difficult concept Ray had ever encountered. A No Thing. The difficulty in grasping the idea that he was not a thing—*he was a nothing*—did not lie in the intellectual challenge. The difficulty came from how it made him feel: engulfed by nausea, he was shadowed by a terror he had rarely, if ever, experienced, the kind of terror that sent brave men hurtling out of their dreams drenched in cold sweat, hearts pounding. The light in the cabin dimmed; the room grew dark. The spinning sphere of his awareness churned with splotches of black energy. He was being sucked into a dark abyss.

Alice had led him too quickly through the distortions of the looking glass; now that he was sinking into the quicksand of unconsciousness, she didn't ridicule, she wrapped him in a hug.

Instantly, well-being flooded Ray's awareness and buoyed him, halting his descent. He was suspended in a globe of other-worldly light emanating from Alice. The light flowed through his awareness and erased the swirling dark splotches. It could only be described as love, or grace. The experience was nothing short of extraordinary, beyond anything Ray had ever encountered.

"I almost lost you," Alice said. "The candle almost went out."

Clinging to Alice, Ray wondered what the hell he had got himself into.

11

As they reached the lobby, one floor above the cafeteria, Randi apologized, "Sorry. I blew it with Seidman. I had no idea he was on the Board. You probably think I—"

"Don't worry," Hal said. "I'm sure he understands. Who would not be a little stressed if..." He wasn't a wordsmith and even a professional scribe would need more than a thesaurus to negotiate a tactful linguistic path around the hard-to-accept truth that her son was dying. "Listen, you could probably use some sleep."

Randi wondered if Hal, reacting to her blunder, was employing the damage control strategy of sequestering the old lady. She jettisoned the paranoia; Hal didn't think that way, he was incapable of duplicity.

"Guess I am starting to get a wee bit blurry around the edges," she said. "I'm about as much help as a lifeguard in the Sahara."

Hal smiled weakly. She poked him in the ribs. "Lighten up." She turned to Chase, "I'll need to find—"

Chase pressed a key card into her palm. "We held a room. At the Marriott. Under your name. Get some rest and we'll meet up later. Try not to get down on yourself. We must remain positive."

Hal hugged Randi—a strong-yet-gentle young bear comforting a wounded old mama bear.

For a fleeting second she imagined it was Ray hugging her. She pushed the thought away, admonishing herself to stay firmly in touch with reality; there was no room for flights of fantasy.

Chase took Randi by the arm and escorted her to the

hospital entrance where they shared a parting hug. For an instant, Chase feared the emotional damn she had engineered to restrain her emotions was about to burst; it was becoming harder and harder to cloister her secret. She wanted to reveal the news, she wanted support, encouragement, guidance, and, yes, even sympathy. She stood back from her emotions, let the urge to spill her guts die down, then hailed a cab.

"The driver will know the hotel," she said, guiding Randi into the cab.

The taxi slowed as traffic thickened. Randi stared out the window. They were passing through a gentrified district. Both sides of the street were lined with two-story brick buildings adorned with decorative awnings. Charming period architecture housed stylish commercial enterprises—clothing boutiques, shoe stores, florists, trendy restaurants, a tattoo parlor, and outposts of the ubiquitous corporate behemoths, Kinkos and Starbucks. She felt strangely removed from the bustling crowd, patrons and clerks and merchants, from the daily hum of buying and selling. She saw only empty motions, hollow concerns, and daily routine that lacked import; the activity, on an ordinary day, was inflated with manufactured meaning, now it appeared banal, boring, meaningless. She was invisible, wondering how many others, like herself, passed through the crowd with heavy hearts, present and accounted for in the flesh, missing in spirit, disconnected from the flow of life.

She felt acutely alone and lonely. Hers was not the brand of loneliness occasioned by the absence of civil company, but rather the profound loneliness which attests to our fundamental separateness, loneliness born out of the solitude of our individual consciousness. Though we were destined to seek our survival in a tribal brotherhood of commerce, we were also sentenced to remain forever isolated in our personal consciousness, island universes in a river of shared space and time.

Would she have felt different if her husband was there to share her grief? Yes, different; much worse. Even now his abusive nature was a source of confusion. For years, she attributed his boorish behavior, foul attitude, and insane rants to the blows and insults his inner world had suffered at the hands of sadistic others when he was too young and too little to defend himself. She imagined he simply played back the inner record of the abuse he had suffered. She sought to silence his angry inner voices, to calm the raging storms darkening his mind, but the task proved too difficult and she began to wonder if there was such a thing as pure evil. Was it always what had been done to us that made us who we were?

Or, she wondered, were we all magicians, each assigned the task of turning life's lead into gold—our real worth determined by how we transmuted life's events into new and beautiful forms? And, if so, did there exist, among us, errant magicians driven by innate evil desire, magicians who churned life's events into a poisonous broth, a vile toxin to be spewed on their fellow man? She didn't know for sure, but, if there were such black magicians, her ex-husband was one.

Her failure to track him down had brought a sense of relief, but now she doubted herself: had she really done her best to find him? When she reached the hotel, should she make another call? No, it would not matter. There was nothing he would or could do to change the situation. She could not transfer to his shoulders the terrible responsibility that came with the decision she would have to make: the decision to terminate life support. She might be faint of heart, but she was not derelict in her responsibility to her son. Besides, if Ray regained consciousness, he would not want to see his father. Of that she was sure.

She closed her eyes and commanded the noisy chatter rattling about in her head to be still. When she opened her eyes again, the taxi was pulling up in front of the hotel. A door man with a pleasant smile and a slight limp carried her bag and escorted her to the registration desk.

Fifteen minutes later, she was alone in her room, collapsed on the bed, but, before sleep could come, guilt paid her a visit and prevented her from drifting off. She had been feeling sorry for herself, had been wallowing in the pain of her loneliness, when, in truth, she wasn't alone. Father McCarty and Dr. Seidman had been there. Chase and Hal, too. She had failed to appreciate the kindness they extended in her direction; she had been ungrateful, unappreciative, and was now ashamed. She drifted into sleep vowing to remedy her callous oversight.

12

With Alice's help, Ray pulled himself out of the abyss. The swirling, black clouds dissipated and she released him from her embrace. She was at a loss; nothing she explained seemed to make sense. She was failing in her attempt to rescue her slow student.

Ray, still shaky, vowed it was time for him to depart; whatever effort it took, whatever risks he faced, he must find his way down the mountain. He hoped the smothering clouds had cleared so he would have the moon to light his way, but even if conditions remained adverse and the journey would consume many hours, he must depart. He would do anything in his power to avoid re-visiting the mind- blotting terror his chat with Alice had spawned.

He grabbed the coffee pot and poured a cup. The liquid streaming into the cup was thin and pale yellow, not rich and black, tea, not coffee. Had she spiked his drink, slipping him a hallucinogen which routed his neurochemicals into a firing frenzy that lit the fuse on his bad trip?

Alice smiled. *"Mad, isn't it?"*

"Puzzling, and a bit curious," he replied with sarcasm, returning her line from Alice in Wonderland with another.

Nothing was what it appeared to be. He was past wondering if there was something strange about this young woman who had more than a few tricks up her sleeve; the question now was the purity of her intent. Was sinister magic her game and had his naive trust landed him in mortal danger? Should he escape and beat a hasty retreat down the mountain, or stay and expose her evil intentions, ripping the veil off her secrets?

"Doubt. It's a curse, is it not?" she said, anticipating his morose mood. "Was there something you didn't understand?"

He pushed the tea away and leaned forward. "Okay, if the spirit is not the body, what happens when the body dies?"

"The spirit separates from the body."

Her answer was simple and to the point. In his present condition, with his reality badly shaken and his suspicions on alert, even the simplest idea took time to grasp.

"I got that. I mean what happens to the spirit without a body? Can it perceive?"

"Why not? Spirits existed long before there were bodies."

One look at Ray's puzzled expression and she knew she was losing him. She went to the screen and began to sketch.

"Imagine a car. No, let's make it more substantial. Let's make it big and sturdy, so the driver can ride hidden safely inside— how about an armored vehicle? A tank. Now imagine that inside the tank screens display signals from video cameras mounted outside."

She sketched interior and exterior views.

"Imagine the tank is outfitted with dozens of sensors: temperature and altitude gauges; gauges that measure water pressure, engine heat, speed, compass direction. The gauges and sensors transmit information to a central processor which stores the data and processes the recorded information for the driver."

He could imagine the analogy, but he wasn't sure where she was going with her example.

"To make the analogy clear, let's put a body side by side with the tank. The central processor for the body is the brain. In the tank, it's a computer. Both receive information from sensors and gauges."

She illustrated a figure climbing into the tank, then sketched a "sphere of awareness" overlapping the body standing next to the tank.

"Just as the tank driver climbs inside the vehicle, you, the spirit, climb inside the body. The driver operates the tank, while you, the spirit, operate the body."

Though it was simply an analogy, Ray followed her meaning. There was a mechanical device, a vehicle, and there was a driver who was not intrinsically part of the vehicle, a driver who could come aboard.

She continued to sketch. "The driver can put the tank on automatic pilot, if he wishes. He can pop up through the hatch and look out as he rolls through the countryside. He can even climb out, if the tank is parked. Or, using a remote control, he can operate the tank as he runs alongside."

"The vehicle has complex sensing, processing, and operational capabilities. These are separate and different from the capabilities of driver. You agree the tank and the tank's driver are not the same, correct?"

"Yes, of course," Ray replied. "The driver makes decisions, determines what the vehicle does, though, at a mechanical level, the tank is capable of operating independently."

"A body is similar. Capable of basic mechanical operations independent of the spirit, but driven, operated, by the spirit, like the vehicle is operated by the driver."

"A crude analogy—"

"Crude, but it illustrates there's a machine, the body, that possesses its own functions and capabilities, and there's a spirit, separate from the machine. This driver, this spirit, makes decisions—what we call exercising free will."

Damn. Ray felt he had slipped under her control again, mesmerized by her patient tutelage. He was being led, with his critical faculties on snooze, down a path not of his own making.

"Are you paying attention?" she asked. "If we are going to make progress, we have to—"

"Go on," he replied, commanding himself to be more alert and astute. Accept no bogus logic, he vowed. He was uncertain why he was suddenly so intent upon protecting his beliefs. He had always assumed he was open-minded, now he could not help but recognize the emotional defenses springing up unbidden, latent sentries stationed to protect a mind should it come under siege.

She continued, "Study the body and its central processor, the brain, and you discover mechanics and function, but you do not discover free will. You do not discover an agent possessing deliberate intention. Those qualities reside with the spirit."

"Spirit controls the body—"

"Spirit can only make the body perform tasks of which it's mechanically capable. For example, it can't make the body fly, at least not with very good results. The body, on the other hand, lacks free will and the ability to reason, so a body without a spirit is very mechanical, machine-like."

The analogy made sense, but, still, Ray had questions.

Alice, however, was having fun with the screen, driving the illustrated tank and operating the illustrated body, apparently oblivious to his ongoing confusion.

He swirled the tea cup and studied the contents as though reading tea leaves; he was actually trying to detect traces of foreign substances, signs of drugs. Then he remembered most drugs are colorless and odorless. *She could have...* He stopped himself in mid-thought. *What the hell was up with this paranoia? She had hugged him, hadn't she? She had cleared his mind with—was it not love that he felt emanating from her in his darkest moment? Not passionate love, but compassion.*

No, he realized, the dark terror that had stormed his world was not her doing. Most likely that terror had been his constant traveling companion for a long, long time, residing in the depths of his mind, quietly entombed in his unconsciousness until summoned to the surface by events out of his control. The thought of an unseen terror lurking in the basement of his unconscious mind launched a new round of paranoia into motion. Slithering and coiling through the passages of his mind, the constricting loops of fear squeezed the air from his lungs, leaving him light-headed. His mind, it seemed, had been diabolically transformed into a fun house mirror through which he viewed a distorted and disturbing world.

He forced his attention back on Alice. Focusing on their debate was becoming a tactic he used to keep crazy thoughts at bay. Reasoned madness he could tolerate, the random emotions that threatened to overwhelm him were quite another thing.

"What about memory?" he asked.

"The vehicle has its own mechanical memory, a central computer which stores input from the sensors and gauges. The mechanical memory can be processed. Programmed routines, involuntary responses, can be created."

"Yes, I'm aware the body is pre-programmed," he added, referring to the genetic code.

"We also train or 'program' the body to act on an automatic, stimulus-response basis. For example, learning to ride a bicycle: after you have learned the skill, when you ride, you no longer think about what the body is doing. Your attention is on your destination. The mechanics of riding the bicycle are automatic. This is true of many physical tasks."

Ray considered the idea: the body possessed genetic memory which came with the package, a program built up over eons of evolution. Like a home computer, the hardware came with programs pre-installed—programs which monitored biological processes, programs which directed the construction of the basic building blocks, the cells, programs like a computer's operating system—but focused on biological operations. One could further program the machine by training it to perform repetitive actions which became second nature: riding a bike, hitting a baseball, driving a car. With practice and repetition we could build programmed routines into the body that no longer required our constant attention.

"What about the driver's memory?" he asked. "Is that different?"

"Recall the analogy of the tank and the driver. The driver's memory is not the vehicle's memory, right? The computer in the vehicle records physical data that arrives from its sensors, the driver, on the other hand, experiences his own perceptions and his own mental activity, which includes his decision making."

She grabbed a matchbox car and drove it in a circle on the

table, demonstrating as she spoke. "You have the conscious experience of driving a car. The car's computer tends to its mechanical operation and keeps a mechanical record, while you, the driver, make decisions, about where to go and how to get there. Your memory of the drive, while it includes your perception of the car—turning the wheel, pressing on the brake—is not the same as the car's memory. Your stream of consciousness differs from the mechanical record of events in the car's computer."

"In that example, a dual system makes sense," he said.

"The machine's memories are recorded in its structure—on its hard drive, so to speak. The same is true of the body."

She parked the toy car and crossed to the screen.

"The spirit's memory consists of mental images. The spirit creates and collects mental pictures of all its experiences. This memory is not the body's memory."

"They're separate, but interlinked, systems," she continued.

"Scientists consider only the body's computer, the brain."

"That's where they go wrong. They don't recognize that two systems are linked and operating as one. This oversight explains their failure to explain consciousness and much of human awareness and behavior."

"Let me see. The brain functions as a mechanical computer, similar to any other computer, and lacks free will or intention. The spirit exercises free will and intention, and possesses memory which is separate from the brain's memory."

"Right. The spirit creates energy pictures of the physical world. It does so automatically, compulsively. These mental images make up the mind. When you daydream, for example, you are looking at your mental pictures. When the spirit departs the body, the mind, which is not the brain, goes with it. The spirit's memory remains with the spirit."

"This isn't science—"

"Scientists can be likened to a primitive tribe. They look at the body and attribute to it all manner of magical powers. They invent myths regarding its origins. They view the brain as a black

box out of which, magically, pours consciousness and our awareness of self, but, in spite of all their efforts, they can't explain how a
lump of neurons and synapses creates consciousness. In fact, they
never come close to an explanation, they simply claim miracles rise
out of the black box."

It was true; when it came to the brain, the standard sound
bite was, "We don't know what happens, or how it happens, but
we assume—" Ray knew this, but didn't want to cede the point to
his young mentor. He preferred clinging to a scientific assumption
rather than acknowledging her hocus-pocus.

Besides, what was she up to, really? What did she hope to
accomplish by tearing down the ideas he had come to embrace?
Professor Kidner's probing debate he could understand—that was
his career—but what was her motive?

"There are many examples of autonomous systems that
come together to form one composite system," she said. "If not for
the prejudices of materialism, we would have explored dualism
two centuries ago."

Alice became sadly introspective, then flashed an enigmatic
smile as she said, "Your science has been hijacked by prejudice and
bias and is being dragged down a back road into the swamp. It's
gone mad."

Ray had the fleeting thought that it was he who had gone
mad listening to her. Nonetheless, he asked the question on his
mind, "If spirit leaves the body, as you describe, does it get another
body? You know, reincarnation."

"If your overcoat wears out, do you get a new one? If your
car rusts and the engine fails, do you get another?"

"A body is different. It *is* a person."

"You make the mistake of thinking I am the body."

She grabbed a toy car, a replica Volkswagen Beetle.

"The driver may become attached to his car, a huge part of
his self-worth and identity may become tied up in that physical
object, but, still, we do not consider the driver to be the car."

"Yeah, that's fine, but no one has seen a spirit get out of a body."

Alice tilted her head, searching for a bottom to the well of her patience. She eyed Ray critically.

"What? What's wrong?" he replied. "Okay, some people claim they've had the experience—"

"Do not forget there is a difference between the material and the immaterial. As the spirit is immaterial, one does not see it in the same way one sees a body. But we can see its mind, the mental pictures. Remember, spirit, though not material itself, can create and project mental images."

That's what a psychic medium sees? he wondered. Not the spirit, but its thoughts and memories, its mental pictures?

"The spirit surrounds itself with its memory. Not a good idea, but the spirit does it anyway. It accumulates its history like adding overcoats, and sweaters, and shirts, layer after layer after layer. Spirit shrouds itself in the physical to gain an identity. That's true whether it surrounds itself with a body, or a body made of mental energy pictures. Remember the spirit is nothing—"

Ray looked down nervously, recalling the last time they hit upon the topic of nothing—he didn't want any part of it. Though Alice was slightly amused, he wasn't, he was ghostly white with fear.

Alice rolled out three matchbox cars: a VW, a '57 Chevy, and a Mercedes 450sl. "The cars are the body—"

"—and the spirit changes cars," he added.

"You will want to understand reincarnation. Such knowledge could be very important to you."

Important? How? he wondered. How could such a distant and esoteric concept be important? "Perhaps, one day, if I take the path of which you speak—"

"If you choose to walk the path, you will discover your past and will be given a chance to disentangle from the burdens you carry."

"Karma?"

"In a manner of speaking. What some call karma is the past

you carry into the present, the cumulative record of your entanglement with the physical universe."

"The spirit's memory."

"Yes, the part spirit cannot easily see. But that's beyond the scope of our discussion. First you must realize you're a spirit and you have a past. What point is there in trying to free you from your entanglement with the past if you do not even know you exist?"

"But I—"

"If you don't know you're in a trap, what would motivate you to free yourself?"

Ray downed the cup of tea and stared into her eyes. They were clear, a transparent portal into worlds Ray was loathe to visit. He looked away.

"This has been one mad tea party, hasn't it?" he joked. A line from *Adventures in Wonderland* came to him: *"I don't want to go among mad people."*

"Oh, you can't help it. *We're all mad,*" Alice fired back with a wink. She, too, had read the book, and apparently, unlike Ray, she had no fear of madness.

13

After Randi departed, Hal and Chase rode the elevator to the fourth floor in silence, lost in their private thoughts. The time for small talk had passed and neither had insights of consequence to share. As they reached the door to Ray's room, Hal pulled up, looked both ways, and half-whispered, "I don't know how you feel, but I find it hard to stand around waiting for the doctors to do something. It seems they're just waiting for something to happen."

"Uh oh, what are you up to?" She knew Hal needed, craved, constant action. Being forced to sit still, forced to wait, was not in his nature.

"There's this odd fellow, lives alone in a cabin on the other side of Gold Hill. On occasion, Ray and I hike up that way. Sometimes we stop and visit. Nice enough guy. Into a whole lot of mumbo jumbo. I was thinking maybe that's what we need here—some good ol' witch doctor mumbo jumbo. Anything but standing around. Wanna come?"

"One of us should stay."

"Makes sense. I'll be back in a few." He squeezed her hand, then departed.

Chase dialed her cell phone. When her boss came on the line, she let him know she wouldn't be in, not tomorrow, not the following day—she needed time off. Though disappointed, he understood. Chase sold industrial water treatment and waste removal systems; she was making the world a cleaner place, she often joked. But, for at least a few days, the world would have to get along in a less tidy condition. Ray used to kid that cleanliness was next to godliness, which put her near the top. She wished, at this moment, as she ducked back into ICU 7, that she was a little closer to godliness.

At last, for the first time since Ray was admitted, she was alone with him. She found hospitals annoying. If you needed to work on a problem, quietly, a hospital was the wrong setting. And she was working on a big problem: *Ray was dying*. She didn't need distractions, like the fact that her feet hurt. She stripped off her shoes and rubbed her aching soles, and considered borrowing a pair of those ugly-but-oh-so-comfortable shoes nurses wore. She closed her eyes and let the memories and worries churn, hoping they would soon dissipate, leaving her with enough of a clear mind to formulate a plan.

Waiting for the mental noise to subside reminded her of their nightly ritual: she and Ray took time, each evening, to "clean house," sweeping away mental baggage that had collected during the day, baggage dumped by individuals eager to unload their thoughts, their desires, their opinions, and their needs. To an outsider, their ritual would appear as nothing more than a lively chat, but Chase and Ray understood they were exorcizing mental and emotional debris. Although Randi was sweet, Hal was helpful, and the doctors were professional, she knew they all toted emotional and mental baggage which cluttered the space.

Now that she was alone with Ray, she wondered if she could break through, if she could slip through a tiny portal into his consciousness and lead him back. She quickly dismissed the idea as childish fantasy; and yet, she needed that fantasy. Fantasy was better than defeat. She wasn't ready to consider defeat.

Why? Why him? What had happened? Some accidents, she knew, were not really accidents: the victims were predisposed and heading for a crack-up long before disaster struck. But not this accident; Ray wasn't that kind, he was a long-term player. They had delayed setting the wedding date because he wanted to "get his ducks in a row," wanted to peer down time's tunnel into the future and know with certainty that success was ensured. He built his future with painstaking care and would not, consciously or subconsciously, plant the seeds of his own demise. He would not booby-trap his own future. He had been driving over the mountain in a light snow, something he had done hundreds of times, this time to bring her the good news that the contract was signed, the funds approved. At long last, his "ducks were in a row." Was God so malevolent, such a bullying tease, that he would entice a man to reach for success and then, when it was in sight, chop off his out-stretched hand? It seemed to her, at that moment, the universe was rigged that way.

But Ray was not the kind who waited for God. He believed in a rational universe, a universe evolved out of chaos into the complex wonder we observe through our telescopes and micro-scopes. He believed there was an answer for every question, one just had to ask. And ask he did. He asked so many questions he drove her batty; he was like a precocious kid who discovers the infinite regress of *Why*. It was no longer necessary for him to voice the *Why*. The *Why* was a given, it was ingrained in his personality.

Now, Chase thought, he had happened upon a *Why* to which there was no good answer; there was no good or rational reason for him to be cocooned in a coma's numbing silence, a prelude to the eternal silence of death. He had arrived at a place beyond questions and answers, where only *decisions* mat-tered—decisions without reference to facts and figures and prior conditions, simple, powerful decisions, such as the decision to be or not to be. As much as she knew she couldn't make that decision for him, she tried.

At the hotel, Randi, refreshed after a two-hour nap, phoned Father McCarty to ask for directions to the church. She had not embraced his theology, and for that she felt no regret, but she did regret not having been more open to his help. The same went for Seidman; she had been rude and wanted to make amends.

Her new outlook had gelled during her nap. In the state between dreaming and waking, she revisited her messy divorce, and the time when young Ray—buffeted about by the stormy emotions of her less-than-amicable parting with his father—had offered his heartfelt advice. Her unthinking response had been to snap back curtly, informing him he was too young to know anything about divorce. Ray, eleven and on edge emotionally, lost his composure, and delivered an impassioned outburst: though he might not know anything about divorce, she should listen when someone tried to help, because help could come from places one might not expect.

In the years since, her son's impassioned plea stayed with her, it was a lesson that resurfaced from time to time. Though Father McCarty did not know her heart when it came to religion and Seidman offered theories she found repugnant, both had offered help. When one stripped away theology and theory, one was left with the simple fact that a helping hand was extended. Ray had taught her to grasp that outstretched hand.

Father McCarty came on the line. "I'm glad you called. I wasn't sure we would speak again. I was afraid I hadn't provided much comfort."

She had made the correct decision; Father McCarty was a caring man, his offer of help was genuine.

"Then I got to thinking," he continued, "there's someone you should meet. An old friend of mine. Where are you?"

"Downtown Marriott."

"Do you mind if I send him to see you?"

"I suppose I don't mind. But who is—"

"This is a bit irregular, so I wouldn't object real hard if it slipped your mind who sent—this fellow who researches the paranormal. The Church is not officially into—"

"The work of the Devil?" she said, poking fun.

"That captures the situation quite well." His smile, the twinkle in his eye, came through in his voice. "In my line of work, cavorting with the horned one can be bad for job security."

"Father."

"Yes?"

"I want to tell you I appreciate how much you care. You know for one person to help another..."

"Yes..."

"It's special. My son Ray taught me that."

"Your son is very wise, and he has a lovely mother, with a heavenly sense of humor."

Twenty minutes later, Les Carson phoned from the lobby. Randi met him in the coffee shop. They slid into a booth; he ordered a Coke, she ordered apple pie a la mode and a coffee, decaf.

The first thing she noticed was the pin on the lapel of his dark blue suit—a pink unicorn. Her gaze lingered on the mythical figure with a single horn protruding from its equine forehead.

"Pink unicorns," he said, "don't exist, except in literature and in our imaginations. Skeptics take pleasure in ridiculing those of us who research the paranormal. They belittle our claims as being the equivalent of pink unicorns. The pin is a mocking salute."

Randi smiled at his self-deprecating humor.

"I'm starting the I Believe in Pink Unicorns Club, he said. "Would you like to join? You'd be the first charter member."

His smile was slow to take shape, as though bubbling up from the depths of a reservoir of good nature. Randi could tell he was a man on good terms with humor, but also one given to adopting a stand-offish posture for professional reasons. As he would later explain, skeptics often approached with the open hand and easy smile, only to later turn mild wit into a humorless and scathing attack. He explained how groups of skeptics banded together, not to study the paranormal, as they claimed, but rather to belittle efforts to understand the phenomena. In the media, they openly attacked paranormal research. Their attacks on religion and the spiritual ordinarily might cause them to be labeled hate groups, but, by justifying their vitriol as science, their hate escaped censure. If one checked closely, Les told her, there was little or no science

taking place within these groups, only expressions of bald prejudice.

Les, recognizing Randi was neither a radical skeptic nor a
naive believer, loosened his tie and relaxed. He found it a pleasure
to discuss his work with the unbiased.

"Father McCarty explained your situation. He felt I might be
able to offer more reassurance than he could."

"He's a kind man. Have you known him long?" she asked.

"We were roommates in the seminary, headed in the same
direction, both obsessed with the spiritual life. Then we turned in
different directions."

"What happened?"

"In our senior year, we landed jobs at a hospital. That was in
Chicago. Mercy Hospital was on the South Side, close to the lake.
They called us orderlies back then. Essentially, we were go-fers. We
transported patients, equipment, supplies. One of our tasks was
transporting...those who passed on...to the morgue."

As he said "those who passed on" he realized his story
might upset Randi, but, if it did, she didn't show it, so he continued.
"So, at night, in the hospital, we confronted death, we went face to
face with the reaper. When we were buzzed on the intercom, we
would wheel a gurney up to the room of the deceased. The nurses
would leave a plastic bag for the body and a tag"—he exhaled—"a
tag we were to affix to the toe of the corpse. That was our job—tag
'em and bag 'em." Les was obviously deeply affected by the
memory; he stared into space and appeared to drift back in time.
"One night, one of our errands started out in the usual way, then
something quite out of the ordinary happened. When McCarty and
I reached our destination and entered the room—where the body
of a deceased woman awaited us—we felt a strong presence. It
wasn't like we saw a ghost or anything, but the presence we felt
was unmistakable, as though the lady who passed had a whole lot
of attention on us and wanted to know what we were doing. Like
she was looking over my shoulder, being fussy, almost bossy, but
kind, too. If the experience had happened to just one of us, we

would have brushed it off as bogus, as the product of an overly active imagination. But, as it was, we both felt exactly the same thing. Our attention would go to exactly the same place in room, at the same time, and we would get the same thoughts. Creeped us out a bit. Made an impression."

He sipped his Coke, let the memory recede, then continued, "During the day, McCarty and I would meet in the chapel and try to sort out what it all meant. You know, the big picture. Divinity students playing philosopher kings."

The waitress delivered their order and, aware she had interrupted, thoughtfully dispensed with the customary small talk.

"Sitting there in the chapel," Les continued, "looking up at the figure of Christ on the crucifix, I began to realize the emphasis—on death and sacrifice—was wrong. The real message, the important message, was that we survive death. The crucifixion and resurrection, taken together, was an elaborate demonstration that we survive death, that we are spirit. In most traditional religious settings, that message didn't come through strong enough—for me."

He smiled to himself.

"What?" she asked.

"McCarty was more old-fashioned, conservative, but even he saw the flaws. One day, while we were alone in the chapel, we got to discussing resurrection, you know, the misconceptions: corpses rising out of their graves, not spirits, mind you, but bodies rising up like the zombies in—what was the name of that famous low budget horror film? *Night of the Living Dead.* That's what it was called. Something like that.

"McCarty slipped away—I didn't notice—and flopped down in a pew, out of sight. When I looked back, he rose up, slowly, stiff as a corpse, a zombie. It was absurd, and terribly inappropriate. Cracked me up. You know how you laugh when something isn't really funny, but it hits a nerve? Pretty soon we're laughing ourselves sick, playing zombies, popping up all over the chapel. We needed a release, you know, from the tension that built up at night with us trying to come to grips with death."

He paused, sipped his Coke, and smiled.

"We were laughing so hysterically we failed to notice a priest walk by. But he noticed us. Got ourselves banned from the chapel for the entire semester."

Randi smiled at the unlikely idea of a young Father McCarty banned from the chapel.

"That day marked an important turning point for me. It was clear the important questions in religion had to do with the existence of the spirit and survival beyond death, the Afterlife, and I wasn't certain I was going to find real answers within the church. McCarty saw things differently, but he's remained a dear friend and we still get together a couple times a year."

"So, tell me, what have you found in your research?"

"Our focus is on survival of consciousness."

"What's that?"

"An academic way of saying life-after-death. Do we survive death? Is there an afterlife? We avoid the word spirit. Over the years, the word has accumulated negative connotations. You're right, though, consciousness that survives death of the body is what has traditionally been called a spirit."

"So you study spiritualism. But you divorce yourself from the public image of spiritualism."

"We're trying to garner acceptance within the scientific community. A foolish goal, perhaps. Maybe there's wisdom in keeping science and religion separate, but I believe that's impossible. Ultimately, science and religion study the same thing, life in this universe. Both pretend they do not encroach upon the domain of the other, but that pretense is giving way to the realization that there will come a day when spiritual beliefs are confirmed empirically. Or be shown to be fiction."

"You believe science and religion will overlap?"

"Our research hastens that day. Though we're in the formative stages, we're confident the evidence will support our hypotheses. It will turn out there's no conflict between belief in spirit and science."

Randi wondered what it was Father McCarty thought Les would say that would allay her concerns or provide comfort. Hopes and dreams of creating a scientific program to establish the existence of spirit were just that, hopes and dreams.

"We have evidence, collected over decades, that supports survival of consciousness. The anomaly that first caught our attention was the near–death experience. Here were hundreds, thousands, of reports from subjects who had experienced being separate from their body."

Randi felt a presence over her right shoulder; she turned and was surprised to find Dr. Seidman approaching.

"I'm sorry if I'm interrupting," Seidman told her. "Chase said I would find you here. I wanted to apologize."

"No, *I* want to apologize," Randi said, leaping to her feet. "In fact, I'm so glad you came, you were on my list of official apologies. Please, be seated. This is Les Carson."

Though they shook hands, Randi was acutely aware of a forced politeness that tempered their greeting.

"You know each other?"

"We haven't met," Seidman offered, "but I'm familiar with Mr. Carson's work."

"C'mon, sit down. How can we apologize standing up?"

She waved to the waitress, turned to Seidman, "Doctor, coffee?"

"With cream, please." He slid into the booth.

"Les and I were talking about the near death experience. People who experienced being outside their body," Randi said.

"Oxygen deprivation," Seidman interjected.

"Some have advanced that explanation, but it doesn't add up," Les said. "There are out-of-body reports associated with NDEs without oxygen deprivation. It fails as an explanation."

Randi gestured for him to continue.

"One has to consider all the data. When you have cases that do not include oxygen deprivation, you must set it aside as *the* cause. You must look further."

Dr. Seidman sipped his coffee, nodded almost impercepti-bly, conceding the point.

"When one studies the NDE, one finds different kinds of trauma precipitate the event. The question becomes what do they have in common? You see, in science, as a rule, you have to account for *all* the data, you have to dig to find a common factor."

Seidman nodded again, almost imperceptibly. "And you have found this common factor?"

"Yes. In all cases, we find a threat to the survival of the body. Any threat."

"So the bottom line is..." Seidman prompted.

"If consciousness exists as something different from the body, something in addition to the body,"—he paused, wondering if it was worth debating with the psychologist—"if we have both spirit *and* body, we would expect, at death, to find spirit separates from the body. And that's *exactly* what we find with near–death experiences, no matter which trauma precipitates the condition. The person approaching death experiences separation."

Dr. Seidman nodded. Randi couldn't tell whether he was silently agreeing, or mute in protest.

"So what you're saying, Les," she said, "is the cause behind NDEs is no one single type of trauma, it can be any trauma."

"Right. In NDEs with an out-of-body component, we have a separation of consciousness from the body happening across a wide range of precipitating traumas. So the cause of the NDE isn't one specific type of trauma, it isn't to be found in any one set of physical particulars. The cause, the common factor, is simply facing imminent death. This is precisely what we would expect if body and spirit are intrinsically separate and merely co-exist, tempo-rarily, in a composite form."

Randi was beginning to see where Les was going and why Father McCarty had sent him.

"The clincher," Les said, "is the out-of-body experience with no physical trauma. If spirit and body are truly separate, one would expect to find some examples, even though rare, of separation when no trauma was present—and we do."

"All explained by altered brain chemistry," Dr. Seidman interjected.

"Another argument," Les countered, "that fails to hold up. How does brain chemistry explain a person perceiving physical events from positions outside the body?"

"What do you mean?" Randi asked.

"Subjects describe perceiving from a position near the ceiling, looking down on doctors operating on their body. Or they describe family in the waiting room, or persons at distant locations. Neither the brain nor any of its sense organs are in a position to view from those vantage points."

"Imagination cobbles together memories," Seidman said.

"Doesn't fit the evidence. Subjects describe events they've never seen before, so it can't be memory. Details often match unique events that took place on that one occasion. In science, the explanation must fit the evidence."

"Extraordinary claims require extraordinary evidence," Dr. Seidman replied, as though the axiom trumped all further discussion.

Les, however, had had that phrase tossed in his face too many times to let it unsettle him. "That's just it," he said. "The claims aren't extraordinary. We have similar claims throughout recorded history. Very ordinary. Common. Only within the narrow paradigm of materialism do such claims appear extraordinary."

He suppressed a smirk.

"What was that? Was something funny?" Randi asked.

"I was considering what *was* extraordinary. Some scientists, in an attempt to refute reports of NDE subjects perceiving from elevated vantage points, argue that people naturally recall events from a birds-eye view. What are they thinking? In order to recall something from a bird's-eye view, one has to have seen it from a bird's-eye view in the first place. People do not walk around with their eyeballs floating above their heads. It seems skeptics make extraordinary attempts to dismiss the evidence."

The waitress refilled Les' Coke, eavesdropping. Les thanked her with a nod and took a sip. It appeared he was just getting warmed up. "I'll give you another example of the poor science that floats around in skeptics' circles."

"I don't defend those guys." Seidman objected.

"Doctor, don't take it personally. I'm merely providing examples of common misconceptions used to dismiss a topic that deserves serious research. Like the myth that free will is an illusion. The myth that the brain makes decisions without our knowledge and we only imagine we exercise free will."

"Sir, that's no myth," Seidman replied. "Experiments demonstrate the brain executes a decision, without our conscious knowledge, and, then, after a delay, that decision becomes conscious. We fool ourselves into believing we consciously make a decision when the decision was already made in the brain."

"Not true. One or two psychologists, grabbing at straws, trying to defend a weak theory, made such a false claim, citing experiments in their footnotes. Other researchers, reading their work, repeated the claim without checking the original research. Then someone else passed the error along. A false claim became 'established' science. If anyone had taken the time to check out the original work, they would have discovered the experiments failed to show any such thing. Even those who ran the experiments would not make such a claim."

"If what you say is true," Seidman responded, "it is a black mark against science, but in the long run science will—"

"Long run? How long shall we allow prejudice to determine the path science takes?"

Randi enjoyed the back-and-forth—the banter had taken her mind off her troubles—but found her thoughts drifting back to Ray.

"If you're right," Randi said, "Ray, in some way we don't yet understand, is still conscious. Even though he's unable to communicate, he's still..."

Seidman clenched his jaw and looked away, his disgust obvious. To his mind, this kind of talk was heresy, or worse, the barking of a carnival con man.

"Dr. Seidman, there's no reason to show disrespect," Randi said. "I made that mistake with you. My son taught me that if someone tries to help, even if they don't have all the answers, it pays to listen, because the desire to help is all that is important. I don't know if Les has any answers, but I'm not going to be rude and close myself off to the possibility."

"Pardon my rudeness, but I happen to know where he's going with this and the use of mediums is something I won't condone on my watch."

"We have used mediums in research," Les said. "They have provided experimental support for the survival-of-consciousness hypothesis. I have not and do not recommend using mediums in situations like this. I take offense you would assume—"

"Once you're involved with mediums, my friend, you're on the slippery slope to la-la land," Seidman countered.

"I admit it's a difficult discipline to research," said Les. "History is filled with examples of fraud and quackery. That, however, does not mean there are not those with legitimate ability that can be tested in the lab. If the survival-of-consciousness hypothesis is correct, communication between the deceased and the living should be possible."

"Fortune-telling is not science."

"We don't engage in fortune-telling. You may wish to reconsider your sarcasm. Those who resort to ridicule often do so out of a need to reject that which frightens them."

"What frightens me is you—bringing a medium into my hospital."

"He said he had no plans to bring anyone to see Ray," Randi countered. "I understand what he's telling me. His research shows there's evidence that consciousness survives death and this evidence, however preliminary, should be considered. If a medium can communicate with someone on the other side, we all should be able to do it. Maybe not now, but some day. So, if we don't close our minds, maybe we can—"

"Do you have any idea what a medium does?" Les asked Seidman.

"Commits fraud?"

"In my investigation," Les continued, ignoring the dig, "I've discovered mediums see mental pictures. The same type of mental images you or I look at when we imagine something. Close your eyes."

Randi closed her eyes. Seidman hesitated, then acquiesced.

"Now see the image of a horse. See its color. The breed. Is it a thoroughbred? Or maybe a pony?"

Both Seidman and Randi nodded, then opened their eyes.

"That's a mental picture you can see," Les said. "Mediums see mental pictures just like that, but they see pictures others create as well. When we look at NDE reports we find the content of those experiences includes mental images, not always the subject's own mental images. Often NDE subjects perceive the thoughts of others they encounter. It occurred to us this is how the spirit communicates, with mental pictures. Mediums are simply those who are good at seeing the mental energy of others."

"Could anyone do the same thing?" Randi asked.

"If this is the natural way a conscious being, separate from the body, communicates, if seeing mental images is natural, it would make sense it's an ability we all possess. Perhaps we fail to cultivate our natural ability. It may turn out what mediums do is not extraordinary, but natural. Our research shows seeing mental energy pictures is an ability one gains, or perhaps regains, when one separates from the body. It's an ability which diminishes while we're inside the body. Mediums are individuals, it appears, who retain some ability to see the mental images of others while incarnate."

The waitress, eavesdropping, reacted with a raised eyebrow—*"you guys are out there."* When they looked up, she blushed and busied herself folding napkins.

"The problem we encounter," Les continued, "is the noise-to-signal ratio is very high."

"Noise-to-signal ratio?" Randi asked.

"Imagine watching six television programs at one time while trying to describe what you see. It's difficult to sort out the thoughts we receive."

Les had said more than enough to convey his ideas to Randi, and doubted there ever would be enough to convince Dr. Seidman.

"Interesting theories," Seidman observed. "There are many who accept NDE reports as proof of survival, proof there's an Afterlife. Such a belief is an interesting social and cognitive phenomenon. Popularity of a belief, however, does not attest to its accuracy."

"We're not talking belief, we're talking evidence," Les replied.

"Oh, it's a belief, one of the most ancient and widespread human beliefs, a deeply-held belief that appeared long before NDEs became a topic of interest," Seidman asserted.

Les swirled the ice in the bottom of his glass, a gesture meant to convey his restraint and dedication to reasoned thought. "Did it ever occur to you, doctor, there's a solid reason behind such beliefs? That perhaps such beliefs are supported by experiences that have been common for thousands of years?"

"Right," Seidman replied. "People saying 'I could see myself lying on the ground.' But we must ask, who is observing whom? This split between 'I' and 'me' is something we should treat with skepticism. When they report 'I saw me dead' we have to wonder, don't we? Precisely who is dead? Me? Who says so? 'I' do. We have a living 'I' proclaiming a dead 'me'? Hard to accept."

The tension thickened. Les studied Dr. Seidman, his weary look posed the rhetorical question: could he really be this dumb?

"In most cases," Les said, "the person correctly makes the distinction. They say I saw *my body* lying on the ground. And they realize the body is not the conscious 'I'."

"I've no objection to you pursuing your line of inquiry," Seidman said, bristling, "but understand this—no mediums at the hospital. Mrs. Carte, there would be no point in my discouraging you from considering these ideas. They may even help. But I hope you consider all options."

Randi could tell he was employing extraordinary effort to affect a calm and reasonable demeanor, while, in fact, his objections were emotional and visceral.

"I'm not ignoring your advice," Randi replied. "But I also have to listen. I don't have the luxury of tossing out a single good idea. I want my son back. That's all that matters. I'd better go. You two stay and sort out your differences."

As she stood, Les slipped her his business card, emblazoned with a pink unicorn, sending the unspoken message that she could call at any time.

Seidman climbed out of the booth; there was no way he and Les were about to convene a summit on the paranormal.

Randi thought it sad that such intense acrimony surrounded the subject; the constant warring no doubt detracted from serious efforts to probe the truth. But, she thought, that's human nature and all scientists are human.

As she reached the door, the eavesdropping waitress shot her a supportive wink. Randi returned a smile as she stepped out onto the street. She decided to walk back to the hospital, at least part of the way. She needed the air after what seemed like close quarters in the exchange between Seidman and Carson. Maybe it was a guy-thing, warring over details, wrestling truth to the ground to count its teeth, precisely, exactly, scientifically. Maybe women were different, maybe women were given to decorating their worlds with pink unicorns, maybe Les was on to something with his new club. She would be pleased to be the first member, because she did believe in the reality of the mythic figure, not just the unicorn, but any mythic figure. They might not be real in the sense Seidman demanded, but they had a reality in people's minds, and that reality was not something to be easily discarded.

Unlike the taxi ride to the hotel, when she felt alone, isolated, and depressed, now that she was walking with the crowd, she felt connected, a new sense of belonging. She imagined she could feel the pulse of life humming through the strangers she passed. Yes, they were all islands, but the common river of life flowed strong enough and wide enough and deep enough to encompass them all and connect them to one another.

14

"Reincarnation is a simple idea," Alice said, clearing the screen with her unseen wand. "It's only made to seem difficult by those who are not prepared to consider—"

"Like me? That's who you mean, right?" Ray asked.

"Yes, you are one of my most difficult students."

"Now I'm your student?"

"Yes, and I've not given up hope for you. Even if I had, it probably wouldn't matter. What you fail to learn from me, life itself will teach you—eventually."

"The fact is I don't recall a prior life," he said. "Not a one."

"Your lost memories will be addressed when you decide to walk the path in earnest," she said. "That time has not yet come."

"Right. What we're doing here is strictly remedial."

He promptly regretted the quip; it possessed too much truth.

"We're engaged in what you might call an intervention. If you pay attention, perhaps, in the future, you won't be so forgetful." Her warning sounded like a reprimand.

Ray's suspicions were confirmed: when it came to the wisdom department, Alice considered herself his superior. Her arrogant impatience with his apparent lack of insight was annoying, and, for an instant, he vowed he would refuse to suffer her attitude for another minute. But, once again, creeping doubt undermined his posture: maybe *he* was the arrogant one, the one suffering over-inflated pride; maybe the raw nerve she hammered with her attitude was nothing more than his ego. *Had she not demonstrated her purpose was not to taunt and debate, but rather to impart information vital to his well being?* Besides, there was no hurry, he did not have to leave quite yet, he had time; often, when he hiked into the mountains, he would not return for two or three days. No one would miss him. He ignored his bruised ego and nodded for her to continue.

"If we start with a dual system, a body and a spirit, as we have discussed, we find it easy to understand reincarnation."

She sketched a crude body on the screen. Then she added a glowing sphere. It represented the spirit.

"We've been here before. We're circling the same block." He was becoming impatient. One look at her arched eyebrow, however, convinced him to rein in his emotions. "Sorry, go on."

"With reincarnation we find spirit inhabits the body and assumes the identity of that body. For that lifetime. You—who you really are, the spirit—inhabit the body."

The idea made sense, logically, but he failed to find an emotional connection. How could he wrap his mind around such a bizarre concept? How was he supposed to keep from snickering at the innate absurdity?

"At first the spirit may simply float in the vicinity of the body." She illustrated her point, moving the sphere.

"Often the spirit occupies more space than the body, being both outside and inside at once. As the spirit gradually assumes more and more control, spirit and body become entangled."

She illustrated her point, bringing the sphere over the top of the illustrated body and letting it disperse into the body's contours.

"Wait a minute," Ray said. "You haven't explained *how* the two are connected."

"The interface is the mind. Notice I didn't say the brain."

"So mind is the glue that binds spirit to the body? But how?"

"The spirit has many prior lifetimes. It has been entangled with many other bodies."

"Theoretically."

"Okay, consider it to be theory. Do you recall when we

spoke about the mind being made up of mental pictures, energy pictures, created by the spirit? Remember, spirit makes mental copies of everything it perceives and experiences. It creates a 3-D moving picture memory."

"Spirit compulsively copies everything it experiences?"

"Good. You were listening. So the spirit experiences the body it inhabits. It creates mental copies of the body with which it is entangled. Let me show you."

With the wand, she transformed the sphere into geometric patterns, a network of connected lines and shapes conforming to the shape of the body. It was a skeletal pattern, not of bone, but a pattern of standing waves of energy. The sphere represented the mental energy of the spirit and was transformed into a mental body—a body of subtle, patterned energy.

"If one accepts reincarnation, one can see that, over a very long period of time, spirit, living many lifetimes, has been entangled with many bodies. In each of those lifetimes, spirit collected mental facsimiles of its body, it created pictures of its body just as it creates pictures of all its experiences. When the spirit entangles with a new body, the old energy patterns overlap with the new. If you can, imagine the old mental body docking with the new flesh body."

She illustrated the concept. "As this mental body, this collection of energy pictures that is the mind, often works autonomously— and on automatic, so to speak—one can consider it to be a kind of 'mental machinery,' something we need not pay attention to all the time. These energy patterns, these standing waves, thus become part of the composite system of spirit, mind, and body."

It made sense, conceptually. Scientists were familiar with autonomous systems entangling with one another to form a new composite system. In biology one theory had parasites combining with their hosts to form a completely new composite organism. In such cases, evolution was not the result of mutation, but rather the result of a symbiotic relationship between two organisms who combined to fashion a totally new organism. In the case of the spirit-mind-body, if he was to believe Alice, the composite was temporary, a symbiotic relationship between a spirit and a body that was terminated upon the death of the body.

Alice's earlier comments regarding evolution and Intelligent Design began to take on new meaning: if spirit and mind were entangled with a body, the body's survival would be altered by the combination. The spirit, conscious and intelligent, would exert a "designing" influence on the body; its decisions would guide the survival of the organism. The mind, with its pictures of the past that traveled with the spirit, would impinge on the body and exert a "designing" influence.

If one accepted Alice's model, the metaphor of the Watchmaker tinkering at his workbench was no longer accurate. The designer was no longer a Big Watchmaker In The Sky, instead, the one designer became multiple designers, individual conscious spirits entangled with life forms. There were billions and billions of watchmakers designing from within, designing the forms with which they were entangled. It was the long, long history of this designing influence which created more and more complex forms.

Alice's model contradicted the commonly accepted view that consciousness was an emergent property of brain cell activity. This contradiction was not an automatic deal killer for Ray—she might be right, he told himself—as the commonly accepted view of emergent consciousness presented a serious problem: no one had been able to figure out just *how* consciousness could emerge from brain cells. The consciousness–emerges–from–brain–cells conjecture had not won its popularity on its merits, it had simply become commonly accepted wisdom by default. Scientists were loathe to consider the existence of spirit, therefore, the only solution was that consciousness *must* emerge from the brain. Alice's concept solved the dilemma of the origin of consciousness. Her model postulated an intelligent spirit that was added to the body; her model was based on addition, not emergence. The analogy of a car and a driver illustrated the difference between the two models. The emergent model postulated that if you left the car sitting on a race track long enough, a driver would magically materialize. Alice's model postulated a driver arriving at the track, stepping into the car, and taking over the controls.

"Even though all evidence points to dualism, to a composite system, scientists choose to remain blind," she said.

"Choose? You can't mean they choose not to see—"

"That's exactly what I mean."

Ray knew, instinctively, that her indictment was aimed at him. By now, he understood she could care less about scientists in general, she was interested in *his* progress. Just why this was so, he had no clue.

"Our emotions and beliefs affect what we observe," she continued. "Emotions can prevent us from conceiving an idea, they can block us from seeing what is possible. Emotions pressure us to ignore that which we cannot easily accept or understand."

Ray thought back to the literature on consciousness—the writings of cognitive scientists, neuroscientists, philosophers, and psychologists—and realized the texts had one thing in common: they summarily dismissed dualism as an out-of-fashion superstition, and yet, not one author supported this "no spirit" claim with hard evidence. A few were honest enough to admit they could not disprove dualism, that they were merely dumping the model as result of personal prejudice. The texts usually included a disclaimer: although the equivalence conjecture that stated brain activity was equivalent to consciousness was not supported by empirical evidence, and might never be supported by evidence, the author would *assume* that such equivalence was a fact. This disclaimer would be followed by three or four hundred pages in which the author treated the unproven conjecture of equivalence *as if* it were fact.

It became clear, once he thought about it, that researchers had garbage-canned a valid theory, dualism, without reason, and had replaced it with conjecture, the brain model. In straying from the evidence, they inadvertently made the decision to be blind. Ray was forced to admit to himself he was guilty of the same kind of thinking.

"I understand their prejudice," he said. "I can see how they could have ignored a possible explanation. I'm guilty of having done the same thing myself. But I'm not sure I understand what emotion has to do with it."

"Emotion dictates 'don't look here.' It causes us to avert our gaze. To look in the wrong places for the truth—"

"Because?"

"Hidden in our minds, we find pains, upsets, loss, negative emotions, traumatic experiences, moments of unconsciousness—things we don't want to look at. So what do we do? We protect ourselves by blacking out negative content with forgetting and unconsciousness."

He recalled the sticky, engulfing blackness that had threatened to shut down his awareness. He found himself wondering what it was he didn't wish to see. And there was also the puzzling matter of his missing memory.

"That's why I have no memory of past lives?"

"You're catching on. Your mind contains pictures of bad experiences as well as good. For this reason there are few who remember their past. Though some do. There's research—"

"I read about children recalling past lives. Some have birthmarks on their bodies where they were injured in the past life."

She turned to the illustration on the screen. "The mind, with its pictures of past bodies, contains pictures of past injury to those bodies. Sometimes these old pictures impinge on the new body and the result is a mark or an illness that echoes the past."

"The past affects the present?"

"We carry, in our minds, the cumulative record of all our pasts, but we find it difficult to confront the upset and pain and confusion."

"So we become amnesiacs."

"Basically. We avoid looking under rocks where we may find the past," she said. "That's one reason scientists dismiss dualism and reincarnation out of hand. Emotionally, they're unprepared to look under those rocks; if they even walk near a rock, they experience extreme trepidation. The emotional content of their minds diverts them away from logical paths."

It was clear why she considered him slow: his intellect was a victim of this forgetting, this amnesia. The more he considered the possibility, the more he probed to uncover that which was hidden, the darker the room became. *He was fading, going out like a candle.*

"Whoa. Don't go there. Not yet," she warned.

The room brightened as she recaptured his attention.

"We're strictly remedial, remember? Uncovering the exact details of your past is something you will do on the path to self discovery. You're not ready."

"So when we place attention on an area of past trouble, we go unconscious?" he asked.

"For now that's all you need to know about why you suffer amnesia," she said.

It was obvious she did not wish to elaborate, and, frankly, unearthing troubled thoughts wasn't all that inviting for Ray. And yet, he couldn't let the sleeping dog lie. "So this hidden stuff...is it what we call the subconscious?"

"If it's hidden from your awareness, then, yes, it would be below, or sub, conscious. But do not think of it in the way the term is commonly used. For now, consider it to be those memories you would rather not look at."

A fleeting memory flickered in his awareness. It was a pleasant memory, not one so horrible it must be buried or banished. He and his partner, Hal, had been hiking, and had befriended an eccentric hermit living alone in a mountain cabin. Over freshly-brewed tea, they had discussed metaphysics, including reincarnation, and now the words came back to him, *"We are trapped on the wheel of birth and death, reincarnating again and again."*

The memory prompted his question, "So when I die—"

"You will always be you," Alice interjected, "even as you assume the identities of different bodies like an actor assumes roles.

Always, you are you. Unchanging. Identities, on the other hand, are like a flowing river."

He clinked his tea cup against hers, a toast that echoed his toast with Hal and the hermit. And then, as happened on that day in the hermit's cabin, he was overcome with embarrassment; he felt ridiculous even discussing the subject. It was a topic for fools. Reincarnation was not something he knew to be true, and not something he believed. He even agreed with critics who joked and ridiculed the idea. "Critics poke a lot of fun at reincarnation," he said. Adopting the sarcastic tone of a critic, he continued, "It makes one wonder, if mediums see fully-dressed spirits, where do the spirits buy their clothes?"

"Now you're being silly," Alice replied. "When we see spirits, we see their thought projections. Spirits can appear dressed, or undressed, or however they choose to represent themselves, because that which one sees is merely a projected mental image. Critics raise silly objections because of their failure to consider the model in its entirety."

"They suffer from the emotional decision to look away."

"Exactly," she said. "You must get past that emotional impediment. The important thing to understand is you are you, no matter what body you inhabit. When it is time, you will move on to a new body. You will enter a new vehicle. You will come to learn that such changes of identity do not negate who you really are, you are you, that which does not change."

"So who we were in the past, our past identities, do not matter."

"Who you were, as a body, is less important than realizing who you are as spirit. The body may change, like we may change the cars we drive, but you are always you."

"But our past must shape—"

"That's right. Who we were in the past shapes the mind, the collection of mental pictures of the past we carry with us into the present. That past, if it is not recognized and discarded, can shape who we think we are in the present. It can confuse us. That's why it's important for us to recognize we're not the roles we have played, we are not the vehicles we have inhabited. Those identities are transient, ever-changing, while spirit is unchanging."

"But I like who I am: Ray Carte. I have things I want to get done. So, if you don't mind, I don't even want to think about reincarnation."

Alice's ironic smile implied graduation day was a long way off. She refilled their cups. He eyed them suspiciously.

"Did your friend, the sage who lived alone in the cabin, speak about attachment?"

His recollection was hazy. Perhaps they had discussed attachment; if so, it had meant little to him at the time. As he pondered how she knew about the hermit James, she interrupted.

"Attachment is the source of all suffering," she said.

15

"Do you care if Ray passes on?"

The question caught Hal off guard. "Sure I care," he responded. "I care a lot."

James Perspy stroked his beard a few times, then added, as he ambled away, "That's unfortunate."

Hal slid out of his Jeep and quick-stepped after James, following him to a modest cabin nestled in a meadow a few miles west of Gold Hill, five-hundred yards from a stream that flowed year round with the melt-off from snow-covered peaks straddling the Continental Divide. The cabin—after surviving fifty rounds of winter's crushing snow drifts and spring's blasting chinook winds—had nearly crumbled and disappeared, only to be rescued like a stray dog by James Perspy four years earlier. The renovation had taken the better part of five months, the window between winter storms.

Hal wasn't sure if James had gone to the trouble of securing legal claim to the property, most likely he was a squatter. Hal didn't ask and he supposed other people didn't ask either: *if James wasn't harming anyone, it wasn't any of their business.* That was the way mountain folk reasoned.

Though a recluse, James was not inhospitable. Ray and Hal had visited the cabin a number of times, shared pleasantries, then hiked on. One time, when Hal was suffering with a nagging bruise, the result of a climbing mishap, Perspy concocted a medicinal poultice, a dressing saturated with herbs, that worked a miracle. The annoying ache and debilitating stiffness vanished within twenty-four hours. As a result, Hal and Ray proclaimed James

Perspy to be their personal medicine man.

Perspy led Hal inside his cabin. Bookshelves lining the walls were filled with volumes on metaphysics, Buddhism, quantum physics, and holistic medicine. Hal squinted at the texts and, for a fleeting moment, was intimidated. He had grown up in Montana, the grandson of a veterinarian who was one of the last true horse doctors, a vet who still made house calls, motoring out to ranches scattered throughout the county on healing junkets. As a boy, Hal had accompanied his grandfather on these calls and, though he was barely able to see over the dash of the 1950 Dodge whose odometer had clocked over two-hundred thousand miles, most days he drove, chauffeuring the old doctor to his appointments with hideously bloated steers, victims of too much fresh grain; cows having difficulty dropping their calves; horses suffering from cuts and lacerations, wounds inflicted by encounters with barbed wire and other hazards; unlucky bull calves whose owners considered testicles unnecessary accessories; pigs who protested with ear-shattering squeals as vaccines were administered; and a host of other members of the domesticated animal kingdom that required medical attention. With his early hands-on experience with nature's creatures, Hal had acquired a keen sense of the flow of life and death. On the other hand, philosophical writings on life and death, pages of abstract pondering, were beyond his ability and his tolerance. *Big ideas crammed into too little space* was his take on erudite tomes. The books were, in his opinion, a vain attempt to reduce a dynamic world to static words; in his eyes, such reductionism was an unnatural act.

On the bottom shelf, medical books stood at sloppy attention, their spines bent, leather covers aged and cracked. Hal and Ray once speculated Perspy had been a doctor, then quit the profession, or was run out. They made a game of guessing the nature of the events that precipitated his departure from medicine, but never summoned the nerve to ask Perspy directly, face to face, what had happened—or even if he had been an M.D.

They had played another guessing game: fathoming the

reason James lived alone in an isolated mountain cabin. The
Unibomber came up; but James was no disturbed crackpot, he was
caring and a gracious host. He enjoyed the company of his fellow
man, he just didn't go out of his way to encourage it. His pointy
beard, shoulder-length hair, and old-fashioned granny spectacles,
along with his collection of esoteric texts, led Ray and Hal to joke
he was a reincarnated alchemist who had spent most of the
fifteenth century in Prague turning lead into gold and now found
himself plunked down in the twenty-first century.

Eccentric he was, but, to Hal's way of thinking, that didn't
excuse his earlier comment about Ray's passing. Hal pressed the
matter, "Unfortunate? What do you mean? Of course I want Ray to
make it."

"Have you read the *The Tibetan Book of the Dead*?" James
asked.

"Heard of the book. Never read it."

"It's a manual that explains how to assist the recently
departed through the transition we call death."

"Ray isn't dead."

"In the Bardo—that's a name they give to the stages after
death —the deceased remains aware of the emotions of the living.
The manuscript warns we should not allow our emotions, our
desires, our clinging, to encumber the spirit as it makes its way
through the Bardos on the Other Side."

"I'm not tracking. What does this Bardo thing have to do
with Ray?"

"He's in a coma?"

"Right."

"Perhaps already in transition," James stroked his beard
thoughtfully. "In that state, one can experience much confusion. It
can be similar to death. He might even have to struggle with the
decision whether to return, or not."

"Wait. Back up. How does this book work?"

"Tibetan Buddhists believe one's thoughts at the moment
of death play a role in determining one's future. One can gain

enlightenment, one can return to the cycle and be reborn, or one can fall lower into regions of hellish existence. After the person's death, a monk reads passages every day for forty-nine days in order to assist the deceased navigate the post-mortem state."

"A monk communicates with the dead? How's *that*?"

"It's a form of meditation. A monk guides the departed soul through the stages called Bardos, based on descriptions in the ancient text."

"Descriptions? Of what we see when we die? That's a big–ass leap beyond haggling over whether there's an Afterlife or not," Hal said, his sarcasm pushing him away from the emotional edge on which he found himself teetering. "We're getting a bit out there, James. Maybe we should reel it in, get the old feet back on the ground."

"For many the survival of the spirit is a practical matter. It has been that way for thousands of years."

James removed a pot from the cast iron stove and poured hot water into cups filled with hand-tied bags of green tea. It was a ritual Hal had been through before, when he and Ray had visited the cabin. After the tea service was carefully arranged on the sawed-off mahogany table, they sat cross-legged in silence. Hal knew if he was to entice medicine man Perspy to help Ray, he must go along with the ritual, nonetheless, the silence wore on like a winter storm that refused to break.

Ten minutes later, James asked, "What do the doctors say?"

"Ray took a blow to the head. He remains unconscious. There was some bleeding. They're mainly worried about swelling. The doctors don't feel the damage is permanent, but, sometimes, they said, the system never comes back on line."

James seemed to understand. "If it's best for Ray, can you allow him to go?"

"If I could imagine a way that it would be best for him, it would be okay with me." He reflected. "But I'm not sure about his girl or his mother. It won't be easy for them, if you know what I mean."

James closed his eyes and appeared to meditate.

Hal wanted to leave; coming here was a mistake, an act of desperation. He had felt the need to do something; standing around the hospital was driving him crazy. Now, however, he realized the idea was inherently silly. Though doctors moved slowly, often appearing as if they didn't move at all, it was for the best. There was nothing else to be done.

"Drive me to the scene of the accident," James said.

"Oh, geez, James, that's okay," Hal replied. "Seems like I'd better get on back to the hospital."

James locked a probing stare on Hal. "What? What did you say?" He used non-verbal intention to wrestle Hal's errant thoughts under control.

Hal hated silent confrontations, particularly when he was up against a master like James. Without much of a fight, he caved. "We can take my Jeep."

The broken and battered tree bled sap which hardened in the sub-freezing air. Snowflakes swirled at its base, filling in the gash the runaway SUV had carved in the frozen soil.

James, closing his eyes, ran a probing finger over the tree's wound.

Hal puffed nervous, impatient breaths, forming vapor trails that quickly dissipated. The crash site spooked him, and James' weird behavior didn't help.

James lowered himself to a squat at the base of the tree, his eyes closed, a blind man fingering braille, reading a world not visible to the eye.

Hal kicked at a snow drift and studied the distant peaks where plumes of dry snow swirled. Occasionally he shot James an irritated glance. James, eyes closed, was oblivious to his presence. Hal, in a cynical mood, wondered if he had accidently stepped onto a Twilight Zone movie set. He half-expected James to levitate and disappear into a sci-fi multi-dimensional astral plane in his search for Ray. Hal ordinarily viewed himself as a down-to-earth, take-care-of-business guy. His random decision to pay James a visit must have been an adverse side effect of sleep-deprivation, he concluded; he promised himself a much-needed nap once he had chauffeured James into town.

Five minutes later, though it seemed an hour to Hal, James uncoiled his legs and rose. "Let's pay a visit to the hospital. I need to meet the mother and the girlfriend. Maybe we will be able to do something after all."

As they turned to go, Perspy's boot struck an object—a stray piece of accident debris buried in the snow—accidentally punting the object down the slope. He started after the crash artifact.

"Hey. Leave it. It's junk, a piece of the truck or something," Hal called out.

Perspy, bending over and stepping cautiously like an Indian tracker, followed skid marks etched by the object in the surface of the powdery snow as it had skipped past. He dug the debris out, blew away a dusting of the snowy crystals, and discovered the little monk that had once dangled from Ray's mirror. He fingered the small icon and held it up for Hal to see.

Hal recognized the monk. "You gave that to him, didn't you?"

"I thought he threw it away. He didn't seem interested. How curious."

On the ride down the hill, Hal probed, trying to entice James into revealing the sights he had witnessed using his "inner eye."

James, sensitive to Hal's latent sarcasm and doubt, was not forthcoming; he simply admitted to entertaining an intuition, a hunch, that Ray had not intended to make such a rapid departure from the world and the outcome was still very much undetermined. Studying the monk, which now dangled from the Jeep's mirror, he mumbled cryptically, "The future is what we make it."

16

What had Alice meant? How did attachment lead to suffering? Ray was pondering the question, a question that had launched an entire religion, when he heard Chase call to him. He knew it had to be his imagination; there was no way she would be on the mountain in the dead of night. And yet, once again, outside the cabin, her voice called to him. He scrambled out the door, not bothering to explain his actions to his hostess.

The low clouds had thickened; they nearly obscured the forest with their damp blanket. The night was oppressive, suffocating, lacking even the faintest breeze. Something vaguely threatening, an impersonal menace, permeated the forest; a sly presence refused to make itself known.

Ray admonished himself. *Being afraid is ridiculous.* He was perfectly at home in the wilderness, the out-of-doors was a womb that comforted and nourished him. From the time he was a small boy, he had felt at one with nature. He had even imagined he could perceive the primal, living and breathing energy that emanated from the soil, from the bark and leaves of trees, from the blossoms that decorated flowers and spread their seed. The life-endowing energy flowed through him, saturating his body, filling him up, energizing his mind and emotions. He had, on many occasions, savored the exhilarating at-one-ness with all living things—which made his present sense of estrangement all the more bizarre.

The forest, he sensed, had become accusatory, piqued, angry. Not only was he locked in a debate with a fairy-tale Alice, but the woods, too, had taken on a fairy-tale quality. Yes, he admitted to himself, playing along with his hallucination, it was true that lately he had taken nature for granted, had suckled at her breast and enjoyed her riches, then failed to protect her vibrant life. When she became worn and battered by the constant assault of a teeming and ever-expanding human population, he had failed to come to her rescue. He had considered he was past the stage of youthful environmental concerns. He was older now, more pragmatic, focused on his own human survival.

He wiped a tear, surprised at the raw emotion his rambling thoughts unearthed. He vowed to reform his callous ways and treat the environment with considerably more care in the future. It was an odd thought as he was not at all what one might disparagingly call a tree hugger. The weighty guilt he experienced was foreign. Playing the role of a sinner brought low was new to Ray, as was propitiating and promising to make amends. An inner voice, the voice of conscience, accused him of confessional theatrics. It had taken suffering and self-loathing to drop him to his knees and force him to vow to mend his ways. Why had it not been lofty principles, aesthetics and compassion, that fueled his transformation? An even deeper remorse overcame him. What kind of man was he?

Inner voices ping-ponged, from pole to pole, slamming back and forth between good and evil, black and white, threatening to undermine his sanity. He shut off the voices and turned outward. His concern, when he strayed from the cabin, had been for Chase —he needed to focus.

He listened. Silence. Chase's voice had, no doubt, been his imagination. Then, clearly: "Ray, please."

The voice came from his left, but, as soon as he ran in that direction, underbrush snagging his pants, slowing his advance, the voice sounded behind him. He doubled back, only to hear the voice once again behind him. Someone or something was playing tricks on him. Panic threatened to rout his mind. He closed his eyes, forced a deep breath and listened. What was Chase doing up here? He had been gone one evening; they would not have formed a search party. It didn't make sense. She wouldn't look for him... unless she was the one in trouble, unless she was the one who needed his help.

He retraced his steps and stumbled upon a fallen tree he didn't recall having been there. But he had been in a hurry and no doubt there was a lot he hadn't noticed. He heard a whimper. There. Behind the log. It wasn't Chase; it couldn't be. It was the sound of a small dog, like Biscuit, the precocious cocker spaniel that had been the family pet when Ray was ten, the tumultuous year before his parents' divorce.

The voices of doubt hammered him: *Why was he besieged by ominous fantasies? Was he driving himself crazy? Would the psychedelic bizarreness never end?*

Again, the whimper. The dog was hurt, or perhaps only cold and lost. That couldn't be—Biscuit died years ago. Ray leaped up on the fallen tree trunk, fully expecting to find Biscuit on the other side, cowering.

The cocker spaniel was there, wet and shivering with fear, cringing in a pose Ray thought he had flushed out of his memory long ago, the same pose the little dog assumed while being beaten by Ray's father. As Alice had taught, painful memories—for Ray felt Biscuit's pain as though it were his own—were often not really flushed out of our minds, they were merely covered up in an act of forgetting.

Before he could explore the nuances of his epiphany, a throaty growl demanded his attention. He looked up and discovered the source of the growl, the source of Biscuit's distress. The creature's jaundiced eyes were bloodshot; foamy saliva, streaked with blood, dripped from its jaws; the flea-infested, coarse hair on its haunches bristled; its thin lips curled, exposing yellowed, but glistening wet, canines. The creature sank into a crouch, muscles tensed, poised to attack.

At first, Ray imagined he was facing a wild dog, then he realized it was worse, he was squared off against a rabid wolf. His training kicked in, there was a rule: don't turn your back on a predator, don't run; face him square on, stand tall; make yourself appear as big as possible, be unafraid. His intellect reminded him a wolf was not the vicious, mindless predator often portrayed in literature; but this was no ordinary wolf. The beast's illness transcended the natural realm: something inherently evil afflicted the creature, something beyond the mundane, something archetypal. When it came to such evil, rules dictating patience were simply an invitation to disaster—Ray hit the ground running with the crazed creature in close pursuit. As he ran, he thought how odd it was that he had never been chased, never run, except in childhood dreams. Except for now.

His foot came down hard on a fallen branch; the rotted wood crumbled, his ankle turned, and he pitched headfirst into the unforgiving trunk of a forty-foot pine. The impact dropped him to all fours; blood trickled down his forehead, its sticky warmth flowed with a dLjB-vu familiarity. A cracked windshield flashed before his eyes. Staring back through the shattered glass was a friendly gnome with a pointy beard—his eager face and whimsical, startled eyes bordered on high comedy. It was someone Ray knew, but couldn't place. He couldn't help but break a smile. The gnome mis-read the gesture and assumed Ray was telegraphing that he was fine. The gnome promptly disappeared.

The wolf lunged. Ray spun left. Jagged, worn teeth narrowly missed Ray's thigh. He kept on spinning, barely evading the jaws that slammed shut with a sickening wet slap. He scrambled to his feet, zig-zagged between the trees, slid down a gully slippery with mud-covered pine needles, jumped up and continued his mad dash. Reaching out and snagging a tree, he catapulted himself on a new tangent and promptly slammed into a foul-smelling figure draped in an over-sized threadbare black overcoat. He had no doubt this ghoul was the beast's master; his grayish complexion and yellowish eyes were symptoms of the same sickness which infected the beast.

"Get your animal under control," Ray screamed, realizing immediately his plea was both comically pathetic and in vain. This was not a delinquent citizen allowing his pet to run off leash, this was a malevolent force that meant him harm. With anguished dismay, he recognized the grotesque man with the sardonic features—his father. He hadn't seen, nor heard, from the man in years. With macabre curiosity, he wondered how the old man had fallen into such an inhuman condition. How had he managed to track Ray to this mountain, this evening? Why?

Ray's curiosity cost him: the man belted him with a backhand that sent him reeling. The back of his head hammered into a tree trunk, he lost his footing and ended up on the ground, staring up at his bizarre adversary. He could see his own fear radiate into space, like ripples on a pond.

Before he could sort out his confusion and devise an escape strategy, he spotted, through an opening in the dense forest, a female figure that appeared to be Chase: a wispy phantom attired in a snow-white lace wedding gown, her face hidden behind a veil. Dragging behind her was an enormous, billowing satin train.

It made no sense. His father tracking him down. His girlfriend, in the woods, wearing a wedding dress.

He trusted Chase—more than he could ever trust his abusive father—to tell him honestly what the hell was happening. As he clambered to his feet, he nimbly side stepped an open-fisted swipe, then ducked a second punch launched by the ghoulish figure with the frozen sneer. He sprinted toward Chase. For a second he lost sight of her as she vanished behind a tree. When she re-appeared, she was pushing a baby carriage, a sturdy gray affair with black, hard rubber tires.

He slowed his advance, willing his brain to process the experience, trying to force logic over the top of insanity. *A baby carriage?* This couldn't be real, he must be experiencing a nightmare hallucination. Perhaps Alice *had* spiked his drink. He willed himself to wake up, to sober up, but there was no relief, no change of scenery. The problem with nightmares, he mused, was you were inside the event, with no way to step outside until the altered state ran its course.

Chase tripped on the gown's hem and staggered to her knees. The carriage caromed off a tree and rolled to a stop. The deranged wolf—though Ray was now certain the beast was not actually a wolf, but rather a hybrid creature wandering the nightmare realm—circled and planted himself between Ray and Chase and the baby carriage.

The carriage needed no defense, Ray assured himself. As he and Chase were unmarried and childless, the carriage must be empty, a cruel symbol Chase was using, along with the wedding gown, to jump-start his give-a-shit meter. Maybe it was her way of informing him it was time to get his act together, time to end his waffling doubt and bring to an end the tedious delay he had put her through when it came to their marriage plans.

Once again, he identified with the Kafka-esque character—the distraught amnesic husband wandering the supermarket trying in vain to fire his memory, clueless as to the nature of his errand. His memory was riddled with gaps, huge gaping gaps he seemed powerless to mend. Hallucination or not, however, he knew he must protect Chase. That was a given.

The cabin was visible, off to his right. If he made a dash for safety, the creature would no doubt pursue him and leave Chase alone—but running was absurd, he should confront the creature, challenge it to do its worse. Being a phantom, it lacked power beyond that which his imagination granted. *What did it matter if he was mutilated in a dream?* He fingered the blood drying on his forehead, felt the throbbing ache in his jaw where the sadistic ghoul had belted him; the blood was real, the pain in his jaw felt real enough. He couldn't take a chance that Chase would be hurt.

He sprinted toward the cabin, creating a diversion, offering himself as bait. When he was three-quarters of the distance across the clearing, the soil softened into mud. He slipped and fell, then scrambled to his feet and willed his legs, which burned with exhaustion, to churn through the slop. He crawled onto the porch, rose to his knees, lowered his shoulder, and body-slammed the cabin door. The wood splintered and the latch gave way. He rushed inside, heading straight for the fireplace, where he armed himself with an iron poker and swivelled to face the demon. But the animal was no longer behind him. His strategy had failed; the beast, apparently, had turned on Chase.

Alice covered an amused smirk with the back of her hand.

"Quit laughing," Ray screamed. "Quit with your silly games. My girl—my future wife—is out there with a rabid animal."

He charged outside, certain he was heading into a violent confrontation he could not possibly win. To stay inside and not go to Chase's aid, however, was unthinkable. As he scanned the clearing and the woods from the porch, there was no sign of the predator, no sign of Chase, no sign of the ghoul who was his father. He puzzled: *if this was a bad dream, it was time to wake up.* But this couldn't be a dream, in spite of its dream-like quality, as he was wide awake and fully alert. A different waking state to which he could escape did not exist —this was it.

A man's voice, faint but recognizable, called for help. This time it was Hal. Ray leapt off the porch and sprinted into the woods, failing to notice how quickly the mud had dried. He followed the sound of Hal's voice until he encountered a steep rocky ravine blocking his path. Through the mist, on the other side of the chasm, he could make out a sheer granite cliff glistening with dewy moisture. Dangling, at the end of a yellow nylon climber's rope, was Hal; his left arm was limp, apparently dislocated, the humerus bone separated from the shoulder socket; his right knee was damaged, twisted at an unnatural, stomach- churning angle; a gash in his scalp oozed dark blood into his sandy hair.

Ray strained in order to see more clearly, assessing the situation. Hal's expression telegraphed "save me." An instant later, his features broadcast: "Let me go, save yourself."

Save him, or let him go? A rescue attempt could prove futile, an invitation to his own death. The image of Hal's tortured face flashed before him—pleading to be saved, then pleading for Ray to leave him and save himself. The dichotomy rendered Ray immobile. He squeezed his eyes shut. He could not depend upon

Hal's judgment. His injured friend was delirious. He was forced to make his own decision, to face his own doubts and fears. Hal was his best friend—he had no choice.

He inched down the slippery ravine and encountered a six-foot drop. He searched, but found no detour around the yawning obstacle. He turned to face the rock and lowered himself, his strong climber's grip supporting his weight. He stretched his body to its full extension and felt for the ledge below with his toes. Out of sight, coiled in a rocky alcove worn into the rock a foot above the ledge, a rattlesnake, defending its shallow home against invasion, struck once, hammering its venomous fangs into Ray's calf. Reptilian nerve-agent flooded human flesh. Years of rock climbing had conditioned Ray's arms and sharpened his reflexes. He used a combination of strength and speed to yank himself straight up, off the ledge.

He inspected the bite. The wound, saturated with poison, swelled rapidly. He glanced across the ravine at Hal, dangling on the cliff. Hal's eyes were shut tight in defeat, in acceptance of his impending demise. For Ray, it was a bitter defeat. In the rescue attempt that meant the most to him, he had failed. His will to continue on was sapped. On his knees, he leaned forward and retched, as though he was vomiting everything in his life that had been a failure.

From the direction of the cabin, Chase's voice echoed, "Ray, it's going to be okay."

Ray pulled himself together and, on his hands and knees, rummaged through the debris on the forest floor until he found a sturdy branch to serve as a walking stick. He struggled to his feet and hobbled across the clearing, the painful swelling in his leg unabated, the snake's venom ravaging his nervous system. There was no way he was going to get down the mountain to a hospital stocked with anti-venom serum in time to deter the poison from its fatal course. He came to grips with the fact that he was as good as dead. All he wanted was one last good-bye, a final chance to apologize to Chase for having messed up, for having entangled himself in such a fix. If he could only reach the cabin...

Off to one side, the disgusting ghoulish figure, the pathetic, hostile, remnant of his father, and his attack-dog stared back at Ray, apparently deriving a full measure of satisfaction from Ray's distress.

After what seemed an eternity, he crawled into the cabin, continuing his desperate search for Chase.

She wasn't there. It was only Alice that stood before him. Her coy smile was replaced by an expression of sympathy so profound it nearly reduced Ray to tears: she mirrored his pain, his desperation, his frustration and loss.

"Your friends are okay," she said. "But we have much to learn and time is running out."

The odd mix of youthful innocence and steely intention catapulted Ray into confusion. His body shook from the adrenalin and venom coursing through his veins; he was edgy with desperate emotions. It was obvious he'd been wrong about Alice, who she was, where she came from, and her intentions.

"No more lessons," he said. "I don't have time, I've been bitten. I don't know—"

"I know you don't know!" she snapped, losing patience.

Ray was startled into temporary silence.

"We talked about the mind," Alice said. "Think, Ray, think. The mind. Mental images. They stay with the spirit when it departs."

She illustrated the body. Then drew the mental body to one side, separate from the flesh body.

He tried to grasp her point but failed. He was trembling and his leg hurt something awful. "What does that have to do with me? I don't grasp what you're saying."

"The spirit, entangled in mental copies of its former body, can still believe it possesses a body, even when it separates from its physical form. It mistakes the mental copy for the real thing."

She held up her arm—it disappeared down to her elbow. Flat out disappeared.

The shock jolted Ray out of his pain-induced stupor. She was dead! He was face to face with a disembodied spirit. No wonder he couldn't figure her out. The astounding revelation rolled through his universe, an 8.0 earthquake rocking his world.

She read his horror and continued, "The spirit, after it departs the body, lives in a world of mental forms, an idealistic world of thought forms."

Her entire arm disappeared, then reappeared.

Ray was only slightly less stunned. He was seeing spirits. He had somehow developed the ability to perceive the spiritual realm. He must have bumped his head and not known it. He'd read about psychics gaining their gift after such an injury, and now he had the gift. That's why Alice had seemed so strange, he was communicating with a being on the Other Side.

"Now you try. Start with making your hand disappear."

When he looked down, to his amazement—no, it was much, much more than amazement—his hand disappeared. The full significance of his new understanding hit him—HE WAS DEAD.

He had never felt as sick as he felt at that moment. Nausea flooded his consciousness; his vision disintegrated; his world shattered into a thousand thousand pieces. Pictures. Memories. Thoughts. He was pummeled by the equivalent of a hundred television signals broadcasting into the center of his awareness at once. He was literally coming apart.

In the midst of the chaos, Alice's face appeared, steady and clear and loving. An act of pure will, an act of pure intention, placed her image there. Solid. Sturdy. Stable. Something to which he could cling. An inviting icon in a sea of disturbing images.

He vowed that, if the chaos ever subsided, he would pay close attention to her lessons. It was clear he needed her. The lessons now made sense: she had been trying to help him come to grips with his post-mortem, end-of-the-line, passed-away, disincarnate condition. She was there because he was dead.

In the back of his mind, all along, it had been there, a haunting suspicion that something was terribly, terribly wrong. The gaps in memory; the haunting, dream-like forest; the apparitions in the fog; the black clouds that threatened to drape him with veils of forgetfulness; the roller-coaster emotions; the grocery-list errand he could not remember; the important message he must deliver that skirted his awareness, eluding his grasp, refusing to be cornered; Chase, in the wedding dress, with the baby stroller; Hal, broken and limp, hanging from a cliff; the archetypal creature and the ghoulish figure that was his father. He had grown suspicious, but the dark heart of that suspicion was a truth from which he had run as hard as he could—he had refused to face his own death.

As Alice warned, emotions and desires had blinded him. She had also warned that attachment brought suffering, and now he understood—he was attached to his body, to his life, to the people in his life. And they all had been taken from him. He knew suffering.

The terrible truth had made its appearance and reality had delivered its painful message: *he was dead.*

17

Chase, asleep, her head resting on the edge of Ray's bed, startled when Randi entered. Her eyes were puffy, her skin creased with bedspread-pattern wrinkles; she was groggy and disoriented, the plight of the overly-tired when suddenly awakened.

"You okay?" Randi asked.

"Yeah, sure. I'm fine."

"Liar, liar."

Chase smiled shyly, through a yawn. "What a strange dream," she said. "Ray could hear me, but couldn't answer. It seemed so real. A frustrating dream."

Randi brushed a stray hair from Chase's face. She didn't know what to think about Chase's dream. Lucid dreaming, like most paranormal phenomena, was saddled with uncertainty, fleeting perceptions, faint hints, elusive intuitions. Many rejected the paranormal solely and entirely as a result of their strong need for certainty, their need for a reality map complete with marked boundaries. Researchers, like Les, couldn't provide that degree of certainty, they worked in the land of *maybe*. Though Randi hated to give Chase a *maybe*, she also didn't want to appear rude. "Maybe he *can* hear us," she replied.

"Really? Do you think it matters?" Chase asked. "I mean if we can communicate with him, will it make a difference?"

"Oh, Chase, I don't know. I have no idea." She didn't like the sound of her pessimism. "It couldn't hurt. The nurses might think we're nut cases, but I'm sure they've seen worse. Well, maybe they've seen worse."

Chase, emerging from her groggy state, smiled. "Imagine being a nurse, in intensive care. Oh, my God. Must be tough. To watch patients teeter between life and death. Dealing with families, like us, clueless, clinging to hope, scared out of our minds."

Randi studied Chase. "If things were different, we would be spending this time worrying about each other. You know, fretting over first impressions, tip-toeing around opinions."

"Yeah, you're right. I would probably be worried about what advice you would give him: 'Stay with her, kid, you got yourself a winner' or maybe something less flattering." She studied Randi, seeking a clue, any tiny hint. Would her future mother-in-law award her a thumbs–up or thumbs-down?

"Ray doesn't need my opinion when it comes to who he—" Randi trailed off. A beat later, she continued, with an ironic grin, "How long *have* you been dating?"

So, Chase mused, Ray hadn't told his mother everything; maybe he told her very little. Should she value the unexpected privacy? Or should she worry because he had not said more?

"Two, almost three, years," Chase answered. "Seems longer. We made plans once. Ray was going to phone you. Then we decided to postpone the Big Day until funding for the new business was in the bank."

"That's him. Always cautious. As though he expected fate to toss him a curve he couldn't handle." She glanced at his unmoving form and her voice cracked. "Maybe he was right."

Chase had no easy response, no words of comfort. Covering her distress, she navigated past tubes and wires and fluffed the pillow supporting Ray's head. She wasn't sure the nurses would approve. She didn't care, she had to do *something*.

"Questions," Chase said. "He always had questions. About how things worked. Why things were the way they were. There had to be a master plan, a reason behind everything."

"I suppose I didn't help. I never could answer his questions about my divorce. He had a difficult time understanding our little domestic disaster. Guess I never really understood it either."

"He never talked about your divorce."

Randi failed to hide her surprise. The marital break up had been a source of considerable upset, the cause of persistent turmoil. "Maybe I didn't screw him up after all," she said. A beat later, "Who am I kidding?"

"Hey, quit with the guilt trip. It's hard enough being responsible for our own actions, so don't even start thinking you're responsible for how someone else turned out. Ray always preached we decide who we are, we're not victims. Nobody creates us, not even God."

"He lost his faith, didn't he?"

"He didn't lose his faith, he tossed it. Dropped back twenty and punted. Too many gaping holes in the God logic for his taste. When it came to philosophy, he belonged to the school that claims if you kick it and it kicks back, it is real."

"A die-hard pragmatist."

"We disagreed on that. I'd rather not think that's the way life is," Chase said. "I'd rather hold out for a miracle." She took Ray's hand in hers.

"Me, too, dear," Randi responded. "Me, too."

They looked up in unison as Hal ushered James Perspy into the room. Perspy looked over his shoulder, checking to make sure he had escaped notice. If Hal was out of place in the hospital, a tree in an industrial park, James was a weed. Open-hearth cooking imbued his clothes with a persistent smoky aroma, his beard and hair were coiffed in hermit style, and his manner was reminiscent of an animal sniffing out its surroundings.

Chase offered her hand in greeting. James shook it absently, his attention zeroed in on Ray.

Randi shot Chase a frown. Chase, in turn, flashed Hal a look— *what the hell are you doing?*

Hal shrugged, then turned to watch Perspy probe Ray's anatomy with a gentle but professional touch.

When Perspy was satisfied with his exam, he squeezed between the head of the bed and the wall, cradled Ray's skull in his hands, gently massaged Ray's temples with his thumbs, and... hummed.

Or was he chanting? Hal wondered.

Chase, who had retreated to the far corner of the room, gestured impatiently to Hal: *get your ass over here.*

Randi also flagged Hal, mouthing "What's up?"

Hal gestured—*it's okay*—and returned his focus to Perspy as though telepathically tracking the unconventional guest, which, of course, was well beyond Hal's abilities. When it came to detecting psychic blips, he consistently struck out, failing to rise beyond wishful thinking.

James cocked his head, examining Chase and Randi. "Come, come here," he commanded in a gentle, but firm, voice.

Chase crossed the room, flashing Hal the evil eye: *you'll pay for this.*

"The thoughts and emotions of those close to him are very important. Grief, sadness, clinging—negative emotions—all impede his progress."

"Progress?" Chase whispered.

"James studied the Book of the Dead," Hal interjected.

Chase and Randi stared at Hal with slack-jawed horror.

"It's a book that prepares monks to guide departed souls as they leave this plane and go to—"

"Oh. Good. Just what we need," Chase snapped. "You did mention a little mumbo jumbo." The meaning of her look was clear: *Not what we need, Hal.*

Randi edged toward the door, on a clandestine mission to summon the head nurse. She figured the nurse's presence would discourage their unorthodox guest from engaging in any extreme mumbo jumbo, but, before she could slip out the door, Dr. Seidman entered. Randi immediately recognized she had encountered a be-careful-what-you-wish-for moment.

Seidman, spotting Perspy, scanned the proceedings-in-progress with a deliberate and suspicious gaze; a half-dozen unacceptable scenarios popped into his paranoid mind.

"Sssh," Randi hissed, her finger to her lips, nodding toward James. "Massage is the one therapy Ray insisted he couldn't live without—we figured it couldn't hurt."

Seidman regarded James with skepticism-on-steroids.

"No mediums, like we promised," Randi added.

Seidman raised ten fingers, mouthed "ten minutes," then spun smartly on the heels of his loafers and exited.

James followed the psychologist's departure with bemused disgust, then closed his eyes and concentrated. He reached out and placed Chase's hands on Ray's head, then covered her hands with his own. He gestured for Randi to hold Ray's hands and motioned for Hal to grab Ray's feet, which were secured to the bed with ankle braces to protect against involuntary spasms which might cause him harm.

"He seems to have very little attention on the body, almost none. He's lost, disoriented, trying to figure out what happened. I don't know for certain that he will return."

Randi bit her lower lip, fighting back tears.

"I wish I understood more...about the events taking place," James continued. "On a few occasions I've been able to establish communication with those who have passed on. For short periods. I can only imagine the same principles are at work with those stuck in between."

For the next five minutes, the room was silent, they were at a loss for words. As unorthodox as James appeared, they figured they had nothing to lose by letting him stay. At the very least, they were doing *something*. In the end, no one would criticize them for acting human, no one would criticize their desperate, futile, wacky attempts to handle their hopes and fears. Later, they might look back on this moment with embarrassment. When they recalled their emotional weakness, they might feel they had acted unwisely, might feel they had succumbed to a desperate silliness, might feel they had been the collective victims of a brain fade episode, but, at the moment, the unspoken consensus was *what the hell*.

Dr. Seidman reappeared in less than ten minutes, and, with

a brusque gesture, signaled the end of their little séance. His thinly-veiled disgust showed he was well aware no massage therapy had taken place; they had been engaging in tomfoolery which had no place in the hospital, in *his* hospital.

Hal thought he witnessed James' placid features harden with stony intention. He made a mental note: if James' mojo was working, Seidman's ass would end up in ICU within twenty-four hours. The hard edge disappeared and James, once again the chilled-out hermit, ushered the entire group, including Seidman, out of the room.

"Let's give him some peace and quiet," James said. "There's nothing to be gained by our crowding around. Is there a venue where we can purchase a spot of tea?"

Hal knew, intuitively, that James was shepherding Seidman's bad vibes out of Ray's room; he also figured out it had been *his* thoughts, not James' intentions, that willed Seidman's demise and it dawned on him that such thoughts would only muddy the psychic terrain Ray must navigate in his disembodied state. Seidman, himself, was incapable of hampering the healing process, but the negative thoughts he provoked in others were land mines strewn about the psychic landscape. Hal smiled, pleased with himself — he was figuring out the esoteric realms.

Chase checked out his grin, curious. He wrapped a big arm around her shoulder, but said nothing. Perspy slowed and looked to Seidman who lagged behind. "Are you coming?"

In the cafeteria, James charmed the help into locating some green tea, although it was the chilled-and-bottled variety, not the traditional bag designed for brewing. Chase, watching, discovered James possessed a fair amount of worldly charm under his fresh-out-of-hibernation appearance. Did he hide his true nature on purpose, or was it out of neglect?

Once they had settled at a table, Seidman pressed James, "Sir, what line of work...are you in?"

"Pediatrics," James replied.

Seidman's cynical look took on the intensity of a laser. *Was the peculiar man mocking him?* "Pediatrics?" he challenged.

"I was a practicing physician, for many years, then I concluded something was missing."

Clearly, Seidman had not anticipated discovering an M.D. lurking beneath Perspy's scruffy beard. His surprise took center stage.

"We fail to treat the complete patient," Perspy continued. "More and more, we simply medicate the symptoms and ignore the underlying causes. I sold my practice and traveled. Spent time in the Orient where I became conversant with alternative treatment modalities."

"Holistic medicine," Seidman said, his tone colored with a faint hint of disdain. "You no longer practice?"

"No, as I said, I decided to take a few years off. Followed the edict 'heal thyself, physician.'"

"And how's that going?" Randi asked.

"Quite well. I'm pleased. Within a year or two I anticipate opening a new practice."

"You'll return to treating children?" Chase asked.

James responded with an enigmatic grin, "Given we're all children, I guess you could say that."

"So, Mr—er, Doctor—" Seidman stammered.

"Dr. James Perspy," James introduced himself formally.

Before Seidman could continue, Eva, Chase's sister, arrived with Bren, her daughter, trailing behind. Eva squeezed Chase's hand in a silent gesture of sympathy, not wishing to interrupt.

Bren, a free spirit unshackled by conventional constraints and not yet programmed into the straitjacket of tact, took one look at Perspy, squinted, and raised her lip in an exaggerated *who the hell is this guy?* greeting.

Perspy flashed her a "goofy face."

She shot him a *yeah, right* look.

He countered.

She fired off another volley of dismissive expressions.

He "rapped" awkwardly for comic effect, "I'm looking at this ugly face, thinkin' what a waste."

"Seein' your pose, makes me think you got beat with an ugly hose," Bren countered.

"You better leave post haste, or find some better taste."

"For all that you knows, I am the one with the best...best, uh...toes." She giggled, pleased with her silly rhyme. She slapped the low five Perspy offered, followed by a high five. In a matter of a minute, they had become solid pals.

It was clear Perspy was not only a pediatrician, but a pediatrician with a remarkable bedside manner. When it came to rapport with his young patients, it was obvious he was a grand master.

A nurse eating at a nearby table, overhearing the rap, flashed James a smile and rendered a verdict, "Better keep your day job."

James winked in acknowledgment.

Eva, uncertain whether she should be pleased or dismayed with her daughter's behavior, inched in Bren's direction, seeking to regain control by re-establishing proximity. Bren inched away. For a second it appeared they would circle the table in their covert game of chase. When Eva realized the mother-daughter drama had become the center of attention and the subtlety of her pursuit had failed to fool anyone, she stopped and whispered to Chase, "How's Ray doing?"

Seidman raised his hand, signaling his desire for a halt in the conversation. He turned to confront Perspy, "You're the doctor here, what's *your* prognosis?"

James ignored Seidman's latent hostility and searched for a truthful, but tactful, response. "It's too early to make a definitive prediction. We do not possess sufficient data. We should pay a visit to the scene of the accident."

His suggestion was met with blank stares. "In order to assess exactly what happened to Ray, we must start at the beginning," he explained.

18

Ray's abrupt discovery of his post-mortem condition set his universe spinning; if one modeled his awareness using Alice's illustrated sphere, that sphere was now glowing and churning, a roiling globe of mental energy. The only way to ride out the storm—the images, thoughts, and nightmares besieging his mind—was to go face to face with Alice. He did his best to anchor his consciousness to her compassionate presence.

Stealing a glance at his hand, recalling its previous disappearance, he faced a terrifying realization: the body he now possessed was nothing more than an idea. He was clinging to his imagination.

This body he was "dreaming" was nothing more than a mental construct fading like aging emulsion on degraded film stock, leaving nothing but... Nothing. If the physical body was gone, dust to dust, and the mental body was a chimera, what was left? Nothing? No thing? Once again, he faced the unsettling idea of the No Thing—it was an idea that stalked his sanity in the darkest recesses of his unconscious.

"It's not easy to confront the idea of a no thing," Alice said. "So let's start with somethings."

Her matter-of-fact and cheery attitude slowed his mind's frantic chatter. Apparently, she was no stranger to this surreal outpost of Purgatory; she was an experienced guide on Dante's tour. No longer did he resent her overbearing attitude: that which angered him previously was now his life raft. No longer did he look for cracks in her argument: that argument was all that remained to sustain his sanity.

She smiled, reading his thoughts.

He realized, for the first time, that his inner sentiments, his very thoughts, were on public display in this post-mortem realm—that was how she had been able to keep one step ahead of him, anticipating his arguments and his emotions.

"This is quite unexpected," he said. "I must admit, it is also terribly upsetting. Someone should warn people. Someone should help." He had been a slow learner, but now, finally, he understood. "That's what you've been doing, isn't it?"

He hadn't said a word, it was as though his thoughts were spoken. *Was that how telepathy worked?* he reflected. Perhaps this was a natural state of affairs that was hidden from our ordinary and limited human awareness.

Before he could sort out the mechanics of telepathy, a glimmer of an idea, a slippery, hard-to-grasp, twinkling notion skimmed through his consciousness, a smooth stone skipping over a glassy pond—*he was responsible for the condition in which he found himself.* His own actions and decisions had landed him in a state in which he could be shocked, confused, and disoriented. He had, ironically, set himself up for this moment and now he was paying the price.

"Are we ready to continue?" she asked.

"I have a choice?" he joked, secretly hoping there was a way to turn back the clock, an option that allowed him to step out of the nightmare. His communication was instant, telepathic; though he had only thought the words, it was easier for him to consider he was speaking them.

"The transition from nothing to something is as simple as a thought," she said, clicking her fingers. "All things you perceive are thought forms. When you see me, you are looking at a projected thought form."

She disappeared, then reappeared next to the fireplace, disappeared again and reappeared by the door.

"You see how easy," she said.

He nodded, but assured himself *he* was not about to try any disappearing tricks.

"Get the idea of a balloon. Place it out here." She pointed to a spot a foot off the table.

His initial attempt was tentative, half-hearted; he antici- pated failure. And yet, his imagination conjured into existence a balloon, a wobbly, sickly-shade-of-purple balloon, floating above the table. But was it really there? Was it in any sense real?

"Very good. I could see that," Alice said, encouraging and gently leading. "That's all there is to creation. Project a thought and perceive that thought. You are the Nothing that creates the Some- thing."

Ray puzzled, though he was not totally unfamiliar with the concept. After Professor Kidner resigned, Ray had looked into the philosophy called Idealism. There was Platonic Idealism: Plato imagined the universe was constructed from ideal forms, primal thoughts; physical manifestations were a poor copy of these primary ideal forms. Then there was Bishop Berkeley, the seventeenth-century Christian philosopher who argued we live in a subjective universe and participate in creating the world we experi- ence; he advanced the philosophical argument that everything we know is subjective and further postulated that God had created that which we held in common, the physical universe, in his role as Supreme Thinker, Master Creator of thought forms.

Buddhism, which pre-dated both Plato and Berkeley, taught something quite similar: the universe was an illusion, it did not exist beyond our thoughts; we all shared in the illusion, one gigantic virtual reality.

In spite of his hitting the philosophy books, Idealism remained difficult for Ray to grasp; its premises were slippery, hard to hold onto in the face of the harsh reality of the physical world that not only did not appear to respond to our thoughts and wishes, but which seemed to make a habit of crushing our dreams. In contrast, the materialists rested their argument on solid ground, literally.

"Though I've heard of Idealism—" he said.

"Only now have you begun to experience it." She searched for the word-pictures that would make the idea easy to grasp. "You have become confused by your entanglement with the thought forms that have become our physical universe. It is a case of a creator becoming confused with and identified with that which he created. A form of attachment."

"Attachment?"

"Yes, for example, you're emotionally attached to your physical body, which is why you cling so passionately to a copy of it."

He dared a glance at his hand. It appeared more solid than the pathetic balloon he had dreamed up—*but was it, really?* As he considered the thought, his fingers became transparent, then started to disappear altogether. It was an experience sure to launch a materialist into a world-class nightmare, an experience that purchased Ray's imagination a ticket on the express train to delirium and insanity.

"This is not a dream," Alice said. "It is as real, even more real, than what you previously considered to be your waking life. Over a very long period of time, there's much you have forgotten: you have forgotten who you are and you have forgotten it is your thoughts that create the world in which you live."

"That doesn't make a bit of sense. Did I make you up? No, I don't think so."

"No, you didn't. We agree to see thoughts. I see thoughts you create. You see thoughts I create. We live in a universe we create together."

"So I'm dreaming, but not dreaming alone."

"When a person departs the body, like you have—"

"When someone dies," he interjected, though a part of him still challenged the reality of his own passing.

"Yes, when they die, they're released into a world that consists of their thoughts, their memories, their fears—"

"The wolf chased me. But I'm not terrified of wolves. Nature's creature are a valued part of my life."

"But was it really the wolf that terrified you?"

"No, you're right, it was the—I feared the sickness consuming the beast." His thoughts hung up, he couldn't muster an explanation. "The ghoulish man. I feared him. When he struck me, I felt it. The blow was real. The hideous figure, who was my father, was really here in this realm or plane, or whatever you call it. He was here, wasn't he?"

She nodded. "He was here. And in his case, as well, it was the sickness that repulsed you and made you afraid. In this stage of your journey, fear finds a life of its own. You see what others intend more clearly. There's a transparency to their thoughts and intentions, though, even here, not everything is as it seems."

"It's not all angels and peace and love and light in this place, is it?"

"No, it isn't. It's a world as complex, with as many faces, as the one from which you departed."

"But *you* are here to help."

"Yes, I am." She appeared to glow with compassion, a grace Ray had never before witnessed. She continued, "There was an even greater fear you could not face: the fear of losing those close to you."

"Chase? You mean Chase? Yes. I am afraid of losing... She was here, also, but not like my father. They were different."

"That's right. She wasn't here in the same way he was."

He didn't want to think about Chase. Contemplating losing her was more than he was prepared to handle, but he was left with no choice: a flurry of mental pictures chronicling the entire time they had spent together flashed before him, scene by scene, as though an unseen cosmic projectionist decided to screen Ray's favorite home movies. Fear of losing Chase *had* clouded his reason, inhibited his perceptions, slowed his thinking. Now, a numbing emptiness, a vacuum of regret, threatened to suck him into its barren embrace. He knew, intuitively, that once he entered the vacuum, he faced doing hard time. He would serve a lengthy sentence filled with grief and despair. The baby carriage, he speculated, represented—in some other-worldly language of symbols—their unrealized dreams; the carriage symbolized opportunities he had failed to bring to fruition. He could have and should have had a child with Chase, but his all-consuming business concerns, his incessant craving for worldly security, his obsessive planning and compulsive need for control, all defeated his dreams—as he had defeated her dreams. He was sucked into a vortex of guilt and regret. As the swirling tunnel gained momentum, it pulled him down.

Alice snapped her fingers, "Whoa. Stop. Let that go." She captured his attention and moved in front of the teaching screen, which, it occurred to Ray, was part of his imagination as well.

"The mental body in which you wrap yourself is a memory, a memory so solid, so dense, it appears real. It seems to exist on its own, separate from your attention, without your involvement, but, as you have seen, you are creating the mental body and you can make it disappear. Frequently, the recently-deceased, like yourself, suffer horrible confusion. Though they seem to possess their earthly body, they find themselves in a world of images. They cling desperately to the image of their old body, holding fast to the old identity, while all around them, reality is fluid and constantly changing. The afterlife resembles a virtual reality created by their thoughts co-mingled with the thoughts of others. It is a condition which confuses them to the point of despair. We have become so attached to our physical bodies, that, when we are set free, we continue to conceive ourselves to be weighed down and unable to create freely.

She illustrated the energy body, the mental body, separating from the physical body, with the spirit encompassed in the disincarnate mental energy body.

"Those who depart the flesh body—"

"Those who die," he added for emphasis.

"—also see thought forms projected by other disembodied spirits. At times the images are welcoming, at times frightening, at times meant to confuse, to trick, to deceive. A recently disembodied spirit can find himself in a condition that resembles the traditional concept of hell."

"One *can* feel a little queasy," he replied, imagining himself teetering on the edge of a precipice, staring down into the mythical hell, vertigo raging. It was there, far below, that the vortex of guilt and regret and shame had sought to transport him. If not for Alice, that was where he would have ended up. He wondered if that was the fate that awaited those in his condition who were not fortunate enough to enlist Alice's help. Was he looking at the fate that befell those who walked past Alice without bothering to stop and chat?

"The recently-deceased must quickly become oriented or fall into a hellish state where uncontrolled images and thoughts and emotions drive them a bit mad."

"Unless they meet a guide like yourself."

"Unless they are aware enough to control their thoughts, they may fall prey to deception."

"Do you deceive me? You could be a devil pretending to be an angel, or a pathological invention of my sick imagination."

"That's right. That's why, some day, you must walk the path yourself. If you do not know your own mind and your own history, if you fail to 'know thyself' intimately and fully, if you are unable to control your thoughts or recognize the thoughts of another, if you are unable to disentangle from the physical and unable to end compulsive attachment—then you shall suffer, and you shall continue to suffer, on the wheel of birth and death."

The slippery thought that had appeared earlier and refused to be cornered—the idea that somehow he was responsible for his own condition—took the stage for an encore. He was a willing passenger on the wheel of birth and death as a result of his own actions. Our choices in the present created our future and led to the cause and effect relationship some called karma.

The idea took on shape and ballast, but then vanished. He understood how he could create a mental image; his imagination was fine. In his head, in his personal subjective universe, he *was* a creator, but that creation, that subjective reality, was not really real.

Or was it? He was no longer certain. In this cabin, on this mountain, with Alice, his subjective world seemed plenty real. Alice, too, seemed real. If he was seeing her thoughts, if the Alice he saw was nothing but the projection of a projection, then he was sharing in *her* subjective world. And the cabin...hadn't they agreed it was real?

"That's right, this cabin is a subjective reality we share. Together, we create the walls of the cabin, we agree to see the walls, and we agree we occupy the space between those walls."

"Agree? We didn't sit down and plan this. It doesn't make sense to say we agree."

"For the most part, I'm agreeing with you: agreeing with the subjective world you make real, automatically, subconsciously, the result of memories you summon back into existence. Like screening an old film, only, in this case, we exist inside the film."

"I'm with you—if this all takes place in imagination—but what about the real world, the objective world?" he asked.

"An objective world separate from our subjective awareness? That is fantasy."

She had said something very much like this earlier; he didn't get it then, he didn't get it now.

"Our combined thought, when agreed upon by many, many conscious beings, becomes solid. That our combined thought is solid and persists through time, however, does not make it objective. It remains subjective, what we call the inter-subjective. The inter-subjective is the combination, the sum, of many subjective universes acting in concert."

"But objective reality—"

"When people say 'objective reality,' they really mean the inter-subjective," she said. "Though this cabin appears solid to you... Look at that wall. If you look closely, you will see how it is only our thought."

He looked closely. The wall grew thin, transparent.

"You are accustomed to agreeing that walls are solid, you constantly agree that it is so. That is reality for you. Over a very long time, agreeing with a great number of others, you came to accept

the existence of the physical, as though the physical existed independent of any thought on your part.

"You agreed, little by little by little, and those agreements
added up, one by one, and became more and more solid and you
considered, more and more, that the world 'out there' existed
independent of your participation. In Idealism, what you consider
to be true becomes your reality. If you believe, more and more, that
the world exists independent of your involvement, that belief
becomes manifest. After a while, you find you have agreed to play
no causative role, you have agreed to become the effect of that
which you helped create."

Ray nodded, only partially understanding.

"The physical becomes an automatic creation, created by
you and for you, so that you might share a common world with
others, a common playing field."

"A playing field that doesn't disappear easily."

"What good would it be, what fun would it be, to have a
universe that was always disappearing? It would have little use. In
order to achieve a common universe that we can share, we must
create that universe so that it persists, so that it appears solid, so
that it looks the same to all of us. It is a very precise creation, it is not
in the least haphazard, random, or coincidental."

"A giant virtual reality," he mumbled, thinking to himself.
We're disembodied programmers creating a vast virtual reality in
which we play games with one another. That's what it all amounts
to, if she's right. And the virtual reality looks the same to everyone,
he thought, reminding himself of Relativity, the theory that argues
the laws of physics appear the same to all observers in their reference frame.

"Any one observer must observe the same laws as other
observers or we do not have a common universe," Alice said. "It's
that simple. You have your own universe, your personal subjective universe, in which you can create anything you want, in which
your imagination can run wild. In the worlds you can dream, there
are no laws of physics to be obeyed."

She sketched the sphere. "But when you and I create a world together, when our worlds overlap"—the two spheres she sketched overlapped—"we create an inter-subjective world. We must have laws to tell us how that overlap region is going to look, how it's going to work. We must be in agreement."

"Yes, I understand, but—"

"When it comes to our physical universe, we have a huge, huge number of participants, an incredibly large number of beings creating together. So the laws must be precise and we must have a beginning so simple we can easily agree—"

A simple beginning? Some scientists argued our complex universe started from simple patterns, simple laws called algorithms. From such simple beginnings arose complexity. Maybe they were on to something, Ray mused.

"That's right," Alice said, completing his thought. "Similar to a computer program that starts with simple patterns and simple rules for how those patterns multiply, generation after generation."

"From simple creations and simple agreements, a complex universe evolves," he added, for the first time getting a handle on the concept.

"Yes, complexity arises from simple rules followed over and over again. These few simple rules—rules based on the patterns consciousness creates—when combined and mixed and repeated, over and over again, generate a vast number of forms."

Ray struggled with the idea. It seemed she was describing how one simple thought, a simple shape, for example, like the sphere of the balloon, could combine with another simple shape, like a sphere created by another spirit. Those two spheres could be co-mingled to bring about additional forms, the collision and inter-section of the spheres bringing about new shapes. He listened as she continued.

"Many creators, working with the same simple shapes and simple rules, cause the number of forms to mushroom beyond our ability to keep track."

"And..."

"Spirit becomes lost, disoriented, entangled in the vast multitude of forms. Spirit, besieged by complexity, is soon overwhelmed and becomes forgetful, loses track of who it is and where it is, becomes lost in its own creation."

"You mean spirit becomes lost in the creation it shares with others," Ray added, imagining what would happen if hundreds of beings, like himself, were to fill the cabin, each one creating balloons, spherical thought forms, and how those spherical energy shells, intersecting and interacting, would result in a myriad of complex shapes.

"Yes, spirit conceives itself to be trapped inside the common universe, the physical universe."

"Surely you have told me more than you intended. Is that which you are telling me not the beginning and the end of the path?"

"No, we are nowhere near the end, you must walk the path yourself. My description may dispel confusion, but it is you who must untie the knots of entanglement that keep you chained, the knots that bind your personal subjective universe to the collective physical universe. Each individual must free himself. There's no magic wand one waves over the universe to rescue its inhabitants from their entrapment in their convoluted creation."

"It is impossible to walk the path for another?"

"For a spirit to disentangle itself from its own thought forms, a spirit must discover the exact path that led it to its present condition. You have a great deal of work to do, my friend."

She winked, not unkindly.

Once again, when she explained the workings of the universe in detail, the explanation made sense. Ray, however, was left with an uneasy feeling. Though he knew she painted a picture intended to assist him, there was still the practical reality of his unwanted situation, a daunting reality he found almost impossible to face: *he had died.*

Was Alice drawing a map to the next life? he wondered. Had he crossed the threshold past which there was no return?

19

Snow tires armed with porcelain studs gripped the ice as the four-wheel-drive Jeep wound through the pass, climbing switchback after switchback. Hal was at the wheel, while James rode shotgun. Chase sat in back, taking in scenery: bluish-green pines silhouetted against blazing white snow, the outlines of their dark green crowns stark against azure skies, as though they were pasted on, cutouts in a school kid's montage.

The cold air whipping past chafed Chase's fair complexion. *It feels good to be alive*, she thought, a sentiment which unleashed a flood of guilt—feeling alive was something Ray could no longer share with her. For the first time since the accident, she slip-slided into the shadows of doubt. James was right: Ray's recovery was uncertain; he might never regain consciousness. She was plagued with questions: *could she live with that?; what about her unborn child?*

Hal executed a controlled skid off the main road. The Jeep bumped and slid down a seldom-used mining road, plowing through foot-high drifts for a quarter mile. He pulled off, stopping downhill from the tree that had broken the Explorer's fall. They hopped out and, without a moment's hesitation, scaled the steep hillside. Hal spotted Chase from behind, providing security in case she slipped; but she didn't fall, she took to the grade with a mountain goat's nonchalance. Within sight of the damaged tree, however, she slowed. Her momentum, which the altitude, the steep grade, and the icy footing had failed to inhibit, was curbed by raw emotion. She paused to quell her rising anguish and whipped out a cell phone.

"Let's make sure we have service," she said. A beat later, she heard the ring and signaled a "thumbs up." She knew that Randi, maintaining a vigil at Ray's bedside, manned a companion cell phone. Perspy had insisted on posting a sentry at Ray's side while they re-visited the crash site. "In the event I need a quick update on Ray's condition," he had explained.

"You okay, Mom?" Chase said, when Randi answered. She had grown comfortable enough to call Randi mom—though she was aware the continued existence of their relationship was contingent upon Ray's recovery.

James and Hal listened covertly as Chase touched bases with Randi.

"We're okay. It's cold. Pretty, but not real friendly." Chase smiled at her choice of words *not real friendly*—an understatement. The site possessed an unforgiving stark reality; *all the hopeful wishes and prayers in the world would not make a dent in this pile of rocks*, she thought. "Well, you let us know if anything changes and we need to get back down there, okay? Bye."

She glanced over her shoulder and found James Perspy hanging the tiny monk on a broken branch. Actually, it was Hal, with his six-foot-four reach, who placed the doll; James directed his efforts.

"Okay. We're here," Chase said with forced cheeriness. "Whazzup?"

Perspy feigned a stern rebuke, then chuckled.

"What's so funny?" Chase shot back.

"You. Me. Mostly how serious we are."

Hal puzzled: *this wasn't supposed to be a picnic, what did James expect?* Was he toying with them, taking advantage of their misfortune? Annoyed, Hal warned, "Don't start in with the 'this is an illusion' speech. Do you have an idea, or not?"

"Mostly not," James replied. He refused to surrender to Hal's plea for a sober demeanor. "We're winging it. Strictly flying by the seat of our pants."

"Wait a second. A little guidance here," Chase interjected. "This stuff you study—"

"Buddhist teachings tell us life continues after death. The Buddha had clear recollections of his previous lives and taught death is not the end of the road."

"Yeah, that's nice." The sarcasm was out of character for Chase; she wrote it off to stress. "Ray isn't dead, unless you know something I don't."

"He's not dead, but history tells us that patients close to death, like Ray, those who experience nearly dying, return with stories of a world very much like the Tibetan Bardo."

"Am I supposed to know what that is?" she asked.

"Bardo. One of the stages after death," James replied. He paused, saw that she demanded more, and continued, "Those who experience near death... The lessons they bring back from the encounter echo Buddhist teachings: the essential qualities in life are love, compassion, knowledge, and wisdom."

"Your point?"

"Ray may encounter a similar experience. At first he will not know where he is or the truth of his condition. Then it will dawn on him that he is dead."

"Nearly dead," Chase added.

"Though we may not see him, he may... He may be able to access our thoughts. What we think—"

"Whatever. What do we do?"

Perspy chuckled at her impatience, appreciated her call for action, and respected her disdain for theory. "His attention may fix on this crash site. He'll try to sort out what happened. All we can do is be here and allow our presence to be a beacon. We'll clear our minds—"

"As if that'll happen," Chase mumbled.

"What?"

"I've never cleared my mind," she said. "I'm not certain I can. Tell someone not to think of a pink elephant and the next thing you know, they can't think of anything *but* a pink elephant."

"Good. Think of a pink elephant, or don't think of a pink elephant. That will be fine," Perspy replied.

Hal puzzled at Chase's sarcasm, her shortness with Perspy. It wasn't like her. One never knew how people would react under stress. "Chase, you and Ray had a ritual for ridding yourselves of the day's distractions, for quieting the noise. He told me—"

"Yes. We did. I'll try that."

Hal and James nodded in unison—*fine*.

"James, this Bardo. What's it like?" Hal asked.

"At first the deceased does not recognize his condition, and he wanders about, confused. When he realizes his fate, he finds himself in a world of thoughts and images."

Chase and Hal traded glances, nodded.

James continued, "Symbolic visions and hallucinations appear. These are karmic reflexes. Thought forms. If he is fortunate, he realizes his thoughts create his world."

"The-world-is-an-illusion bit?" Hal said, feigning annoyance.

"Something along those lines," Perspy responded, returning Hal's smile. "At first there may be happy and glorious visions, then terrifying visions may cause him to flee. He must recognize his own fears."

"And then..."

"He realizes death resembles a flame passing from wick to wick, his future stretches out in front of him. But, before rebirth, he undergoes many trials and views many things that frighten and challenge him. He must recognize karmic creations are the products of his own mind, though this is not as easy as it sounds, as it can be difficult to sort out cause and effect. The manner in which he completes these lessons determines how he is to be reborn, or if he is to be reborn at all."

"Or if he will return and just be Ray?" Chase asked.

"I know very little about those who visit the other side and return. I've heard stories. So I can only speculate," James replied.

"But you know this stuff works?" Hal asked.

"Yes and no. I'm not a master, but I know the principles are sound. My own experience has shown me that. Over thousands of years, however, the original teachings were altered, so it is difficult to find the pure lessons."

"The teachings got watered down?" Hal asked.

"You could put it that way."

"About this Bardo book," Chase interjected, "how can these monks know this stuff unless they die?"

"There's not a one of us that has not died many, many times," James replied.

"We're hampered by rotten memories," Hal chided.

"Very bad memories, amnesia," James added. "To answer your question, the descriptions of the afterlife are given to us by monks who have spent lifetimes perfecting their awareness so they can pass easily from one state to another. After you depart the body, while you are in the intermediate stage, your memory becomes many times more lucid."

Chase toyed with a thought: "So, if this guy, this Buddha, lives many lives, he should still be around. Somewhere. Right?"

"Yes," James replied. "Your point?"

"You were saying the lessons were changed, so maybe it's time for a fresh version. You know, if he's still around."

Perspy smiled. "You catch on quickly. Your suggestion is exactly what I've been thinking, but I've no idea where—"

"Figures," Chase said. "As soon as you get lost, the map is nowhere to be found." She made an effort to resurrect her earlier optimism. "When Ray comes back, maybe he'll bring the map."

Perspy nodded. "Let's be still. Maybe our presence will be a sign he will recognize."

20

"You cannot stay forever," Alice said, "on this mountain, in this cabin. You will grow tired of such a small universe. Besides, there are those who will not allow—"

"I'm not sure I understand," Ray said. "Where I should go?"

"The decision is yours," she replied. "But we must hurry."

"I'm not sure I understand...how thought works."

He had not spoken aloud. He exchanged thoughts with Alice, not words. For the first time, he became aware of how fast she moved the dialogue; she was in a hurry and he was going to have to keep up.

"Let us review. I will try to be more clear."

She sketched an illustration which lifted off the screen and floated in mid air. "The screen was a device to which you were accustomed, it fit within your reality. Now that you know you are viewing my thoughts, we no longer need it."

She created a sphere, then a second. She pointed to the first. "Imagine this sphere contains your awareness, your personal universe. It can expand or contract, holding everything you imagine or perceive."

She turned to the second sphere. "This is my universe. The two universes are separate. My universe is not your universe. I do not perceive what you perceive. You do not perceive what I perceive. We exist in two completely separate universes."

The spheres, symbolic of their respective personal universes, floated toward one another until they partially overlapped.

She pointed to the overlap. "Here a part of your universe exists in common with my universe. In that common space, if we agree, we can create common objects."

In the overlapping space, a cabin appeared, a miniature version of the cabin they presently occupied.

"When we share a space and see one another's thoughts— we have a common universe." She glanced at Ray, hoping to discover comprehension; after all, this was a review of her earlier lesson.

"I don't remember agreeing," Ray thought.

"You don't remember, this is true. Those agreements are as old as the universe, a universe much older than scientists imagine. The original agreements became automatic as, at that time, in the beginning, we agreed there would be time and our basic agreements would persist throughout that time. When the basic agreements were locked in, they became automatic, and one no longer needed to be constantly aware of their existence."

A dozen spheres popped into existence, then a dozen more, all overlapping in a small glowing region.

"Just as you and I can agree, so, too, any number of individuals can agree: hundreds, thousands, millions, and more. In order for such co-creation to work, the universe we share must have specific laws on which we agree."

"The laws of physics," Ray added, starting to grasp the concept, if not the reality.

"That's right. Discovering the laws of physics is a way of discovering the nature of the agreements. They are the same. When we understand the laws, we understand our agreements, we understand why everyone perceives objects in the same way."

Ray recalled the professor. Alice finished his thought, "This is what the Buddha meant when he said our world was an illusion. He did not mean the universe did not exist, he meant the universe was our shared thoughts, a common illusion. It does not exist separate from our collective thought."

The spheres disappeared and were replaced by three overlapping spheres. In one sphere, a purple balloon appeared; in another, a red box; in yet another, a yellow pyramid. The region in which they overlapped remained empty.

Ray understood: three spirits, each creating a thought form in their own universe, a thought form the others did not perceive.

She moved the ball, the pyramid, and the box into the overlapping region.

Again, Ray understood: when thought forms were created in shared space, with shared energy and matter, they became what we call the objective world: an objective world that did not exist, other than as shared thought forms; an objective world that did not exist without the subjective.

She pointed to the common region. "This shared space is what we call our universe."

"What was the purpose? Why did we—"

"To play a game."

"A game? Like I'm going to believe that. Not."

"If you want to play ball with friends, you must all be on the same field, you must agree to the same rules, you must agree to use a ball you can all see, you must play your position. When do we have the most fun? When we are playing, right?"

"Life is not always a game," he argued.

"Life is always a game. When we become unable or unwilling to play, or fail to recognize we are in a game, then life no longer seems like play. But it is still a game."

She waved her hand, the spheres all collapsed into one sphere, a small sphere glowing so brilliantly it was nearly impossible to behold. The sphere expanded and expanded. For a moment, Ray was reminded of the big bang theory.

"The shared universe became so desirable that our attention became fixed on it, we lost sight of our own universes. The collective thought forms became more and more valuable, cherished and desired. The desire to possess these forms resulted in our becoming subservient to the agreements we created with others. It was not long before we became prisoners of our desires, entangled in the collective thought forms, attached to them."

"Entangled?"

"The forms became more valuable than the spirits who created them. That which was created became more valuable than the creator. Desire led to our attachment to the shared illusion, which, in turn, led to our suffering."

She paused to see if he was following, then continued, "Because we create these forms together with other spirits, they do not belong to us alone. They are shared possessions, not private possessions. Thus they can be taken from us, thus we suffer loss."

"So there is a price for creating collectively?"

"Yes. If we create in our personal universe, we own our creations. But when we create shared objects with others, we do not exert full control over them. Thus there may be loss."

Ray saddened for an instant, glimpsing fully, for the first time, the origin of mankind's struggle over possessions.

Alice continued, "These forms, which we do not create alone, may differ from our own personal ideal forms, causing us to suffer displeasure. In our own universe, we create as we wish. When we create with others, the results may vary and we may not like everything that is created."

"Thus imperfection and displeasure are an intrinsic part of the collective universe."

"Only if we fail to appreciate and admire the creations of others," she replied.

Ray sensed there was an important lesson in her simple statement, a clue to the source of her non-critical compassion. *Only if we fail to appreciate and admire the creations of others*, he repeated to himself. That explained so much he had pondered previously. The constant battle between men about who was right, whose creations, whose visions, were to be accepted as reality.

"The forms may be hoarded, creating the illusion of scarcity, leading us to suffer want and envy," she said. "Such suffering comes about when we forget we can create at will, in our own universe, and when we forget we have, collectively, created the forms we covet and are capable of creating an abundance of those forms."

"This does not seem like a game," Ray added.

"It is a game of have and not have. But when we forget it is a game, a game we created, we suffer."

Her lessons were so different, so new, and yet, at the same time, the knowledge was ancient, a river of truth running through all time. For a fleeting moment, the veil parted and Ray's consciousness flowed in that river.

Alice drew a deep breath; her patience was paying off.

"What about God?" he asked.

"If God is a Creator and we are created in his image, then we would be creators as well," she replied.

It was a new concept for Ray. There were those who imagined God created us, as bodies. Which, if one understood biology at all, made little sense. The manner in which new bodies were created was well established, he thought with a smirk. In the past, Ray had little time for such apparently flawed religious concepts. But the idea that a Creator created creators—in His own image, so to speak—was an idea he could entertain. When he had time. He set it aside to be explored later as he turned his attention back to Alice.

"This universe," she continued, "as remarkable and complex as it is, is limited and restricted. The physical universe is the least common denominator of all our creating."

She projected hundreds of spheres overlapping in one small region. "Many creators, one common creation."

A nagging question crept into Ray's thoughts. He had often heard the expression, "We are One. One Cosmic Consciousness." Alice's explanation contradicted this belief.

She anticipated his unspoken question and answered, "You are you. Not me. We come to this universe as individuals. That which comes before...does not concern us now."

The idea that we were one, that upon death our individuality dissolved into one cosmic consciousness, into a sea of energy, was a common New Age belief. At one time, he recalled, he had toyed with that belief; but here he was, on the other side, and he had not dissolved into a blob of oneness. As Alice pointed out, she was not him and he was not her.

What brought about the belief in the One, in monism, as it was sometimes called? He looked to Alice.

This time, she did not feed him an answer. "It's time you started thinking," she said.

What was the All One? If we were not One, if we were not a single cosmic consciousness, what made us think we were? If Alice was right, we created the universe, then deceived ourselves into thinking it created us. What was there about that illusion? What did we share? What did we have in common?

He projected spheres into space, as Alice had done. Multiple spheres representing the overlapping awareness of multiple spirits. He collapsed the spheres into one tiny common sphere. That was it—we have the physical universe in common. That which we share, that which is one, is one universe.

He glowed with the excitement of discovery.

"We created a common universe," he said to Alice. "That's what makes us think we are one. We share *one* universe. If we identify with that which we created—like you said, confusing creator and created—then we think we are one, one universe."

Ray grasped the slippery concept, but expressing it was not as easy. If she was correct, these were the basic dynamics of how we came to exist in this universe and how we subsequently became forgetful and failed to recognize our present condition.

Alice projected another visual metaphor: an hourglass. She vanished the top half, leaving only the pinched opening of the neck and the bottom half.

"Above the hourglass, individuals are separate, creating personal universes. Like individual grains of sand free of constraints. Without a container."

"Think of the tiny opening in the hourglass neck as the portal into this universe. Metaphorically speaking, individuals fall through the tiny opening and into the bottom half. Each one passes through the same narrow portal, a common keyhole into a new universe."

Alice talking about keyholes and portals reminded him of Carroll's book, of Alice chasing rabbits wearing pocket watches down rabbit holes. Were the metaphors of fantasy and fiction our long-lost past resurfacing, poking through the veil of our amnesia?

"Perhaps what we share in common is entering through the same door—though it is not a door at all. Below the neck, in the bottom of the hourglass, we exist in the shared space of a common physical universe. We are still individuals, creating, but now our creations are tied together with the creations of all other individuals. We exist in a state of collective creation. As we pass through the portal, we bind ourselves, through agreement, to the common creation. Our thoughts become synchronized."

"But we're still individuals," Ray noted.

"Which is easy to demonstrate empirically. You are you. I am me. We are not one being. The mystic and philosopher who speak of All One confuse awareness of the existence of a shared universe with the idea all observers are one. They experience a vague memory of the moment they passed through the portal, when they passed through the point of view we all have in common, the moment they came to take part in a shared universe."

She turned her attention to the space above the hourglass, where a dozen free-flying tiny spheres, or particles, collided to form one sphere.

"There were times, before we slipped into this universe, when we would come together with other spirits to create universes. We shared thought creations completely and fully and effortlessly. In those earlier universes we existed in a state of total synchronicity, experiencing the radiant splendor of at-one-ness. Faint memories of these past glories echo in the present and bring us, temporarily, into mystical states in which we experience at-one-ness."

Something totally unexpected and quite odd occurred: Ray found himself inside a blue sphere, not unlike a huge blue balloon. Though he could not see her, he felt her presence as though she were at-one-with his mind, he felt her thought permeate his consciousness.

He sensed her mental command: *Contract*. The balloon walls closed in, in a series of stutter steps he struggled to follow. *Expand*. This time he synchronized with her thoughts and the balloon expanded smoothly. *Contract*. It seemed he was fully in control of the balloon walls, though he could sense otherwise. As though they were one, he and Alice expanded and contracted the walls in perfect synchronicity. The exercise was exhilarating. Without words, she demonstrated the joy of synchronous creation.

The balloon vanished and Alice popped into view sitting before Ray on the edge of the table, the folds of her blue dress gathered about her knees.

"Were we one?" she asked.

"In a way."

"Were we really one?" she pressed.

"No, we *acted* as one."

"Correct."

"*As if* we were one."

"Right. *As if.* We could occupy the same space, see the same objects from the same point of view. *As if* we were one. We could experience each other fully, we could know exactly and precisely what the other was being, doing, creating. In this way, we experience a closeness that—"

"Is love," Ray interjected.

"This is the love mystics experience, the being-one-with-all. That's the experience. As you see, we are not one. As immaterial spirit, we can pervade the space of any material object, a balloon or a flower, and we can imagine ourselves to be that balloon or that flower. We can pretend to 'be' any object in the universe."

"But then we forget what we're doing and think we really are the balloon or the flower or the entire universe," he added, letting her know he was catching on.

"Right. That's the misconception that causes us to become entangled in this universe," she said. "We can pervade the space of any object and 'be' it. We can 'be' the balloon or the flower, we can experience it fully, we can know it fully. But when we make the mistake of thinking we really *are* the object and not ourselves, we face attachment and suffering. We identify with the object, and that identification becomes total attachment."

"The object is a thought," Ray added. "We create the thought, then think we are it. Or we pretend to be it. Is that what you mean?"

"That's right," she continued. "We make the mistake of believing we are that which we created, creator becomes the created. We identify with our creations, we become the object. That leads to our downfall."

"Downfall?"

"When we identify with our creations, we become attached. What is total attachment? It is identifying with the object."

She illustrated the body and the sphere of awareness, as she had done before. Her thoughts flashed through Ray's mind.

"If you identify with the body, if you say 'I am the body,' that is total attachment."

Ray flashed back to his own identification with the body, the attachment that was so complete it had negated his awareness of his existence as spirit.

"We are never truly the form," she continued. "We are the No Thing that creates all forms. Once we have created the form, we can consider ourselves to be the form, but it is never more than our consideration. An immaterial spirit is not a material object."

Ray wrestled with the concept. His thoughts were not as malleable as she suggested. He assumed his inability was a function of his strong attachment.

"When we identify with that which we have created, we suffer attachment."

Ray recalled how attached he had been to the image of his body, he recalled the terror he felt when his hand disappeared. Glancing down at his hand once more, he summoned the courage to look at it for what it was, a construct of his mind. His hand disappeared. This time, however, he merely felt queasy, not nauseous.

When he looked up, expecting an "attaboy" from his mentor, he was greeted by a four-foot-tall rabbit dressed in a waistcoat, fingering a pocket watch. The rabbit promptly disappeared and a Cheshire cat appeared, lounging on the fireplace mantel.

Such events no longer rocketed Ray into mind-numbing confusion, but they did leave him unsettled. He accepted his fate, at least for the moment, but it was still disturbing to have people appear and disappear and turn into fairy-tale creatures. He could grasp, intellectually, the philosophical concept of Idealism, the idea that what you think is what you get, but it was another thing entirely to live in that reality.

The Cheshire cat blinked in and out of existence, then disappeared altogether. An oversized door mouse popped into being, handed Ray a key, then shape-shifted back into Alice.

At that moment, "I think, therefore I am" took on a new and deeper meaning for Ray. Through Alice he had learned about the joy of play, the sticky quicksand of attachment, and the malleable nature of reality.

"We are not forms. We create forms," she repeated. "That we can pretend to be the form, does not make us the form."

Ray mulled over his new awareness, not wanting to lose it in the tangle of mundane thoughts that surely would return.

"You have learned the difference between being entangled in the physical and being free as a spirit," Alice said. "When we believe we are the physical, we identify with our creation. We are no longer free to create and we suffer attachment. That is the problem with the 'all one.' It is attachment to all forms."

Another thought nipped at the edges of his consciousness. *Spirit is energy, isn't it? Wasn't that what most believed?*

"A misconception," Alice's thought hammered Ray. "Energy is a property of the physical. To say spirit is energy is to identify spirit with the physical."

The blue balloon encompassed Ray as Alice projected her thoughts. "Pull the skin of the balloon toward you, now push it out, away from you. Energy moves the balloon. Were you the energy? Or did you create the energy?"

Ray repeated the action, he pushed the balloon away and then pulled it in.

"You see, you are not energy, you create energy," she said. "Identifying spirit with energy is the same as identifying spirit with matter. In the famous equation from physics, $E = mc^2$, energy and mass are equivalent. Spirit creates the physical, both mass and energy. The physical is the created, spirit is the creator."

Her argument, though easy to understand, was difficult to accept. When we speak of something, he thought, we are accustomed to speaking about a thing-ness. Saying spirit exists, but is a No Thing, saying it lacks thing-ness, was hard to accept. The idea spirit was that which creates, but not the thing created, made sense, but was difficult to embrace. No doubt, he thought, his difficulty had to do with his own attachment, which was turning out to be much deeper problem than he had imagined.

"Spirit is the No Thing that creates the thing," she repeated gently.

The Nothing and the Something; the Creator and the Created; the Spirit and the Physical. The Yin and Yang. The differences were becoming clear. It was also becoming clear that identifying with the physical, with the world of forms, was a subtle form of attachment that itself prevented us from realizing we suffered from attachment. If the spirit firmly believed it was the form, the spirit was unable to then stand back and recognize it was merely attached to the form, not identical to it. The trap was subtle; the paradox baffling. In creating this universe, we had created a puzzle so subtle it defied solution: we could be the form, while not being the form.

Ray had been the type of person who insisted either you were something or you were not something. The idea of a nothing that could create something, then slip inside that creation and pretend to be it, was challenging.

"Spirit becomes confused because it shrouds itself in a mind made of energy," she continued. "The spirit identifies with its mind, just as when you were clinging to the mental body."

Ray's attention snapped back on his body, his mental body to be exact. Dark emotions swirled, he suffered a deep sensation of loss. The abyss, exerting its magnetic attraction, pulled him toward its vortex, its siren song irresistible. He was deeply attached and suffering, unable to maintain the detachment Alice had apparently achieved. Though he had soared to new heights of understanding, he could not maintain the altitude. The sticky pull of attachment to earthly life reeled him in. He felt himself sinking.

"We've gone up the path, yet it has not solved my current dilemma," he said.

"You've not been on any path," she said with a chuckle. "I've merely painted the landscape for your consideration. Do not confuse my introduction with the hard work of walking the path."

"What *is* this path of which you speak?"

"When you decide to follow the path, you must look carefully at your entanglement with the physical. You must inspect the personal attachments that bind you to the collective universe. The knots will have to be untied, one by one."

She had taken him on a tour, that's what she was saying; he was a mere tourist, real progress demanded commitment.

"On the path, you will shine light on regions of darkness you fear to travel, you will discover the factors that entrap you. And you will view, once again, decisions that bind you to the physical, agreements that link your fate to the fate of all others."

"But the lessons you have given me..."

"It was important you glimpse the big picture. It was important for you to learn to set your creations apart from the creations of others. You needed to be reminded of who you are, to learn to separate your mind from the minds of others. These are the actions of a spirit on the path, but for you, now, this discussion is simply remedial."

"You've shown me—"

"What lies before you."

"I no longer have a life—"

"You assume you have fallen into an irreversible condition. That was not my assessment, it was yours."

"Wait...being here...like this."

"So quickly you forget," she said.

"Lessons are not easy to learn under duress."

"True. But think back. Did you not learn your thoughts determine your future?"

"I also learned I agree too strongly with the physical, and my former body." *His former body*. He didn't know the condition of the body...there was the impact...he separated...then he had assumed...

"You did not look," she said. "You did not want to see."

"Who are you? Who are you, really? How do I know—"

Alice shape-shifted into a monk: a rotund, kindly monk sitting cross-legged in front of the fireplace, smiling. Behind the monk, flames leapt into the air and froze in the shape of a tree—a Bodhi tree, the tree the Buddha sat under when he achieved enlightenment.

"Who am I? I am nothing. And I am a student of he who was the Buddha," the monk said. "Did the Buddha teach we are not our body? Did the Buddha teach we are also not our mental body, that which some call the soul—that which is not the spirit, but rather a soul identity, a mental energy body, the spirit adopts?"

"I don't know."

"You are capable of forgetting. Good for you. That is valuable. Sometimes."

The monk's sarcasm was unveiled; he delivered his lessons with a sting.

"Was he not a compassionate being?" the monk asked.

Ray shrugged. It was starting to come back to him, but it was so long ago.

"You assume he would abandon those who suffer and not

return to provide a route, a map?"

"I didn't really give it much thought," Ray replied.

"Ah. Emptying your mind. That is valuable, too. Sometimes."

Ray wondered if he should remain silent and refuse to answer any questions. No reason to place his ignorance on display.

"Is there a reason you assume he no longer exists?"

"No reason." Ray paused. "I've never given it much thought."

"That's why I appear to you at this time: to paint a picture which will remind you, so that when you are ready—"

"You speak of that which I do not know—"

"When your heart seeks the lessons, you will find them. They are not hidden, except from those who do not wish to look. When you seek, you will find what you need."

For a long moment they sat face to face in silence. Maybe the monk was right about the forgetting; there was something about the rotund figure that stirred the faintest of memories, hints of a long forgotten era, hints of a past he had lived.

Before Ray could wind his way back to the origins of the ancient memory, the monk interrupted, "Our time is nearly at an end. You have a decision to make. We must turn our attention to that which you did not wish to see."

The smiling monk morphed into a grinning Cheshire cat and scampered up the frozen Bodhi tree of flames. "Follow me," the Cheshire Cat said, winking. "Let us bring your confusion to a conclusion."

21

Randi clutched the cell phone in one hand; with her other hand she squeezed Ray's unfeeling fingers. Her eyes were closed tight, her brow furrowed with intense prayer. She was trying to jump start his body, trying to flow the current of her living consciousness into his unresponsive flesh. For the last hour, without pause, she held the pose, causing the head nurse, Lani, to pace nervously outside the room.

Father McCarty, summoned by the candy striper, Teri, at Lani's behest, entered, studied Randi quietly for a beat, then cleared his throat.

She looked up, tense, prepared to do battle. When she recognized the priest, she relaxed.

"You okay?" he asked. A rhetorical question.

She half-nodded "yes", then shook her head "no."

"They asked you to make a decision?"

"They disconnected the ICP monitor." Seeing his confusion, she clarified, "It measures intra cranial pressure. They said the pressure is down and he's out of danger from the swelling. But he hasn't responded. They want to see if he will—"

"They're going to disconnect the respirator?"

She nodded. "They're not optimistic."

"How do you feel about that?"

She looked out the window, as though the answer was out there, somewhere.

Father McCarty went to her side. "Do you want me to stay?"

"Yes. Until he's gone. If you don't mind."

Dr. Seidman entered, crisp, businesslike. "Mrs. Carte, will you join me in my office?"

She shook her head "no."

"I'll stay with her," Father McCarty interjected.

"I'll be fine," she assured Seidman.

Seidman hesitated, unable to muster a counter argument, unable to simply exit.

Randi reached for a Kleenex with shaky hands. Accidently, she toppled her purse, dumping its contents on the floor. The priest and the psychologist knelt to retrieve the fallen items; among them was a worn copy of an illustrated children's book. Father McCarty opened the dog-eared cover and was taken with the faded, but handsome, color illustrations. He paused to admire the artist's rendering of *Alice's Adventures in Wonderland*.

"It was Ray's favorite," Randi said. "When the call came, with news of his accident, I booked a flight immediately. While I waited for the cab, I rummaged through a trunk of personal belongings he left behind when he headed off for college. I hadn't looked inside before—I figured maybe Ray wanted the contents to remain private. After the news of the accident, it didn't seem to matter anymore, so I looked inside—and found a tattered scrapbook lying on top. When I picked it up, this lovely little book tumbled out. I remembered reading it to him when he was young. He would ask to hear the story, over and over."

She sat down, took the book from Father McCarty, and opened it to "Chapter One: Down the Rabbit Hole." It appeared she intended to read to Ray, though he remained comatose. Seidman flashed a concerned look to Father McCarty. The priest pretended he didn't see the glance and rested a comforting hand on Randi's shoulder.

"Dear, if it would help. Go ahead, read to him. No one objects."

She shook her head and dabbed away a tear, but she didn't read, at least not aloud.

Seidman hovered, not really committed to staying, but not

making his departure either.

Father McCarty recited a silent prayer. The moment when hopes and prayers clashed with medical reality was upon them; it was a moment the priest despised.

On the mountain, the wind died down and the little monk icon, hanging from the tree branch, ceased swinging and became perfectly still. Below, Hal and Chase squatted in the snow and watched James, who was seated under the tree, his legs crossed, meditating.

The prayer-filled tranquility was disturbed by a bobcat streaking gracefully over the snowy landscape, heading straight for them at a dead run. When the cat drew near, it slowed and then continued its advance, inching forward in a predator's crouch. The small, but fierce, cats were not uncommon in the front range, but usually they avoided people, and, as bobcats could turn vicious, people usually avoided them.

Though Hal was caught off guard by the brazen approach of the wild feline, he knew enough to remain still. The cat did not fear them, neither did it intend to make them its prey. Hal's backwoods experience had taught him the wisdom of remaining silent and allowing nature's creatures to follow their instincts. Something, he didn't know what, attracted the cat; he was certain it was not the prospect of dining on three fully-grown humans.

He was right: the bobcat fixed its hunter's stare on the branches of the pine, then exploded out of its crouch and tore up the tree, its sharp claws shredding bark as it ascended. The cat crawled steadily, purposefully, out on a branch, extended a paw, leaned down, and batted the monk.

Hal and Chase traded a smile. James, eyes closed, lost in a meditative reverie, was not smiling. He had become a spectator in the theater of expanded mind, observing the ghostly image of Ray peering through the shattered windshield of the Explorer at his own broken and bloodied body.

Ray viewed the wreck from the same position he had

taken up seconds after the impact—outside the vehicle, outside his body. He was viewing a memory he had hidden from himself. Actually, he was viewing from inside a memory; he was re-living the instant, shortly after the crash, when he found himself outside. It was a moment he had covered with a black cloud of amnesia. He glanced down at his body crumpled behind the steering wheel, blood running down its forehead. He felt no pain, only remorse, regret, and a sickening awareness he had totally screwed up. He couldn't stomach looking at his damaged body. He didn't want to know its pain; he was outside, free—it was over. There was no need for him to torture himself.

Glimpses of events that followed the crash—the arrival of the rescue team in their orange parkas, the chatter of their radios, and the noisy arrival of the helicopter—flickered past in dream-like detail. Viewing the 3-D technicolor memory, he regretted his earlier decision to look away; he had been cowardly and lost his nerve; he had "jumped ship" prematurely.

He re-lived the crash, viewing it again and again. He was immersed in a memory, but that memory was not in his head, the memory played its 3-D holographic pictures in the theater of his awareness. As he viewed the energy pictures over and over, they grew fainter and fainter, then disappeared altogether. The disappearance of the disturbing images, the disappearance of the memories that had once been shrouded in black, revealed those memories had been superimposed over the actual accident scene. He was now at the site.

His recall of how he arrived at the crash site was faint. He remembered leaving the cabin and following his mentor—the Cheshire cat, the Monk, Alice—through a strange world inhabited by wispy, radiant figures beckoning seductively to him. These other-worldly phantoms, their unsung siren songs promising the bliss all men crave, promising succor and escape, would have commanded his obedience, had he not been following Alice, who was playing the Cheshire cat. Her instructions had been clear: these figures, and many others like them he had not yet seen, presented a grave danger, the details of which she had too little time to describe. It was for moments like this she had tutored him, teaching him to distinguish his thoughts and intentions from the thoughts and intentions of others.

In the far distance, approaching rapidly, another peril loomed, a magnificent glowing light, its radiance a magnet for his attention. The Cheshire cat who was Alice warned telepathically: do not follow your desires and instincts, focus on the journey. Ray narrowed his attention and fixed his will, like a bayonet secured for an infantry charge. He had followed the Cheshire cat, which had delivered him to the accident scene and now he sensed he was not alone with the cat.

The bobcat toyed with the monk, teasing it, slapping it. The tiny icon swung in wider and wider arcs until the string broke loose and the little figure tumbled through the air and plunked sharply off the skull of one meditating James Perspy.

He startled, perhaps imagining an invisible Zen master demonstrating "one hand clapping" had selected his head as its target. He ducked and rolled, dodging any follow-up blows the invisible cosmic boxer might inflict upon his crown.

Hal and Chase stifled their laughter, but only for a beat, only until the volcano of their emotions erupted. Tension that had them wrapped in its coils, squeezing the breath out of their emotions, exploded, unleashing a rolling chain of laughter. They rolled in the snow, tossing handfuls of snow at each other, captives of an emotional release chain reaction destined to run its course.

James glanced at his companions, certain they'd gone daft.

Hal plucked the monk out of the snow and lofted it at James, a nonverbal invitation for him to join them in a snowball fight.

James rolled the tiny figure between his fingers and craned his neck to study the bobcat perched on the limb above grinning very much like a Cheshire cat.

Hal and Chase, pelting each other like kids on a school-free "snow day," turned on James and launched a flurry of snowballs, the missiles fabricated with dry snow exploded upon contact into bursts of sparkling crystals. Before the volley was exhausted, James had joined the frenzy, hurling fistfuls of the powdery white crystals.

The trio's uninhibited joy, their expansive spirit of play, delivered a contact high, setting Ray's consciousness vibrating, lifting his spirits. Against the radiance of the brilliant snow, he saw the forms take shape and, as his vision cleared, he recognized his friends tumbling on the ground like carefree children. Off to the side, a faint apparition he recognized, the baby carriage, flickered in and out of focus.

He used his intention to place his mental body into sitting position, his back against the tree, and watched, learning the full meaning of attachment: he ached to join in, to play. He laughed, but they could not hear him; he perceived them, but they could not perceive him. His dilemma opened the emotional floodgates to a beautiful sadness, a dichotomy that vibrated between two poles: between love, for his friends, and the pain brought on by his hopeless separation from them. "It's a game," Alice had taught, and now he wanted back on the playing field more than anything he had ever wanted.

James, on his hands and knees, sucking air, catching his breath, thought he saw something—Ray, seated against the tree, smiling. Lonely, but smiling. James didn't trust his perceptions; he wasn't meditating, so how could he see? Was the phantom a product of his overheated imagination? Had wishful thinking gotten the best of him?

James' arrested motion spooked Hal and Chase, they ceased laughing, and, with concerned looks, queried his weird posture and sudden silence. Chase thought she felt something move inside her belly; but that couldn't be, it was too early in the term.

"James, what's up?" Hal asked.

The radiant sprites whom Ray had passed earlier were not to be denied, their invitation was not to be spurned. They circled and grasped Ray gently by the elbows and levitated him to his feet. Alice had warned he could refuse the next step in his journey for only so long—his hiatus was up.

The cell phone's sing-song ring crashed the party. The Nokia had fallen in the snow. As each successive ring hammered the trio with increasing dread, Chase searched frantically.

The bobcat arched its back, snarled and hissed, then dropped from the branch and sprinted gracefully across the snow field and disappeared into the rocky landscape.

James and Hal shared a look: something had happened. But what?

Chase dug the phone out of the snow. In the quiet of the mountains all three could hear Randi's voice on the other end, "They're taking Ray off life support. I gave my approval."

It wasn't Randi's voice alone that grabbed Ray's attention; it was her presence, encompassing space like the spheres Alice had illustrated. He wanted to see her before he left, for good, on his journey. The thought sent his consciousness hurtling through space in search of his mother.

In less than a millisecond, he found himself inside a hospital birthing center in the company of one very pregnant woman, a mother-to-be on the verge of giving birth. Sweat dampened her brow, labor pains quickened her breathing.

He was confused, had the thought of his mother translated, in the symbolic realm of the Afterworld, into a Platonic ideal of a mother, any mother?

Perhaps, in an ironic twist of fate, the thought of his mother had sent him hurtling into the presence of his future mother, delivering him to be reborn. Was it time, so soon, to climb back on the merry-go-round of birth and death? Apparently, his immediate future held diapers and blended beets. That must have been the meaning of the baby carriage: an invitation to begin his earthly life once again as an infant. He was confused, one thought connected to another connected to another in a giant web of meaning. His mother, all mothers, a new mother.

He wasn't listening as much as simply perceiving thoughts when the mother-in-labor battled her frazzled husband between bouts of Lamaze panting. The overwhelmed father-to-be was lobbying to name the new baby Jeff, while she preferred Darian. The names appeared, embroidered on imagined articles of clothing; at first, it was toddler wear, then on football and baseball jerseys.

Ray pouted, pretending to himself to be upset that neither of his new parents had consulted him as to whether he wanted to be a Jeff or a Darian. In fact, he wasn't ready to be reborn as either Jeff or Darian. It was his mother, Ray Carte's mother, he sought. Refreshing the thought-intention sent him space-shifting to a room where Randi, cell phone pressed to her ear, tried, but failed, to avert her eyes as two nurses and a doctor leaned over a lifeless body.

His mother's emotions, focused on the bedridden figure, motivated him to inspect the body closer. At first, he didn't recognize himself. When he did, he was not prepared for the shock. The body, drained of life, looked cheap; it was pale and inanimate, as one would expect, but there was something else, something oddly wrong—the form was no longer dear to him. It was just a body, not him, really. He was sickened, the body looked like a...a thing. He was strangely unattached and wondered why it had ever been otherwise.

He watched as the doctor eased the respirator out of the thing's throat; watched as a nurse disconnected an IV; watched as another nurse removed a feeding tube. He almost turned away into the embrace of the radiant ones, but before he could—

The heart monitor bleeped, then hummed a steady warning. The body was flat-lining.

On the mountain, Hal, Chase, and James recognized the sound issuing from the cell phone and bowed their heads, not so much in prayer, as in defeat. James thought he heard the tree sigh, but this time, he knew it must be his imagination.

Father McCarty secured Randi in a comforting embrace as her sobs, which began as small gasps, grew to chest-wracking gulps. Seidman, watching from outside, in the hall, was rendered still and silent. There was nothing he could say, nothing he could do.

Alice appeared to Ray. Her penetrating eyes locked on him; she was no longer teaching, no longer playing. "Ray, you have a decision to make, and no time to waste."

He looked at his mother and felt the combined emotions of Randi, Hal, Chase, James. His decision was instantaneous. Immediately, he hit a black wall; the gut-wrenching impact left him uncertain he was even conscious. Slowly, however, he became aware of an all-encompassing pain and an enormous weight that rendered him unable to move. The flesh body was incredibly heavy, deathly inert. The sensations filled him with terror: it was as though he had been buried alive. Then he realized what had happened: he had returned to a state he previously considered normal.

The heart monitor beeped to life. The nurses, already half way out the door, spun around, startled and panicked more than surprised. Randi looked for an encouraging sign from the doctor, a victory sign from Father McCarty.

On the mountain, the "beeps" were carried by the tiny but clear sound of the Nokia. "Is that what I think it is?" Hal asked. James nodded. They held hands, waiting for confirmation.

Randi leaned over Ray's body, searching for signs of life. His lips quivered, then went still. A finger moved, *or did it?* Randi tossed the phone to Father McCarty, freeing both hands for her search. Dr. Sloane and Lani and her staff of nurses worked around Randi, joining the search for vital signs.

On the mountain, Hal, Chase, and James listened as Father McCarty told them to get their blessed butts down the mountain. They half-ran, half-slid down the grade to the Jeep, but then James clambered back up the incline, panting with exhaustion. A minute later he returned, clutching the monk.

Ray transited the dark portal, and gave in to the weight, the anchor that was his body. He was back. He had to let them know.

Randi sensed Ray was trying to say something. She wanted so much to hear what he had to say, anything he had to say.

Ray battled gravity in an attempt to raise an eyebrow in a struggle that resembled a scripted bad dream; it took all his strength to raise one eyelid. The task accomplished, he found himself peering into his mother's eyes while he marshaled his remaining strength to satisfy the impulse to communicate. That which had been so effortless a short time before, when he was outside, now required Herculean effort.

"There's life after—" he whispered.

Dr. Seidman cut him off, "Oxygen deprivation can cause some pretty horrendous hallucinations. But don't worry, you're in good hands now. You'll be on the mend."

Randi and Father McCarty regarded Seidman with stark disbelief.

"I want to speak...before I forget," Ray stammered.

"I know, I know, but we're a lot more interested in your recovery than in your story," Seidman said. "It's important you rest.

When we get you back on your feet—"

"Don't worry," said Father McCarty, kindly, stepping forward. "we are interested. You get a little rest, then you can tell us everything." He winked. Ray winked back, setting his scalp on fire. The price of his decision to return was going to be pain, lots of pain, but he was willing to pay the price. With his mother holding his hand, he fell into a deep restful sleep.

Later, Chase would arrive and hold Ray's other hand. Hal cradled one of his feet in his big grip.

As Ray napped, vaguely aware of their presence, all he could think of was telling them all he had learned. He had returned with good news.

22

That evening, after James left, Hal and Chase, barely able to keep their eyes open, maintained a vigil by Ray's side, while Randi sat in the corner reading *Alice's Adventures in Wonderland* to Bren, who had dropped by to see for herself that "he was back."

Chase fretted her niece would be emotionally scarred by her earlier visit, but the child was blasé and matter of fact with regards to the entire drama. She was happy Uncle Ray was on the mend, but he was sleeping most of the time and wasn't much fun. Randi, on the other hand, was willing to read to her, and the illustrations in the book were captivating.

Randi was grateful for the opportunity to practice a little mothering. While she was reading to Bren, she even imagined she saw Ray smile once in his sleep. Life was good, her disillusion and doubt had been merely a test of her faith.

Chase, watching Randi and Bren bond, found her thoughts wandering to her impending motherhood. Her pregnancy remained a secret, and, though she longed to share the news, she knew it was best to stall the announcement until Ray was well-rested. She had waited this long, she could wait even longer to make sure the moment was right. She knew he would appreciate being the first to share her joy, rather than waking up, late to the party, discovering they had celebrated while he slept.

She admired her niece's bright eyes as the ten-year-old was magically transported into Wonderland by Randi's recitation of Carroll's story:

> *"Lastly, she pictured to herself how this same little sister of*

hers would, in the aftertime, be herself a grown woman; and how she would keep, through all her riper years, the simple and loving heart of her childhood; and how she would gather about her other little children, and make their eyes bright and eager with many a strange tale..."

Ray squeezed Chase's hand, causing her to start. He licked his lips, signaling he was about to speak. Chase leaned close to hear his whisper.

"The baby carriage. Why?"

Chase flushed pink with embarrassment. *He knew. HOW did he know?* With others present, watching and listening, this was not the time for her to unburden. She kissed his cheek and whispered, "Not now, Ray. We'll talk when you're rested." She squeezed his hand, sealing her promise.

Ray, medicated with painkillers, battled the drug torpor and strained to remain alert. His question about the baby buggy had gone unanswered and, though he had gained her promise that an answer lay in his future, he was impatient. He squeezed her hand again, wet his lips, but before he could speak an efficient orderly, with the social graces of a robot, arrived, pushing a gurney. He was on a mission, with orders to transport "a Mr. Ray Carte" to the Imaging Department for a series of brain scans. The young man, curt to the point of being rude, replied tersely to Chase's queries: Dr. Sloane ordered the tests; the patient would be gone at least an hour, maybe longer.

Teri, the affable candy striper, came to the rescue. With her bubbly charm, she quashed their concerns while helping transfer Ray from the bed to the waiting gurney, adding a touch of much-needed professionalism to the process.

Within minutes, Ray, whisked away on the gurney, with the gruff orderly at the helm, was embarked on an unwanted adventure, his question regarding the baby carriage unanswered.

After Ray's departure, Chase summoned Bren, "I'll drive you home, kiddo. Your mom will be worried."

"She won't. She knows I'm okay."

"She knows *you're* okay, it's the hospital she's worried about."

Bren play-acted being gravely wounded by her aunt's dig, sweetly kissed Randi good-bye, slapped Hal a low five, then trudged after Chase, a disgruntled-but-compliant baby duck queuing up in momma duck's wake.

Hal soon departed, in search of good night's sleep.

Randi, emotionally wrung out, dozed off, *Alice's Adventures in Wonderland* resting on her lap.

The MRI, a large industrial donut of a machine, an icon of space-age technology, was designed for imaging, not comfort. Though the technicians were considerate and careful, the device was inherently oppressive and uncomfortable, and extremely noisy. When triggered into action and called on to perform its magic—imaging the brain in molecule-thick slices—the huge magnets delivered ear-smacking clangs, the kind one might expect at a construction site.

A half-hour later, the technicians and the radiologist, having studied the cross sections on their raster screens in real time and having seen nothing remarkable, cheerfully, as though working a film set, declared "it's a wrap," and freed Ray from the device that was a first-cousin to an alien probe.

The gruff orderly wheeled Ray out of Imaging. Accelerating too quickly, he missed his mark and the gurney glanced off the door jamb. For a second, Ray feared the vehicle would tip as it teetered then swept out a wide turn in the hall that led to Ray's room.

Ray, fully awake after the rousing racket of the MRI, the effects of the drugs having worn off, lodged a request, "Can we take a detour? There's something I need to check out."

"Nope. No can do. We got pre-set routes. Means no detours allowed," the less-than-pliable orderly responded, obviously having been sternly chastised for prior transgressions.

"Aw, c'mon."

"Nope."

"Look, here's the deal," Ray said, resorting to lying. "I'm dying and I have one last wish—a visit to the pediatric ward to glimpse the newborns. It's important, I need to see life begin as well as end. Seeing those happy little fellas will provide a much-needed lift. You've got no idea how depressed—"

"No can do. Sorry to hear you're not doing so well."

"Okay. I understand. You're a consummate professional. And for that you are owed my gratitude. Not only that, you're a decent gurney driver, who deserves a tip. As soon as we get back to my room, I've got a picture of Jackson that's all yours."

Ray spoke the universal language of bribery, a language the orderly understood. "As long as you stay behind the glass and don't disturb the little fellas," he mumbled, spinning the gurney one-eighty. He navigated up one floor and down a lengthy corridor, which dead-ended in the waiting room adjacent to the nursery. After parking the gurney against the glass partition, he ducked into a visitor's restroom for a smoke. Ray rolled on his side to peer into the nursery, but the gurney was too low; he was forced to prop himself up on one elbow and endure the stabbing pain in his ribs in his effort to view a half-dozen napping newborns, two of them bathed in the fluorescent light hospitals employed to combat infant jaundice. He had wanted this opportunity to reflect on life's beginnings and to confront a nagging doubt—had his out–of–body experience been real?

Two weary yet pleased fathers, maintaining droopy-eyed vigils in the waiting room, stirred at the sight of Ray laid out on the gurney. "What the heck happened to you, pal?" probed the one in the cardigan sweater.

Ray immediately recognized the man, and his sweater: it was the man who had argued with his wife over the selection of their son's name. The nagging doubt retreated. His heart beat fast with the excitement of discovery.

Though clearly exhausted, the new father was buoyed by the giddiness that accompanies the birth of a child. His attempt at humor, however, was stunted by his lack of sleep: "What happened? You try to coach your wife through labor?"

The fathers chuckled. The orderly, who had returned, reeking of tobacco, smirked.

Ray, playing along, laughed, and paid the price—the pain in his ribs painted a grimace on his lips. After the burning sensation subsided, he caught his breath and asked, "Which one is Jeff?"

The father in the cardigan proudly pointed out a contented and healthy pink infant tucked securely in his ward crib. A beat later, the father's expression darkened: how did this wreck of a man, confined to a gurney, know his kid's name?

"Jeff. Good name. Better than Darian," Ray said, with a decided lack of forethought.

"My wife and I...never even discussed the name Darian... before...how did you...?"

Ray had inadvertently waded into territory that required exquisite tact or an insanity plea; he chose the latter. "Don't know. Don't have a clue. Since I got this bump on the old noggin, strange ideas pop into my head."

Strangers, Ray speculated, were more likely to accept a mystery, an unknown, than the truth. That was an axiom he would remember in the coming days. He sank back on the gurney and gestured to the orderly. His wish-fulfillment journey was over, he had overstayed his welcome. It had been a successful mission: he had backed the nagging doubt into a corner, in spite of upsetting Jeff's father. As he was being wheeled away, he waved bye to the suspicious fathers and tried to appear normal, tried to look like anything other than a psycho baby-snatcher on the prowl.

The next morning, Ray's life returned to the humdrum rhythm of a hospitalized patient. His abbreviated waking hours were filled with the hustle and bustle of hospital routine and a flurry of congratulatory visits from friends.

That evening, after Ray's dinner tray and its contents, including an untouched Jell-O dessert, had been bussed away, Randi escorted a polite, reserved fellow into the room. He wore a pink unicorn pin on his lapel.

Les Crane extended his hand in greeting, studying Ray for signs of lucidity.

"If you prefer, I can return later," Les said, in his humble and deferential manner. "Although it's best to document the near-death experience as soon as possible, before the memory—"

"Stay," Ray said. "It's okay. Mother convinced me you were someone I could speak to honestly. Said you had experience, said you weren't likely to—"

"Insist you're crazy?"

"Something like that," Ray said, struggling to sit upright. Randi fluffed a pillow and propped it up behind him. He leaned back, exhaled a breath, and composed himself. "I would like to share my experience. Yet, I know how hard it is for others to accept. I mean, get real—it's gotta sound crazy. I don't expect anyone to actually believe. Yet, it doesn't really matter to me who believes. Because the experience... Well, it is what it is."

Les shed his coat, fetched a tape recorder from his leather satchel and balanced it on the bed, opened a fresh spiral notebook, uncapped his Mount Blanc fountain pen. His precise, practiced procedure and rehearsed exactitude resembled the manner of an overly-conscientious stenographer on her first day in the executive boardroom; it bordered on the comical.

Ray decided the affable researcher was simply intent on making him feel comfortable, setting the stage so he would feel emboldened to talk freely. The man was harmless. But he wondered if Les was eager to listen, or merely eager to believe? Did the man harbor doubts? He should. Ray harbored doubts—and he had been there.

Ray knew that in the sober light of day the story he was about to impart would seem a bit "off planet." In fact, he had serious second thoughts about the interview: why not keep the story of his unusual experience to himself? There were valid explanations for the phenomena he encountered, but his experience was so far beyond ordinary waking life that he seriously doubted it was possible for anyone to grasp what he had been through without also having had the experience. He recalled how, even when he was dead and with Alice, he had a hard time believing. How could he expect anyone to take his word that such strange events were based on anything remotely real? There was no way that was going to happen, he told himself. There was only one way they knew you were sane after you experienced something like this—and that was you kept your mouth shut. You didn't talk about it. That's what a sane person did.

"Dear," Randi said, sensing Ray's doubts, "Les helped me while you were gone and gave me hope. If you could return the favor and help him understand what you experienced... Maybe some day that will help someone else."

"Documenting the near–death experience," Les jumped in, "has been a benefit to a great number of patients. Unaware that others have had the same experience, some patients worry. They fear they've lost their minds. It's nice to be able to let them know there are others—"

"After the crash, after the impact," Ray started, "I popped out. You know what I mean?"

Les nodded; Ray didn't have to explain being "out" to him.

"The experience of being outside the body, and not wanting to see the body, not wanting to feel the pain, was something I didn't... I could not have anticipated."

Les nodded, *go on.*

"Almost immediately, I found myself in a different setting. Someone was there with me."

Les leaned forward, encouraging. "Who was it?"

"I called her Alice."

"Alice?" Les probed.

"Yes, like Alice in Wonderland."

Randi showed Les the book.

The paranormal researcher resisted the urge to express his disappointment, though it was difficult to hide his feelings completely. During the raw data collection stage, it was important that his emotional reactions remain muffled lest they influence the subject and color the report. None the less, a fantasy involving the children's tale *Alice's Adventures in Wonderland* was *not* what he was hoping to hear.

"She wasn't really Alice," Ray continued. "That was just... The story and the character of Alice, being a part of my past, came to mind, it wasn't like... The important thing is there was another being and she communicated using mental pictures. She showed me how we could see each other's thoughts."

The researcher's enthusiasm skyrocketed. "Totally consistent with our research. Something we hear often. Please, go on."

Ray searched his memory for detail, then continued. "She was like a teacher, but much more than a teacher. A spirit. A spirit guide of sorts. An angel. But not really an angel like we think of them."

Les scribbled a note.

Ray continued, "I was in a lot more trouble than I realized at the time. She was patient. She walked me through preparation for some kind of exam. I assume it was to be a test of my character, but that doesn't fully express the nuances, as the trial that lay ahead—I can't report exactly what that test was, because, thanks to her, I was able to return."

"The decision to return. Tell me about that."

Before Ray could respond, Dr. Seidman entered. He was in a dark mood, his clenched jaw muscles rippled with tension as he fixed Les with a commanding stare.

"Sir, can I speak with you? Outside."

Les rose and handed his notebook to Randi, who was busy counting to ten with her eyes closed.

Seidman, who had turned to go, spun around and waggled a finger at Les' paraphernalia—the gesture making it perfectly clear he expected Les to collect his belongings and follow.

Ray scrutinized Seidman, painfully aware of his abruptness, his rudeness. He felt the urge to attack, to give in to "the best defense is an offense" strategy.

Randi, intuiting Ray was about to create a nasty scene,

flashed him a look that warned *let it go.*

Les, too, had no desire to create a confrontation. On his way out, he gave Ray's ankle a squeeze, a gesture that conveyed an unspoken bond, a commitment—we'll see each other again soon.

In the hall, Dr. Seidman berated Les in a whisper akin to a hiss. "What do you think you're doing? We've got a patient who's been through major trauma, a patient who's feeling extremely vulnerable and open to suggestion, and you're feeding him your carnival hocus-pocus. Do you have any idea of the damage you could cause, the confusion you could create? Once my patient is released, I can't stop you, but in here, in this hospital, I'm responsible for the outcome, and your act doesn't cut it. Now, please leave."

He turned away, then turned back. "Let's not make anything of this, okay? You made a mistake, you were presumptuous and I'm willing to let it go. If you just leave. Now."

"Sure. Fine. Whatever you say."

Les exited, the back of his neck glowing with suppressed anger. It wasn't worth doing battle with the likes of Seidman on their own turf. There was nothing to be gained by a show of logic or integrity or reason: Seidman's objections were all about Seidman's emotions. And Les knew it.

Early the next morning, as the candy striper Teri delivered Ray's breakfast, Seidman paid Ray a visit. "Can I join you?" he asked.

"Sure, pull up a chair. Maybe I can bribe the nurse into bringing you a cup of coffee."

Teri smiled an acknowledgment that was cut short by the psychologist's request, "Extra cream, please."

"Uh oh, that'll cost me extra," Ray said, prompting another smile from Teri. "What can I do for you, doctor?" Ray asked.

"I want to make sure my actions last evening were not misconstrued," Seidman replied. "I may appear abrupt at times. Like last night. With your visitor. But I assure you, it's only because I care about my patients."

"Go on," Ray said.

"We've made advances. We now understand trauma patients experience unusual perceptions, we understand the psychological side effects. In the old days, we ignored the side effects. We simply dismissed them as troublesome adverse reactions. If we said anything at all, we assured patients they would forget the experience. If not right away, then eventually. However, they didn't always forget. Sometimes they became confused and upset. Now that we understand more, I like to make sure patients, like yourself, have the benefit of the knowledge of exactly what happened to them so they're able to integrate the experiences into their life. And move on."

Ray paused between bites of bland scrambled eggs, downed a swig of coffee, wiped his lips. "Excellent. Good approach. It never hurts to stay up on the latest."

"We have come to realize the brain is capable of much, much more than we ever imagined. In fact, so much more that we're not certain we'll ever understand it entirely."

"Really," Ray said, "it's that mysterious?"

"Yes, but that doesn't leave us empty-handed. We can start with what we know and go on to make inferences. For example, we understand the brain is capable of cobbling together memories and creating imaginary scenarios."

"Memories? Imaginary scenarios?"

"Yes, imagination. The brain constructs elaborate scenarios in its attempt to reason. It creates fantasies designed to enable us to survive. You see, the complete focus of the brain is survival. If we're dying, or think we're dying, what does the brain do?"

Ray shrugged and shoved his tray aside.

Teri delivered Seidman's coffee and a refill for Ray. He flashed her an appreciative look, an acknowledgment that went unnoticed by Seidman.

"So what does the brain do in those dire circumstances?" Ray asked.

"The brain creates imaginary scenarios that assure us we

never die. It creates images. Sometimes they're images of religious figures promising immortality. Why? The brain is programmed to survive, to do anything it must to stay alive. When it is no longer assured of survival, it invents survival."

"I didn't know that."

Seidman had anticipated more resistance. On prior occasions he had encountered patients who were not so quick to let go of their delusions. They insisted their experience was real; for them, the experience was anything but a fantasy cobbled together in their bruised gray matter. Seidman took this denial as further proof of the marvelous chameleon-like nature of the brain. The old gray matter was a master at disguising its operations.

"Fascinating," Ray said. "I wasn't aware brain research had progressed that far. That they've identified the actual neurons and synapses that fabricate out-of-body experiences is quite amazing. I would love to see the research that identifies these inner programs. Hard to imagine they can read the actual program in the brain."

Was Ray putting him on? Or was he being genuine? Seidman wasn't certain. In spite of his doubts, he continued. "There are places in the brain—stimulating these locations causes the illusion of an out-of-body experience. For short periods of time.

"How long?"

"Two seconds."

"Two seconds? Not too long," Ray said. Then, stroking his chin as though forming a deep question, he asked, "How do they know poking and prodding causes an illusion? Maybe their probing *actually* causes the spirit to separate from the body."

"They stimulate the brain. That's how they know. Simple cause and effect. Probe the brain, get an out-of-body report. Cause and effect."

"No. Wait. That doesn't prove the out-of-body experience is an illusion. For all we know, the probing may cause an actual separation."

"Yes, I see your point," Seidman replied. "But where is the spirit? Nowhere. No one ever sees the spirit. It doesn't exist."

"Ever read Plato?"

"Maybe once. In college. I don't recall."

"You don't recall the story about the cave?" Ray asked.

"I may have heard about it."

"Plato wrote we're like the inhabitants of a cave and what we mistakenly perceive as reality is only our shadows cast upon the wall by light streaming into the cave. Our heads are chained so we are unable to turn to see that light, we see only the shadows on the wall, a shadow reality. But some can leave the cave and go into the light. To see reality, as it is." Ray paused for a beat as a realization took shape. "Plato also warns that when the explorer returns to the cave and tells the others what he has seen, they will refuse to believe him. If he tries to get anyone to go with him, they will attack him."

"Well, brain science was pretty crude back in Plato's day. We call that the age of superstition. Thank goodness, we've moved out of those primitive caves." Seidman's attempt at humor was forced.

"So I experienced a hallucination? My imagination went on tilt, went a little berserk. Is that it? My brain convinced itself it survives beyond death?"

"A patient who recognizes the experience is imaginary can let it go and get on with his life. That patient gains valuable perspective. Last night, I didn't want that fellow confusing you about what was real and what was not. Folks like that have a habit of luring people down some pretty torturous paths, confusing them with all manner of bizarre concepts, leaving them a befuddled mess. I didn't want that to happen to you."

"I appreciate your concern," Ray said. "Wouldn't want to leave the hospital carrying on like a nut case." He smiled ironically and raised his coffee cup, proposing a toast.

Seidman responded awkwardly, sensing his little talk had not gone well. He had good reason to believe this patient was mocking him. Information Seidman had withheld convinced him this patient was considerably more cagey than most, clever enough to play his cards close to his chest.

The nurse cleared the food tray and empty cups, then fluffed Ray's pillow and encouraged him to get some rest.

Seidman, meanwhile, stared out the window, plotting his next move. As he turned to leave, he said, offhandedly, "I received a complaint yesterday. No, I'm being overly dramatic. It wasn't really a complaint. It was an inquiry. Seems an upset father wanted to know how a trauma patient could know the name of his new-born child. He also wanted to know how that patient, whom he had never met before, also knew the alternate name he and his wife had considered, but rejected. In private. This father was a tad con-cerned about hospital security. He was worried the staff might be a bit lax when it came to his family's safety. He managed to upset our administrators. His complaint prompted them to step out from behind their desks. Which is a rare event. I vouched for you and told them the incident was mere coincidence."

"Hmm." Ray replied. "Curious."

"If you want to let me know how you knew those names, how that came about, I'd be interested in hearing. We know you bribed the orderly. Did you also bribe a maternity nurse? Is that how you got the names?"

Ray shrugged "maybe."

Seidman turned to go.

"Oh, say, doctor," Ray said. "Maybe it had something to do with neurons wanting to survive. Might be worth researching."

Seidman didn't particularly like this patient; the man was messing with him. Other patients with delusions sought his help; even if they were adamant about what they had experienced, they were anxious and open to counseling. This patient was different, perhaps worse off.

"Yeah. Maybe that's it," Seidman replied. "We'll look into it. You get some rest now. Listen, if you decide you need someone to talk to, I'm here. If you don't, that's okay. But I don't want you thinking I'm not here for you."

"I wouldn't think that," Ray assured him.

Seidman exited.

Ray inhaled a deep breath and realized he had been breathing shallow, holding his breath, during Seidman's entire visit. The
guy was intense. Not exactly your chilled-out, sympathetic-listener
therapist.

As Ray drifted toward sleep, the weight of his body pressed
down and he longed for the freedom of the out-of-body state. Then
he realized the sensation of pressure was not solely the mass of his
flesh weighing him down; it was the mass of Seidman's thoughts.
Over the course of a lifetime, Seidman had built, in his mind, a
"cabin in the woods" that was more like a bunker, with thick
concrete walls devoid of windows, and outside that bunker, in his
mental landscape, it was always dark, a perpetual night. If Seidman
had the misfortune of being hurled into the near death Ray experienced, the outcome would be a horrible affair, with the psychologist suffering the pains and terror of his unwanted condition in total
blackness. He would suffer without vision.

Ray knew this with certainty. While they were conversing,
he had visited the dark "cabin" of Seidman's mind and the visit had
been depressing. Throughout their conversation, Ray attempted to
light metaphorical candles; Seidman snuffed them out, one by one.
The real danger posed by Seidman, Ray discovered, was not that he
was content to sit in the dark; the danger was Seidman's passionate
mission to have Ray join him in that unlit cave.

For the first time, Ray understood clearly that he possessed
the ability to make choices. He could control his own thoughts; he
was no longer forced to dwell in the dark spaces others projected
around him. If this was a co-created universe, and he now firmly
believed it was, then one inadvertently, unconsciously lent one's
support to the creations of those with whom one had con-
gress—the darkness was contagious. And, only by being aware of
one's own conscious creation, moment by moment, could one
divorce oneself from the dark creations that might besiege and
occupy one's space. The trick was to be fully present and recognize the nature of the creations one faced. Where there was dark,

create light, he mused. Instantly, as a result of that thought, he felt lighter, like a balloon, floating ever higher.

Lani, passing by in the hall, glimpsed his smile and shot him a puzzled look. Ray winked an acknowledgment then closed his eyes and drifted off, knowing he had found a key to making his life, at least in small measure, lighter and brighter, and knowing with certainty the knowledge he had gained from his experience was much more than fairy-tale wishfulness—it was practical wisdom he could apply.

23

In his dreams that night, Ray discovered he could visit the perimeter of the Other Side where he had encountered Alice. He could walk through the meadow, though she would not be there waiting. Not now, not yet. Maybe later, when he was ready to make the final journey, when he needed her again, she would be his guide. Perhaps then, when he left this life, her assistance would be his, no matter what strange land he must cross.

Dreams, he discovered, also partook of the ideational nature of the afterworld. In dreams, however, the disconnect between spirit and body was not as severe as the disconnect in near death; in dreams, the spirit, released in small measure from its hypnotic attention on the body, momentarily visited the world of the mind detached from body. While the body was asleep, the spirit enjoyed a short respite from the enslaving chore of tending to the welfare of the body, a hiatus from the constant need to fix attention on the body's demands. Dreams, it seemed to Ray, were fleeting voyages to the periphery of the spirit's natural habitat. Dream content, not unlike near–death content, included the joyous, the puzzling, and the horrific; dream content, like most content buried in the repository of the subconscious, was mostly obscured and occluded by black clouds of forgetting. In dreams we struggled with the mundane, but also, on occasion, we parted the veil of forgetting and glimpsed the horrific or the spectacular.

Psychologist's attempts to ascribe the genesis of dreams to a reshuffling and optimization of the neuronal hard drive seemed to Ray to be a desperate but failed attempt to justify the brain-only model. It was clear to anyone who paid attention to dreams that the content was not wholly memories of everyday experiences. Dream content often encompassed scenarios and details which could only be accounted for by much richer experience. Perhaps the richness of experience that resulted from the spirit living more than one life, he mused. Scientists, steeped in materialism, were quick to dismiss dreams and imagination as unreliable and unimportant; for them, dreams were scenes to be clipped from the totality of our conscious experience and left on the cutting room floor. In their attempts to deify the objective, they missed the importance of the subjective. With their focus on the body, they missed the continuity of conscious life which extended into the dream world and the afterworld. Ray could see this clearly now, and yet, it was not something that overly concerned him. He was not yet ready for the monumental task of excavating entrenched thought, not yet prepared to change steeled hearts and rigid minds. He let go of the challenge of reforming science and slept well, secure in the knowledge that his near–death experience had opened doors to the totality of his being and broadened the expanse of awareness he enjoyed. Confident that Alice, when he needed her, would be there to guide him through future trials.

Harsh sunlight streamed through the window, silhouetting Randi, making it difficult for Ray to discern her features. He searched for other clues to her mood, all the while finding it odd to be bedridden and under his mother's care, as though he had stepped into a time machine and was once again a young boy sidelined by chicken pox or measles. The time travel moment conjured up old feelings that had hovered over mother and son during his growing-up years like a poisonous cloud; rather than attacking nerves and tissues, this poison wilted the emotions and the psyche. He now understood the origin of that cloud: the encounter with the ghoulish figure in the other-world had unlocked the mystery.

"When I was out," Ray said, "I encountered things...and

saw...maybe you always knew...I never did...as a kid you don't always see...he was ill, wasn't he?"

Randi knew exactly who Ray was talking about; she had waited a long time for this conversation.

"It wasn't a normal illness, it wasn't a medical illness," Ray continued. "It was his soul that was sick—discolored, infected, festering."

Randi fished a Kleenex out of her purse and dabbed a tear. "Thanks. I needed to hear you say that."

"He's no longer with us, is he?"

"I— I don't really know. I haven't heard. I imagine he's still—"

"I don't think so. When I was out, I saw...people. Perhaps it was only their dreams or their thoughts. But he was different. He was actually there, stuck in the dark world, not seeming to mind, like he belonged, like he was at home. Seeing him in that condition was sad. Aw, the hell with sad. It was ugly and disgusting."

Randi nodded, urging him to continue.

"As a kid, when I was afraid, I mistook that fear for weakness and covered my feelings and pretended to be brave. Pretended there was nothing wrong. Pretended he was just like other fathers. I know that made it harder on you." He took his mother's hand. "I'm sorry."

She leaned over and hugged him. He didn't complain about the stabbing pain in his ribs.

Father McCarty interrupted the tender moment, dancing into the room, displaying his soft shoe skills with a light-hearted flourish. He gave Ray a comical once-over. "Ah, the one that got away. For awhile, lad, I was hard at work negotiating for your soul. Had my sights set on saving you for our side. Did yer mum tell you you nearly went to heaven a Catholic?"

"Not sure I came anywhere near heaven. Hope I didn't spoil your quota," Ray kidded.

"Yes, that darn old quota. No rest for the wicked." He turned to Randi. "I'm glad the cheeky lad found his way back. From what I hear, he ventured more than a few steps beyond that locked door. Has he brought back any startling news?"

Ray, matching McCarty's banter, jumped in, "I believe there was some grumbling about the long wait they must endure before they have the pleasure of your charming company."

"Figures. I'll be there soon enough. I would inquire further into the nature of your trip and our ultimate destination, but my employer frowns upon such banter. A recent edict made it clear we're not to engage in such New Age trifles, but, don't worry, I can always count on my old friend Les to give me the skinny."

"Last night, Les was treated rather rudely," Randi said.

"Heard about that. Don't you worry. He's well acquainted with being shown the door. He wanted me to let you know that if you still want to share your experiences, he'd be delighted to listen."

Father McCarty slipped Randi one of Les' business cards. It was the second she had received. She held McCarty's hand for a beat, conveying her thanks.

"Well, must get on," he said. "Quota to fill. When you're ready to make the journey, son, don't forget you're spoken for."

The priest winked and was gone, bustling down the hall with a light step, on his way to spread hope and cheer.

That evening, alongside the well-done roast beef, over-cooked green beans, and cinnamon-topped applesauce, sat the colorful collection of meds Ray choked down every evening. He made a habit of polishing off the pills before he started the meal; his motto was get it over with.

Teri lingered after delivering the tray, which was unusual; meal time was one of the busy periods during her shift. Ray noticed her loitering. She returned a raised eyebrow, "Hey, Sherlock, see anything different?"

He looked her over: was it her hair? had she lost weight? He failed to discern any obvious change. She rolled her eyes and nodded toward his tray. The food looked pretty much the same, unremarkable; the tapioca dessert was a plus. He counted the meds. One, two, three— Four?

"Bingo," she said. "A wise patient always makes it a habit to check his medication."

"What magic pill have we added?"

"Seidman lobbied the doctor to add a little feel-good booster, a little happy times treat." She continued, with sarcasm, "We don't want that dark depression creeping up on us, now do we?"

"Thanks for the tip," Ray said. "I owe you."

She winked and exited, late for her rounds.

Ray buried the depression-fighter in the tapioca pudding and set the dessert aside. He didn't need, nor want, Seidman messing with his neurochemical balance. He resented the covert attempt to fit his mind with cement shoes. Before he could formulate a plan to formally express his dismay with Seidman, Chase, Randi, Hal, and Bren arrived, well-rested and in festive spirits.

Ray despised the role of party pooper, so he dragged his battered frame out of bed, crossed gingerly, grimacing all the way, to the closet where he slipped on a standard-issue hospital robe and slippers and prepared to hang out with friends and family.

Hal stuttered a few false starts, then blurted out, "I'm sorry, mate, but, while you were away, I'm afraid I stole your thunder and let the cat out of the bag."

"Congratulations," Chase said, wrapping Ray in a hug. "I never doubted you would get the funds."

"Hal, thanks for carrying on in my absence. I'm afraid my little encounter with the tree wrecked my timing as well as my truck," Ray said, absolving Hal of guilt.

It seemed like the perfect time for Chase to announce her news, but she hesitated to make a public pronouncement. It wasn't fair to Ray to make the special moment a public affair. Besides, she did not know how he would react. If she could only get him alone.

"How about a stroll, my dear?" he asked, with a touch of melodrama. He hadn't read her mind, he wasn't using telepathy; he, too, had been angling for some one-on-one time, and hadn't wanted to seem rude by ejecting his other guests. "You folks make yourself at home, we'll be right back."

Chase helped him adjust the crutches the candy striper Teri had delivered shortly after he vacated ICU. He swung himself out into the hall on his first athletic outing since the accident.

Hal and Randi busied themselves tidying up the room. Bren eyed the tempting tapioca and pondered what punishment might be meted out to pudding thieves.

"It was the oddest thing," Ray said, as he and Chase entered the nursery waiting room. "If I'm to believe Seidman, the father was a wee bit pissed off."

Chase seconded Jeff's father's disbelieving reaction. The idea of her disembodied fiancé eavesdropping on a childbirth session, wondering if he was being recruited to a new life, was a tad "out there" for her tastes. Unlike the proud father, she had no doubt Ray was telling the truth, the truth as he experienced it. Nonetheless, the narrative landed squarely outside the bounds of her known world. She would have expressed her strong personal reservations had her attention not been snagged by the "bundles of joy" dosing contentedly in their cribs on the other side of the glass.

"They're soooo cute," she exclaimed.

"Yes, they are, though it appears Jeff has left the building."

Studying the peaceful infants, Ray wondered if this next generation was different, wondered if guides like Alice had been making a difference in the between-lives period, wondered if the spirits being reborn, the spirits taking over these little bodies, were wiser, more prepared to make a difference in the world. There were people who said they could sense a spiritual change taking place in our age. The world was becoming more spiritual, they claimed. Perhaps the increase in spirituality had something to do with lessons taking place between lives, Ray told himself, lessons learned during "time-outs" between rides on the wheel of birth and death. During his brief sojourn in the disincarnate state, he had learned more than in the entirety of his schooling. If he had stayed longer, who knows what he might have learned and how well he might have been prepared when he returned.

Chase interrupted his reverie, "If you had to choose a name—"

"Boy or girl?"

"Don't know yet. Haven't had the ultrasound. Figured I would wait for you," she said, matter-of-factly.

Ray replayed her words half-a-dozen times, and still, they didn't add up. "You figured you would wait for me? To set the date? The wedding date, right? I didn't forget my promise: once the funding was approved, we would set the date. Just as soon as I can trot up the aisle without these darn crutches—"

"Don't think we should wait that long."

He *had* heard her correctly. Now he understood her previous question. "If it's a girl, Alice; if it's a boy, Michelangelo."

"You're saying it had better be a girl. Is that it, huh?"

He pulled her close, a bit of a trick on crutches, and kissed the top of her head, then kissed her mouth. Their kisses deepened. Yes, he thought, I am attached, but I'm also creating and happy with my creation, happy with the love I'm sharing.

A new father, at once exhausted and exhilarated by the ordeal and the triumph of childbirth, shuffled into the waiting room and flashed a double-take at the sight of Ray in the hospital robe, perched on crutches.

"Difficult delivery, huh?" the father half-kidded.

Ray smiled and ushered Chase out, not wanting a replay of his last encounter. Some things were better left unsaid.

Outside Ray's room, he and Chase stopped at the nurses' station. He whispered a request to the nurse on duty, a perky young lady with flaming red hair who radiated mischievous good humor.

As they entered his room, Ray spotted Bren, spooning her first bite of the heisted tapioca.

"Put that down!" Ray yelled as he hobbled across the room,

snatched the spiked pudding out of Bren's trembling hand, then dumped the contents in the toilet and flushed, twice.

Bren, stunned speechless and just short of tears, wondered what the hell had happened to Uncle Ray to turn him into such an ogre. It was only a cup of pudding.

The others in the room were as stunned as Bren.

Ray, exiting the bathroom to face a row of tense and serious countenances, realized his panicked reaction excited fears he had not anticipated. Events had stripped away the veneer of social harmony, revealing the concerns and fears of his loved ones: they doubted he had recovered with all his marbles intact. Explaining his need to duck Seidman's drug regimen probably would not win them over. So, instead, he went with the moment and huddled with Bren, forehead to forehead, pretending his pudding assault was only a joke.

He whispered confidentially, "Poison, my dear. Poison in the pudding. The evil forces trying to finish off Uncle Ray nearly knocked off his favorite ten-year-old."

He glanced around, his jittery expression telegraphing raging paranoia. For a moment, everyone in the room doubted his sanity—maybe the bump on the head had consequences the doctors failed to forecast. A beat later, Ray chastised them with a "get serious" smile, letting them know they had been kidded.

Before they could react, Ray was off again, hobbling on the crutches, intercepting the perky redhead nurse who slipped him a cone-shaped party hat and a noise maker, the kind that uncurls when you blow on it. He presented the items to Bren with a conspiratorial wink and drew himself up, posturing for an official pronouncement. He gestured for Bren to make ready the noise-maker.

"Two weeks from tonight, in a location yet to be deter-mined, the lovely maid Chase and our dashing, yet wounded, hero, yours truly, will be joined in holy matrimony."

Bren tooted on the noisemaker and kicked off a one-girl marching parade, her exuberance energizing her high-step march cadence.

For a beat, Randi's mind stalled out trying to process the good news, then she snatched the party hat from Bren and snugged it on top of her head.

Hal, meanwhile, grinning like a five-year-old on a sugar high, wrapped Chase in a congratulatory hug.

Ray felt the full impact of just how attached he was to these people, and, though he knew attachment brought liability, he didn't care. He understood attachment carried pain along with joy, but if one understood the world was transitory, something impermanent we create, and, if need be, re-create, then the liability was lessened. The encounter with Alice had impressed upon him the importance of actively creating the moment.

"Roughly nine months thereafter," Ray added, "our first child shall enter the world."

"Whoa, easy boy, let's not get overly confident," Hal challenged. As soon as the words tumbled out of his mouth, the full meaning of Ray's announcement registered. Randi was only a beat behind him in comprehending the message. Bren was uncertain just what had transpired, but she blew even harder on the noise-maker as Hal and Randi doted over Chase. When Ray proudly rubbed Chase's stomach, Bren's eyes widened with stunned amazement.

When it was all over, the nurses were heard to comment the party was one of the most exuberant celebrations that had taken place on the floor so far that year.

For the next two days, Ray continued to ditch the meds Seidman foisted on him, burying them in various and sundry desserts. On the morning of day four, he was discharged from the hospital and made the trip to the patient-discharge driveway in a wheelchair piloted by the once curt but now amiable orderly, who was hoping to bag another generous tip. At curbside, Chase and Hal greeted Ray and, along with James, helped him climb into Hal's Jeep.

Chase presented him with a balloon purchased in the gift shop. "Here, something to lift your spirits."

He thanked her with a kiss and when he looked up, his gaze locked on James. After a moment of silent interrogation, he said, "It was you, looking through the windshield, right?"

"Something like that may have happened. Hard to be sure. Apparently."

Ray placed his hand on Perspy's shoulder in a gesture of deep appreciation, a gesture also intended as a reality check, a probe to make sure James was real, standing before him in the flesh.

James fished the little monk out of his pocket and passed it to Ray. "Thought you might want to reclaim this fella. He's not much good at preventing wrecks, so I don't know if I'd hang him on your rearview mirror. But you might find other uses for him."

Ray closed his fist around the tiny icon and held it tight.

Hal fired up the Jeep, being of the opinion that the sooner they put major distance between themselves and the hospital, the better

"Place gave me the creeps," he shouted as he accelerated.

24

Hal downshifted as he cornered into the switchback, throwing the Jeep into a controlled skid. Coming out of the hairpin turn, he punched the accelerator, spewing gravel into the air. He was late, racing to James Perspy's cabin for a formal tea ceremony celebrating Ray's return to the living. Ray, Chase, Randi, and Les Crane would already be there. His mad dash, however, was inspired by more than party fever—bad news, delivered within the last hour, fueled his vehicular rage. He tore past the turnoff leading to the doomed pine tree and failed to spot Ray's rented Blazer bouncing down the side road leading to the turnout below the tree.

In the turnout, Chase parked the Blazer. Then she and Ray scaled the slope, not without some difficulty, to stand before the damaged and dying pine that had saved his life. It was the first time Ray had re-visited the crash scene, at least the first time while in the flesh. With a ceremonial flourish not unlike that involved in hanging a Christmas tree ornament or creating a shrine, he hung the tiny monk on a branch. Chase and Ray stood in silence. Ray let his mind shift through the events that had so dramatically altered his life.

The near-death experience had left him deeply moved. He greeted his second chance with unbridled enthusiasm, and yet, there was a downside. He had become painfully aware of no longer wanting to play the game of life—at least not by the rules that shaped the box which defined how the majority of humans lived. Cultural edicts no longer seemed relevant. Social myths that carved the "proper channels" we were to follow in society had lost their importance.

During his recuperation, he spent the early morning hours at the local coffee house, watching people on their way to jobs they hated, saddled by careers that no longer inspired. He had come to fear the mechanical, robotic rhythm that defined their lives. This was not to say he had no respect for the courage people mustered in the pursuit of their daily routines. Day after day, they struggled, like the mythic Sisyphus in the Infernal Region who was doomed to roll a huge stone up a hill only to have it roll back onto the plain where he would once again begin his toil. Ray was willing to put his shoulder against the rock with others, the effort did not daunt him; that which tortured him was the dark mystery in which Mankind found itself—perhaps, like Sisyphus, they were living in a hell. Having glimpsed a larger view of life, it bothered him that such a view was not more widely known. It bothered him that he could not share that which was most real to him. He felt alone in a crowd. His life, his thoughts, were out of synch with those around him. He harbored a secret that few wanted to know. As far as he knew, they were content to let him cling privately to his secret. It was not something they cared to glimpse.

Not that he was disenchanted with his life; to the contrary, he was more enthusiastic than ever, but he found it difficult to engage others, found it difficult to lift their gazes from the mundane to the vision of the world he had discovered. That difficulty was a source of frustration. Acutely aware of the desperate silence of the unhappy, acutely aware of the hypnotic state in which most humans lived their lives, he was moved by compassion to make a difference. At the same time, he was at a loss as to how to effect real change. That quandary created a dis-ease where there should have been only bliss.

He faced the daily realization that the number of players prepared to join him on the playing field he had discovered was extremely limited. As Alice would have pointed out had he asked, the boundaries within which solid citizens lived their lives were...well, quite solid. Once, he, too, had lived his life safely within bounds, with the smug certainty that he was one of the achieving normals, one of those who coped successfully with reality, as though conforming to external reality, catering to reality, was a noteworthy achievement. It wasn't. Now he was painfully aware of the false security his previous smugness had provided. Perhaps, in the end, it was better to be seen as mad. Artists who stepped outside the boundaries often were considered mad, when, in fact, they merely lived within a larger reality, within a bigger box, or perhaps they were closer to realizing they lived within a reality they helped create. For most people, however, there were no such options. As one author had once noted, most men lived lives of quiet desperation.

As Ray stood beneath the pine, sorting through the recent past, he realized Seidman, in particular, had cast an especially dark cloud. The man's thoughts seemed capable of endowing a space with a soiled quality. Ray quickly regretted the unkind thought. There was no need to be negative, no need to harbor critical feelings. From the outset, while bedridden, he had made up his mind to avoid discussing the details of his experience with the psychologist, knowing it would only upset him. There was little or nothing to be gained. And yet, while he was still in the hospital, the more Ray talked about the weather, the more Seidman suspected him of withholding his honest feelings.

The psychologist had made it his personal crusade to heal Ray. He had related tedious accounts of brain-damage research, stories of Phineas Gage's brain-piercing encounter with a rail spike, and other gross tales that, in his mind, proved the brain was all there was to consciousness: if brain damage impaired this or that function, that stood as proof there was no spirit; if autistic kids had difficulty recognizing their mothers, their malfunction proved the non-existence of spirit; if patients whose brain hemispheres had been surgically separated changed their behavior, the altered function was proof there was no spirit. Numerous times Seidman had quoted neuro scientists who fashioned dubious claims from all manner of brain disease and abnormality.

After listening to these arguments for the third time, Ray had lost his self-imposed control; he reprised one of Alice's lectures, explaining to Seidman there were three parts to the composite: the brain/body, the mind, the spirit. He explained how one must understand the function of each individually *and* understand how they worked in unison before one could properly analyze impairment or malfunction.

A damaged body functioned poorly, Ray argued, in the way a damaged race car performed poorly. A race car with a damaged steering mechanism, the result of a high-speed encounter with a retaining wall, might no longer execute left turns—but the malfunction did not provide proof the driver did not exist. The malfunction might only be evidence that the driver's frantic efforts to steer the car were being defeated by the crash-damaged steering mechanism. Furthermore, he argued, another scenario was entirely possible. The driver might have been knocked unconscious in the crash, leaving the car to continue on an erratic path with no driver in control. In that case, the body-machine could still perform, but would perform in an erratic manner as a result of the loss of the driver. Thus, Ray argued, one must be cautious and not draw unwarranted conclusions regarding the existence of spirit as a result of observing a damaged body. One must be careful when one analyzed a complex composite, such as the human being; one must not sign off, prematurely, on false conclusions.

Seidman remained opaque, scribbling notes furiously, finally having ferreted out Ray's true feelings. It appeared to Ray that Seidman failed to make even a cursory attempt to reason though the analogies Ray presented. More disturbing, he detected a strong dogmatic undercurrent in the psychologist's views. Seidman, it appeared, harbored an unstated agenda. Ray concluded this unacknowledged agenda was tied to a perverse need for power and control over other men's lives. If you convinced men they were robots and convinced them you controlled robot technology, you assumed a position of power.

The psychologist, Ray told himself, belonged to a discipline that inhibited spiritual advancement. Some had argued, perhaps with merit, that organized religion placed barriers in the path of spiritual enlightenment, but religion's infractions were minor when compared to the discipline of psychology which hammered away at the culture with its man-is-an-animal "theology." The new field of evolutionary psychology, holding hands with the emerging discipline called cultural biology, flooded the culture with theories of doubtful merit, theories lacking in a role for the spirit. These theories made preposterous claims that events happening millions of years ago on the African Savannah determined how four pounds of gray matter now dictates our hopes and dreams and loves and beliefs. The astounding gap between the capabilities of the lump of brain cradled between our cranial bones and the actual life we experienced, unimaginably rich in conscious experience and spiritual awareness, belied the theorists' pronouncements. Ray snickered at the poverty of thought in the field, but then was humbled when he recalled his own acceptance of those very same theories at a time when he lived safely within bounds.

He vowed to take a more compassionate and a less critical stance toward those who advanced such theories, then balked when he considered the likely response he would receive if he were to attempt to share his insights with them. Still, he refused to cave in to negativity. He would simply avoid confrontation. There was nothing to be gained by wrestling with those who compulsively erect barriers to understanding. He had erred in expressing his views to Seidman and vowed not to repeat the mistake. His vow, fortunately, was never put to the test, as the next day he had been discharged.

During Ray's silent recollection, Chase, watching the monk sway under the branch, re-visited the moment she had considered Ray might not return and recalled her subsequent struggle to come to grips with that awful reality. That he had returned was a miracle, she decided, as she slipped her arm around his waist and turned into his kiss.

Ray's attention snapped into the present; thoughts of
Seidman were left behind. Upon his return from near death, Ray
had discovered an odd and tangential benefit: his bodily sensations
were heightened. Chase was able to light him up with the slightest
touch. Her kiss sent silvery sparks shooting through his awareness
and, oddly, he seemed acutely aware of how her body responded,
as well as his own. As Alice would have said, he pervaded Chase's
form and experienced double the pleasure. The thought brought a
cat-that-ate-the-bird smile to his face, which garnered an inquisi-
tive look from Chase.

Though adversely affected by observing the suffering of
others and feeling at a loss as how to change their lives, an inner
bliss, a lightness of being, filled his days. He often found himself
covering what others might consider a silly grin. He would laugh
for no reason at all. He was inherently happy. He wondered how
long his state of bliss would last. How long would he experience
being attached and non-attached at the same time? He didn't know
and he didn't worry. He was happily parked in the here-and-now
present, enjoying every consecutive moment in time's flow.
    "We better head up to the cabin," he said. "I promised Les I
would give him my undivided attention for the afternoon."
    Chase pouted and ran her hand up his thigh, her fingers
searching for his zipper. "Are you sure that's where you want to put
your undivided attention?" she joked.
    He tossed a look at the monk, "Sssh, he's watching."
    Chase pulled back, embarrassed, then realized she had
been put on. Initiating an impromptu race, she sprinted for the car.
He accelerated quickly, but a bouquet of pains in his bruised and
battered body hobbled his performance and he finished a distant
second.
    "Damn," he swore, "these bodies take their own sweet time
healing."
    Chase backed the Blazer onto the road, tossed open the
door, waited for him to clamber in, then sped off.

25

When they arrived at the cabin nestled in a breath-taking mountain meadow that could have been lifted from a painting by Bierstadt, Randi greeted them with unexpected solemnity. She gestured toward the woods where Hal's angry expletives rent the alpine serenity; each curse was followed by the sound of a rock ricocheting off tree trunks.

"What the hell's wrong with him?" Ray asked. Receiving only shrugs in response, he hiked off to investigate.

Hal was perched on a boulder, swearing and hurling stones. Ray cleared his throat to make his presence known. Hal leapt up and wrapped him in a bear hug. So, Ray thought, at least his anger is not directed at me.

"That sonofabitch," Hal cursed. "You're not going to believe what that sonofabitch lowlife went and did. And I don't want you to think for one damn second you're responsible. In any way. You hear me? You're not taking this personally."

"What sonofabitch? What did I do? Or not do?"

"Man, you won't believe this. They pulled our funding."

Ray was at a loss for words. The question *why* shaped his features.

"Seidman cast some major doubt on your ability to run the program. The freak pissed in the pond of goodwill. He convinced the board you suffered 'long-term effects' from the accident. Said you 'could no longer be counted on to perform.'"

Ray picked up a stone and side-armed it into the woods. It ricocheted off trees and boulders.

"I tell you who's not going to be able to perform when I get done with him," Hal added.

"Whoa. That's cold. I knew he didn't like—I hardly told him anything. The guy copped an attitude. I had no idea he would scuttle our program."

Hal fired another rock, sending it careening off a tree.

"Damn," Ray said. "Man, I'm sorry. This really screws you, doesn't it? You've been waiting and now it comes to this, to nothing. I'm sorry—"

"Hey. Not your fault. Don't go gettin' guilty on me."

"Is everything okay?" Chase called from the cabin.

"Yeah, fine," Ray said. Then, under his breath, "A fine mess." He turned to Hal. "Don't spoil the afternoon for everyone. Don't say anything. Let's go have a nice, serene tea ceremony. We'll think of something. Maybe we'll sue. Nah, we're not going to sue anyone. Damn. I don't know what we'll do."

As Hal and Ray wound their way through the trees on their way to the cabin, they glimpsed Les pulling up in his beat-up, faded Volvo.

"Wonder if Seidman got word I was giving the paranormal researcher an interview?" Ray wondered aloud. "That would piss him off. He's taken a real dislike to the fellow."

"Maybe you should keep a lid on your story," Hal said.

Ray dismissed him with a look, then accelerated his gait, grimacing at the strain it put on his injuries.

When Ray arrived at the cabin, James was escorting Les on the royal tour of his one-room abode.

Randi was tending the boiling water and fussing over the placement of tea bags. Hal went to assist her.

Chase looked up, appraising Ray's mood with open concern. He escorted her outside to a rise overlooking the creek, a glistening crystal ribbon splitting the meadow. The snow on the ground was melting, but spring had not yet arrived; it was one of those days in late winter when the sun shines hot in the mountains, foreshadowing spring, while the frozen earth, not yet awakened to the coming season, continues its wintry snooze.

"What's up with Hal?" she pressed.

"He's coping. With a minor setback. Nothing serious."

"Oh? It's not like him to carry on like a psychopath, so I thought he might have a valid reason for cussing and attacking those poor trees."

"The accident changed all of us," Ray said.

"Yeah. It's been tense."

He was surprised to hear her frank sentiment. He wrapped her in a supportive hug. "I was thinking. We ought to make some changes. You know how easy it is to get stuck. One day follows the next and before you know it, you're caught in the same old rut."

Chase frowned her concern.

"That's one of my shortcomings," he continued. "Getting stuck in ruts. Comes naturally to me. The accident knocked me out of my rut. I don't want to fall back."

Chase studied Ray. *Where was he going with this monologue? Was this about the wedding? Had he undergone a change of heart?*

"Are we set for next week?" he asked.

She nodded, now doubly worried.

"What about Father McCarty? Did he agree to deliver the vows? Even though we're not baptized Catholic?"

"He promised to seek divine intervention."

"It's good we were able to move quickly. While my mother is here. It's not easy for her to make the trip."

Chase nodded.

"And Bren found a dress? Boy, I had no idea she would be so thrilled, so ecstatic, to be a flower girl."

"You have a funny way of getting out of ruts. What's up?"

He responded with a snort, followed with a dismissive shake of the head, an expression of flippant regret. "By the way, they cancelled our funding. We're out of business. The news upset Hal a bit." He smirked ironically at his understatement.

Chase reeled. His best bad-news punch had decked her

emotions.

Ray read her thoughts and fears. He made an effort to set them to rest. "Doesn't mean a thing. As far as the wedding goes. Doesn't change our plans. My decision to get married has nothing to do with the business, or funding. I got jolted out of that rut when I was—"

"When you were in a coma, flitting around in some imaginary world? Not sure that's a good time to make major, life-altering decisions."

"It was the best time. At least for that moment, I had a better vantage point on my life."

He reflected, then said, "At one point, Alice and I...were creating as though we were one. Our thoughts, our minds, were totally synchronized. It occurred to me that a marriage, a good marriage, must be like that. Not just hanging out, but creating together. Making decisions together—decisions that create a day-to-day actual world. You know, if we really do make the world we live in, we can decide to make that world together. I think we can do that. I know we can do that."

Chase nodded, the outline of the picture he was painting was coming into focus.

"When I was coming back and I thought I was starting over as a baby, I watched these new parents experience really amazing feelings. They were watching a child's life begin and sharing in the knowledge they had created a life. Wow. That was a major high. That kind of joy, that wonder, is something we should enjoy every day—"

"Well, duh, we kinda are doing just that," she said, resting her hand on her expanding belly.

"Yeah. We are. But I mean beyond that. I was thinking... As we create our world, as we give birth to life, together, moment to moment—" He paused. "I probably sound like some old time soapbox preacher."

"No, I understand. It sounds wonderful." She drew in a breath, then, "Your mother worried her marriage screwed you up

for good. She worried it would be difficult for you to create a relationship. She worried the trauma left scars that rendered you unfit
for domestic life."

"Yes, I know. We talked. I hope she can let that go. We
talked about my father. He was ill. In a strange way. Like it was his
soul that was sick and festering with evil. For my mom and I, living
with that illness was like living with a rabid dog, that was constantly
circling and circling, threatening. We never knew when we might
get bit and infected with his illness."

Chase simply nodded. There was nothing she could add.
Sympathy wasn't a valid response. She knew Ray had to deal with
the past on his own terms. Late into the night, he had talked with
her about his new views on destructive emotions. How they were
something we could make disappear, if only we were able to untie
the knots that held them in place. He had gone on for hours, talking
about desire and attachment and entanglement. And the knots that
tied us to our past. She hadn't understood much of what he said,
but she could tell he was changed. He had a handle on things in a
way he never had before. And he probably would figure out how to
untie the knot that tied him to this recent bad news.

"Will Hal be okay?" she asked.

"He'll be fine. We put everything into the plan, so we're
screwed when it comes to money. But it'll work out. Seidman
claimed I was unstable. Torpedoed the deal. You know, some
people, once they know you really desire something, work hard to
make it scarce. They work to take your dream away. I suppose
that's just part of the give and take that comes with a universe built
on desire."

"Well, I don't like it. Even if it is built in," she said. "You
think it's wise talking with Les? You don't know him all that well.
You see what happened with Seidman. Maybe you're inviting trouble."

"Just because Seidman screwed us doesn't mean we should
lose faith in our fellow man," he said. "I want to hear what Les has
discovered and I want to share my experience. Mother took a liking

to him, so I'm sure he's okay. Let's get back to the cabin, they'll be waiting for us."

As they walked, he asked, "Are you ready for a James Perspy tea ceremony?"

"Not sure I'll ever be ready."

"It'll be different. It'll keep us out of the rut."

James hosted an elaborate tea ceremony. Ray, during the long stretches that passed while they sat cross-legged in meditative silence, allowed his thoughts to wander—a mental river flowing freely between the banks formed by the sights and sounds of James' cabin: tea swirling in cups; pungent odor of the wood-burning stove; the rumble of the creek; dust motes dancing in rays of light that streamed through unwashed windows. He pondered the quality of the light, that most mysterious of all phenomena. *Sometimes a wave, sometimes a particle; always traveling at the same speed in a vacuum, no matter the speed of its observer. Electromagnetic radiation. An electrical field and a magnetic field in a vibrating dance. Electricity inextricably wrapped up with the push-and-pull of magnetism. The wondrous array of frequencies: gamma rays; X-rays; ultraviolet; visible light in a rainbow of colors; infrared and microwave. Communications and aesthetics. Sustaining energy.* Ray became acutely aware of the mysteries of light. *Let there be light. What was the origin of the first light?*

He focused his attention inward and left his analytical musings behind. He allowed intense emotions to percolate and bubble to the surface, wave after wave threatening to overflow, but inevitably waning, leaving Ray to visit the bliss of just being there.

When Ray looked over at James, he imagined him to be a magus orchestrating the event with an unseen hand. James returned the look, smiling, as though it was Ray who was the magician secretly in charge. Ray recalled Alice's lesson, how together we create reality, one ongoing, never-ending co-creation. In her model, each and every one of us was in charge—together. Ray was pleased to be one among a multitude of creator spectators.

James, it seemed to him, was a friend with whom he could play—one who appreciated the subtle way the world was changing, moment to moment. A kindred soul who also sensed the veil being lifted to reveal our common hidden spiritual nature. Ray promised himself that, when the opportunity presented itself, he would spend more time with James and get to know him. Conversations with James would not be the same as the one he was about to have with Les. James was a fearless explorer, traveling up the jungle river, while Les sequestered himself in his lab, arranging "specimens" in tidy little boxes. His game was categories and classifications, while James traveled to realms beyond category and class.

At times like this, surrounded by close friends, Ray felt at home in the universe, unlike the way he had lived most of his life—a stranger trapped in an inexplicable maze. He surfed the feeling, was content, and at peace.

After the ceremony, Ray toasted their wedding plans. Out of the corner of his eye, he caught his mother dabbing a tear of joy and was pleased. Formalizing the union with Chase seemed to unite those gathered. Two people committing to wedding vows, pledging their mutual support for better or worse, renewed the primal hope all men and women harbored. The hope that this was a universe in which it was possible to find loving agreement and lasting partnership. In spite of any and all evidence to the contrary, it was this hope that kept humankind looking forward to the future, stumbling into tomorrow with heads held high.

On the heels of the feel-good tea ceremony, Hal, purged of inhibitions, his anger having run its course, blurted out the news of the funding collapse, giving the bad news a stoic twist. Events had turned out for the best, he said. He and Ray would have suffered later, once their hearts and souls were totally immersed in Changes. Once they had achieved success, evil forces lurking behind the scenes would have trashed their dreams. It was better their enemies displayed their true colors early in the game. Hal toasted Ray for having smoked out the opposition. Ray, in turn, toasted Hal, complimenting him for having the conviction of a good and decent partner. With irony, Ray vowed they would enjoy their impending poverty as life-long friends.

James lowered his gaze and kneaded a serious thought. "While we're making announcements, I have a little news to add about a little business I've been forced to keep to myself. Until now. This week I completed negotiations for the purchase of the land in this valley."

"All of it?" Chase asked, with unguarded shock and surprise.

"We weren't even sure you owned the land this cabin sits on," said Hal.

"To be honest, we thought maybe you were a home-steader," Ray confessed.

"I've had plans in the works for a couple years. I'm building a spiritual retreat."

Ray initiated another toast. "To the success of your venture."

"I would be extremely pleased, I'd be honored, to have you two work on my dream project. And, given you're both out of work, I figure I can afford you now," he joked.

One of life's mysterious reversals of fortune had unexpectedly transmuted misfortune into bounty.

Ray, stunned, gave the fine-tuned planning that had been his previous mode of operation a rest. He met his good fortune with an open heart and an open mind.

26

Later, as morning became afternoon, Ray and Les hiked upstream to an idyllic setting where the creek widened and carved a sandy beach into the rocky landscape. The beach was dotted with smooth boulders, which appeared to have been positioned by a nature-spirit trained in Feng Shui for the comfort of weary hikers. The sun, ten degrees past its zenith, glinted off glassy sheets of water that curled effortlessly over and around granite boulders and collected in tranquil pools.

Les settled on a rock with his back to the creek, using his body as a baffle to shield his inexpensive microphone from the rumble of cascading water.

Ray selected a smooth, flat-topped boulder, settled in and leaned back; he closed his eyes and turned his face to the radiant energy of the sun, welcoming the solar balm he hoped would heal the scars on his forehead.

Les, a patient listener, took copious notes as Ray recounted his adventures on the Other Side. Though Ray's experience was unique— in the way any personal experience was unique—there were elements common to the near-death experiences of others, strong parallels to cases Les had previously investigated.

Like Ray, many NDE'ers reported an ideational world where thoughts were viewed in picture form and were shared telepathically. Some NDE'ers also encountered guides: some of whom were religious figures, though many were not. Often, when religious figures were encountered, the NDE'er simply assumed he was face to face with a religious figure, as the guides rarely declared their identity. Other NDE'ers were like Ray, Les told him, in that they could change location while in the near-death state—they could appear and disappear—simply by intention, their movements dictated by their thoughts. Often emotional concerns brought the person experiencing near death back to the real world, where they would view friends and loved ones who were unable to detect their out-of-body presence. These experiences, including those in which NDE'ers viewed their bodies from a position outside the body, had come to be called OBEs, out-of-body experiences. Though Les found Ray's experience not that unusual— except for its rich detail—unlike others, Ray was able to articulate insights he had gained. Quite often NDE'ers returned with a sense of awe and wonder, extolling ineffable epiphanies which endowed them with radically altered outlooks on life, but they were unable to explain the how and the why in a manner that made sense to those unfamiliar with the experience. Such stories, lacking in context, confused not only the person who had the experience, but researchers as well.

Les probed Ray's memory, drinking in the details like a derelict stranded in the desert who stumbles upon a cache of chilled Evian. Researching the paranormal, Les explained, involved enduring periods of tedium and boredom—hours spent sifting through existing reports searching for patterns—punctuated by the sporadic excitement that accompanied a fresh report. The survival-of-consciousness discipline relied, for the most part, on field work. The science of consciousness had not matured to the point where controlled lab experiments were possible or fruitful, though such shortcomings were being overcome as more and more researchers devised methods which allowed them to control at least some of the variables. Subjecting individuals to traumatic situations that mimicked real life, or more precisely, real death, was out of bounds, but some researchers were making sure that when such events did occur, the experience was documented with as much detail as possible. In this regard, Ray was a major find for Les.

Alice had transformed herself into a monk, Ray told Les, and had left him with a strong sense that he, too, had once been a fellow monk devoted to spiritual pursuits. For reasons he could not recall, he had broken away from the monastic tradition and lived subsequent lives immersed in the mundane. Perhaps his past was the reason he comprehended her lessons, though, he informed Les, Alice had considered him a difficult student, strictly a rehabilitation project. She had made an appearance, at least in part, he speculated, to remind him of his past and set him back on the monk's path, but he couldn't be sure, it was only a hunch, a vague sense of a past lost to the suffocating amnesia that shrouded all but a few long-term memories.

He explained to Les that all the lessons he had learned from Alice were merely a glimpse, a remedial tour, visits to places he should know but had forgotten. He explained how one must walk a path and unsnarl the karmic knots of the past, knots that entangled the individual spirit's mind with other minds and the collective physical. But he had no idea where to find the trail head to that path, though he was supremely confident such a metaphorical embarkation point did, in fact, exist, and confident he would eventually discover its location.

In spite of Ray's obvious enthusiasm and confidence, Les expressed concerns regarding Ray's future. Some who experienced near death found the transition to mundane life to be somewhat of a trial. He probed, asking about the impending marriage, about the business that had failed to get off the ground.

Ray assured Les he was not facing serious problems or making rash decisions, but he also expressed his upset with the paucity of like-minded individuals with whom he could share his thoughts. He told Les of the times he felt inspired to shake people and insist they wake up. He told him of how sometimes he felt the urge to stand on the steps of City Hall and shout through a bullhorn, announcing the end of The Great Sleep. He was also acutely aware that such bold actions resulted in folks being locked up or medicated by guys like Seidman. In the end, Ray figured, the good news would be relayed, person to person, in whispers, in quiet conversations taking place over coffee, or while walking along mountain streams, or watching the sun set over the ocean. The murmurs of this whisper campaign, he had come to learn, were already spreading far and wide, leaving people with certainty that changes were afoot. The days when monks were sequestered in caves and the ancient knowledge was a cloistered secret for the few were, apparently, coming to an end. And, yet, the gradualism was difficult for Ray to endure; he wanted overnight changes. Patience, he had learned, was an acquired virtue.

Les commiserated, acknowledging the degree to which one was forced to embrace the solitary life—that went with the territory. Luckily, the situation was changing. More and more, individuals were seeking insight into the spiritual realm.

An hour later, in mid-interview, Les rose suddenly, waved, and shouted, "Hey, Kyle, over here."

Kyle Winston, outfitted in hiking boots, khaki shorts, a sweat–stained Stetson, and a faded denim shirt, with a beat-up Kelty day pack slung over his shoulder, slid down the embankment and found a boulder to call his own, as if he was expected. He pulled out a pouch of tobacco, an imported Dutch blend, then snagged a packet of Zig Zag cigarette papers from his shirt pocket and proceeded to roll a smoke. His walking stick was carved out of hardwood not native to the region. Ray shot him a query—*do I know you?*

Les apologized, "Sorry. This is Kyle Winston, physicist, who, many years ago, offered to review my papers, fully expecting to debunk my wacky theories and send me packing with a return ticket to la la land. Since that inauspicious beginning, he's become a minor fan. Though not a soul in his professional life is privy to our dirty little secret."

Kyle licked the cigarette paper, inspected his handiwork, then looked up at Ray. "I'd planned a hike, but Les insisted I stop by to meet you. I don't have much time. I'm hoping to make it over the pass before sundown."

Ray bobbed to his right and found an angle where the sun was not glinting off the physicist's Ray Ban's. Behind the aviator sunglasses, he found the steady gaze of cool green eyes ringed by crow's feet, the lingering tracks of a lifetime's worth of skeptical squints. As Les briefed Kyle on Ray's experience, focusing primarily on Alice's idealistic version of cosmology, Ray realized that with Kyle one quickly became a specimen to be dissected and analyzed. The physicist was one of those poor souls afflicted with the compulsion to strip off the layers of reality in a constant search for a more basic physical reality. He had been a reductionist on a quest for the scientist's Holy Grail, a primary physical truth. As years passed and Kyle pursued this goal with ever-increasing passion, Les told Ray, he had come to doubt the wisdom of old-fashioned materialism. For Kyle, materialistic reductionism had come to resemble myth more than rock-steady rational thought.

"The discoveries of the past century put the old models in doubt," Kyle said. "It seemed the farther we pursued a purely physical theory, the more elusive that goal became. Physicists, like myself, hate to face up to what nature is telling us, so we harden our resolve and blindly plunge ahead on the same path."

"Tell him what upset the proverbial apple cart," Les prodded.

Kyle took a thoughtful puff on his cigarette and shot Les a pained expression. The answer to the question was more involved than Kyle wished to pursue with limited time available.

"It boils down to a new understanding of the observer and the observed. A new understanding of space and time," Kyle replied.

"Oh, is that all?" Ray kidded.

Kyle returned a squinty smile and launched into his explanation. "Special Relativity started the ball rolling with a new look at the importance of how observers view space and time. Prior to relativity, we assumed an absolute space and time. We were taking, more or less, a God's-eye view. In the theory of relativity, the observer, embedded in the universe, plays the central role. Two observers, each in their own labs, both moving at a constant speed, discover identical laws of physics. When they conduct experiments in their respective labs, they arrive at the same results. In addition, they each discover the fact that changed science—no matter how fast or slow their lab is traveling, or in what direction, they observe light moving at a constant speed. The speed of light, in a vacuum, remains the same, no matter how fast or slow the lab travels."

"Constant speed?" Les asked, drawing Kyle out.

"Prior to Special Relativity, it was assumed that if an observer traveled in the same direction a beam of light traveled, the light wave would appear, to the observer, to move slower. For example, if you tossed a rock into a large pond, creating waves that propagated outward at twenty miles per hour, then hopped on your motorcycle and drove adjacent to the pond at ten miles per hour, from your point of view, the waves would appear to move slower. If you traveled at twenty, the same speed as the wave, the wave would appear, to you, to stand still. If you road in the opposite direction, the wave would appear to travel faster. Thus, it was assumed one could add or subtract the velocity of the wave to the velocity of the observer. For light waves, however, that turned out to be wrong. No matter how fast or slow your motorcycle or your lab or your spaceship travels, light moves at the same speed."

"Which turned things upside down," Les added.

"It meant different observers in motion viewed space and time differently. The way they viewed the contents of each other's labs was different. Observer A viewed the clock in his own lab different from the way Observer B viewed the same clock. Special Relativity describes the universe as an evolving network of relationships between observers. The discovery that the speed of light was constant for all observers, regardless of their motion, was revolutionary, but another critical idea, that was only appreciated later, was the importance of the observer. We no longer view the universe from a God's-eye view, but rather as a network of relations between observers."

"Yes, I'm aware the importance of the individual observer

to calculations became apparent, but one could still take the reference frame of a God, if one wanted," Ray added.

Ray was not unfamiliar with the subject, after all, he had
been reading for a degree in the philosophy of science. Kyle nodded slowly, taking in Ray's comment. Les had failed to brief Kyle on
his background. It didn't matter, Ray reflected, each individual
recounting of a story was unique. Each time he heard a description
of relativity, he learned something new. He was reminded of the lit-
erary passage that speculated we would, at the end of our travels,
arrive where we began and know it for the first time. The name of
its author escaped him— *ah, yes, it was T.S. Elliot, wasn't it?*

"It gets worse," Kyle continued, flashing a wry smile.
"Quantum theory further challenged our ideas regarding the role of
the observer. Though many scientists apply the principles of quantum mechanics with incredible precision, they lack a single definitive interpretation of what quantum theory really means in terms of
the underlying reality. We find ourselves grappling with puzzling
and paradoxical interpretations. One model suggests the act of
observation determines what becomes real—observation and measurement determine the state of a system. For example, if our
experiment is designed to measure light as a wave, we observe a
wave, but if our experiment is designed to detect particles, we
observe particles. It appears that only when we observe a system is
its state determined. Some call this a collapse of the wave function—"

"Don't get technical on us," Les chided, painfully aware
Kyle was prone to esoteric descriptions peppered with higher
math.

"Set aside the details of Schrodinger's wave equation for the
moment and simply consider the equation to be a description of the
state of a single particle or system. Now imagine a vast sea of particles and virtual particles, none of them having a definite position or
state— they are simply one vast sea of potential. Imagine a collection of simple pictures, with each picture representing a unique
possible state of those particles. The picture would be what we call

a configuration."

He fetched a deck of cards out of his day pack and fanned them out on the boulder. "Each card represents a possible state."

Ray nodded as, so far, he was tracking with the idea.

"In quantum mechanics, probability plays a large role. We describe what *might* become real in terms of probability. When we make a measurement, we might find any one of these possible pictures," he said, running his hand over the cards. "However, until an observer interacts with the system, the system has no definite state of existence—it could be any one of the pictures—it is as though the system exists in all possible states at once," he said, again waving his hand over the cards. "When the observer engages in measurement, in an act of observing, that is when one picture, one card, is selected and the system takes on that value. That picture becomes real," he said, holding up the deck and gesturing for Ray to select a card. Ray pulled out a queen of spades. "We call the process of going from the set of all possible outcomes to one definitive state, a collapse or reduction of the wave function." He palmed the remaining cards. Ray still held the Queen. "All the pictures, except one, disappear. All possibilities disappear, leaving one result—reality."

"It's as though the universe exists in a state of maybe, a state of continual possibility, until our interaction with it brings about a definite reality," Les added.

"In a way we don't fully understand," Kyle continued, "the act of observation is involved in what becomes real. The observer and the observed are part of one system, but we don't know exactly how that system works."

He paused, struck a match, and re lit his hand–rolled ciga-rette. He squinted and exhaled smoke into the air as he continued. "Dirac came up with a model that may be relevant. Keep in mind all models in physics are analogies, mental models that allow us to picture that which we can't see. We then check to see if experi-ments behave as our models would behave."

Les scribbled down a note. When Ray queried him with a

look — *what did you write?* — Les said, "All physics models are analogies."

Kyle continued. "Dirac proposed a sea of electrons with negative energy. We don't see them. They are part of empty space, the void. Imagine this sea to be the unseen fabric of the shared space of which your friend Alice spoke. When energy is added to the sea of virtual particles, an electron pops out of the fabric and becomes a real particle, with a negative charge. The hole it leaves behind behaves like an anti-particle with a positive charge, the positron. You've heard of electrons and positrons and anti-particles, haven't you?"

Ray nodded.

"When the electron falls back into its hole, both the electron and the positron disappear, giving off energy. You see when these two anti-particles collide, they disappear."

Ray nodded. Les' eyes were beginning to glaze over.

"So, if we allow naked speculation, we might apply this to Alice's lessons," Kyle continued.

"How's that?" Les asked.

"Imagine that we, as conscious beings, create energy, like Alice showed Ray with the balloon. Imagine we project that energy onto this shared fabric and that added energy causes particles to emerge from the sea of virtual particles, from the void, and become real. Thus the pattern of thought we project onto the fabric becomes the pattern of the particles that spring into existence. Our thoughts shape reality."

Kyle's mind hiked through its own high-altitude terrain; he wasn't looking for Ray or Les to follow or to support his speculation. He worked alone on a blackboard in his mind even as he speculated out loud.

"Then we have the idea of a pilot wave," Kyle mumbled, to no one in particular. "Consider we have a large tanker ship at sea, and consider we're able to control the direction of that ship using commands delivered via a radio signal. With an almost imperceptible signal, with almost pure information and no mass, we control a massive vehicle. If our thoughts are like that radio signal, like that pilot wave, they provide the information that determines how matter behaves."

"The problem of coming up with *the* interpretation of quantum theory rattles physicists something terrible," Les interjected. "Some interpretations of quantum theory, it seems, are merely transparent attempts to circumvent the role of the observer. Efforts to remove the conscious observer from the equation."

"When we should be attempting the opposite," Ray noted.

"Observation translates into consciousness," Kyle added, drawing in a breath of smoke as though it fueled his brain. He squinted as he exhaled, prominent lines in his face attesting to a lifetime of cogitation brought to bear on esoteric problems. "In both relativity and quantum mechanics, reality is linked to the observer. We know that, but physics, in its haste to restrict its explanations to the strictly material, fails to fully define this observer and fails to understand consciousness. A mistake is made when consciousness is assumed to be an emergent by-product of the physical."

"We can never take the observer out of the equations, can we?" Ray asked, rhetorically.

"That's right. The observer cannot be subtracted from the equations," Kyle responded.

"No conscious observer, no science," Les added.

"No reality as well," Ray said. "Sounds very much like what I learned—consciousness creates reality."

"Perhaps," said Kyle, seeming to back off. "We don't really know, as a practical matter." He skipped a rock off the glistening surface of an eddy. "I've concluded that, in order to make progress, we have to understand consciousness as something that exists on its own, apart from objects. That's the focus of my efforts, bringing a better understanding of the conscious observer to physics. Not to explore the physics of consciousness—though that figures in—but rather to explore the role of consciousness in physics. I have a hunch we will never arrive at a final theory, a theory of everything, until we factor consciousness into the model. But don't tell anyone I'm working on this, not yet."

If what this physicist was saying was true, even scientists were coming to recognize the idealism Alice had preached, Ray thought. If only she had been their professor. Ray borrowed Les' pad and pen and sketched Alice's model of consciousness overlapping the body. He showed it to Kyle. "What do you think?"

"Possible. Very possible. Nothing in science would tell us it's not possible."

Kyle took a long pull on what little remained of his cigarette, squeezed the ember out with his fingers, and deposited the butt in his pocket. He flashed Les a conspiratorial smile, "You've sworn your friend to secrecy, right? I was never here."

"It's professional suicide for him to be found in our company," Les half-joked to Ray.

"You have tenure, don't you?" Ray asked.

"Yeah, sure, but haven't you heard of shunning? Don't think it doesn't happen. Besides, if they find out, they'll repossess my pocket protector. What's a physics nerd without a pocket protector?" Kyle grinned as he hefted his pack onto his shoulder. "In the old days, you were called before the committee if you were suspected of consorting with communists, like what happened to Oppie. Now the committee searches under physicists' beds for paranormal freaks, like you two." He feigned a paranoid glance over his shoulder. "None the less, we should meet again," he promised as he disappeared up the path adjacent to the stream.

Tacking an addendum on the meeting, Les explained, "He's helping me design new research protocols. I'm helping him with some basic conceptual work."

Ray chuckled to himself. No doubt Les would bring them together again—under the guise of having Ray relate his experience. But Ray doubted he would get in more than a few words as Kyle was a professional classroom lecturer, riding solo on the breaking waves of his inquiring intellect. Ray was encouraged, nonetheless, that at least a few rebels from the establishment were beginning to consider key questions—even if they were forced to keep their illicit musings hidden. He laid back and soaked up the sun's rays, which were weakening as the orb's descent toward the horizon picked up speed.

After interrogating Ray for another half hour and scribbling a few final notes, Les told him, "You've helped a great deal. I'm writing a paper. Outlining a series of hypotheses. I'm calling the work "The Spirit Hypotheses." I would be pleased if you would proof the rough draft."

Ray nodded. A drop of water splattered his cheek. A second drop plunked off the tip of his nose. Quite bizarre, he thought, as there wasn't a dark cloud in the sky. Out of the corner of his eye he glimpsed a flat stone skipping over the creek, raising a fine spray of droplets. Then he heard the tell-tale giggle.

Torturing his bruised and healing body, he leapt up and gave chase. A squeal of feigned panic arose from a nearby bush and Bren, attempting to make good her escape, slid helplessly down the slippery mud embankment into his grasp. He cantilevered her out over the stream, threatening to deliver a punishing dunk in the freezing water. Then he summarily commuted her sentence and lowered her to her feet.

Les, chuckling at her mock distress, enjoying the horseplay, became her next victim. She hefted a fist-sized rock into the pool, creating a splash that doused him.

"You're into all that *weird* stuff, aren't you?" she harangued.

Les might have assumed she was teasing, but wisely observed her intent was heartfelt.

She kneeled and plunked a volley of rocks in the stream.

"Yeah. I research the weird stuff that happens to people. So they can understand it better."

"I understand," Bren replied. "Some people don't. But I know I was here before."

"Here?" Les prodded.

"Yeah, you know, I was someone else before."

"You'll have to tell me all about that. You know there is research on kids who remember past lives. One guy spent forty years studying the subject. He still does, as far as I know."

"It's not something you talk about," Bren replied.

"You're right. Not unless you want to. Ray was just telling me what happened to him."

"I know. When I visited the hospital, I saw he was gone. I could tell. It isn't that hard. But it don't mean nuthin.'"

"It can mean something. Some people have a need to know what happened—"

"So they don't think they're crazy?"

"Something like that." Les turned to Ray. "Which reminds me, would you be interested in speaking at a little gathering I'm hosting next month? Share your experience with a few people."

"A few people?"

"A couple hundred of my best friends show up on a good night," Les replied, collecting his recorder and notebooks, signaling the end of the interview.

Ray assisted Les up the bank as Bren fired off one last missile that splattered them with icy droplets. Together, they hiked toward the cabin, where Bren's mother, Eva, narrowed her eyes and scouted for her AWOL daughter. When she spotted her target, she waved, a wave that was both a greeting and a summons. Bren smirked, they had been there less than an hour and already she was being rounded up and put under house arrest like an enemy prisoner.

"Don't know if I should be putting myself up front like that," Ray said, in answer to Les' invitation. "I'm a lousy public speaker. I fluster too easily. This experience was kind of personal. I'm not sure I'm ready for any penetrating questions. Besides, I've no idea what my calendar looks like. You'll have to speak with Chase. I think I have a wedding to attend."

"Me, too," Bren said. "I'm a maid of honor."

"Thought you were a flower girl."

"Nooo. Maid of honor. I have to get a dress, you know. And

shoes. And we have to rehearse. A lot."

"So you're not available to speak about your past life recall?" Les kidded.

"No time. Do you have any idea how long we've waited for this wedding to happen? It's a good thing it did. I won the bet."

"Bet?" Ray queried.

"With my mother. She said you were never going to pop the answer."

"You mean pop the question?" Les asked.

"Yeah, that's it. Mom said 'Ray's too much a loner, too much in love with himself.' But I knew Uncle Ray would pop the answer. I know things like that."

"How much did you win?" Ray asked.

"Twenty bucks."

"Twenty bucks! You gotta split with me. You know that, right?"

She shot him a skeptical look out of the corner of her eye, checking to see if he might be kidding.

"Did you get cash?" he asked.

She slapped her hand over the pocket of her jeans. "I'm not splittin' anything," she said.

Ray feigned pursuit, sending her on the run, screaming.

Ray drew a deep breath and exhaled. He scanned the scenery, taking in the snow-capped peaks of the Divide and the rolling meadow which would be dappled with wildflower blossoms in a few weeks. He felt detached from his body, at one with all he viewed, as though a burden had been permanently lifted and enslaving bonds had been cut. He knew he was experiencing a small measure of freedom compared to the blissful states Alice promised he could achieve, but, at the moment, even this meager freedom was nearly overwhelming and made him wonder if he could tolerate an even higher high. Emotions which used to weigh him down were now simply rivers of feeling flowing through his awareness, sparkling energy streams he could taste and enjoy but which he recognized were transient and ever-changing. Something to be viewed, not possessed. He had even worked with Chase, teaching her how to become still and view her emotions, both the unwanted and the desirable, and she had caught on quickly.

"I'll do it," Ray said.

Les frowned. "You'll do what?"

"Speak at your event."

"What changed your mind?"

"If I'm not willing to share what I learned, what kind of person would that make me?"

"A shy person?"

"No, a selfish person. We have a responsibility—"

"I'm not sure we owe anyone. But I guess we can choose to be responsible."

"Well, then, I'm choosing to come to your git-together and speak." Feigning a moment of doubt, he added, "Two hundred of your *closest* friends, right?"

Les chuckled. "I'm acquainted with a few of them."

27

Two weeks later, late in the afternoon on an exquisitely perfect day—a day blessed with crisp clean air, pristine blue skies, and radiant sunlight—a day that many would consider a gift from the gods, Hal, shirtless and sweating, swung a double bladed axe, notching logs that would frame the main lodge of James Perspy's retreat. Ray, also shirtless, and quickly regaining his health, positioned the notched logs around the perimeter of the foundation, which had been poured two weeks earlier, the day after the wedding. Pine sap splattered on their skin and collected sawdust. At this altitude, the sun, even in spring, deepened their tans. The spots of sawdust against tan skin created a leopard pattern that gave the men a primitive at-one-with-nature appearance.

James had departed an hour earlier, hiking up the canyon to survey an irrigation system designed to crisscross the property with streams. The plan was that each cabin would be within earshot of a bubbling brook. James' guests, each night, as they fell asleep, would be treated to a subliminal reminder of life's constantly-changing nature.

Chase parked the Blazer alongside the cabin, which now served as a bunkhouse. When the building was completed and the retreat was ready to open, Chase and Ray would have their own cabin, but, during construction, the men roughed it, bunking together. Chase hopped out, carrying Ray's newly-pressed suit. He should have been waiting at the cabin door, showered and ready to go, but was nowhere in sight.

She hung the dry-cleaning bag on a branch and followed the

sound of an axe blade biting into a pine log. Half way up the trail to the lodge site, she bumped into Ray as he sprinted past, tossing a kiss, double-timing it in the direction of the makeshift shower outside the cabin. *"I'm late, I'm late, for a very important date,"* he mumbled as he hurried down the path, his crutches now a memory.

Chase pretended to scold him with a shake of her head, and then, with time to kill, continued up the trail to the lodge site to watch Hal notch logs.

"Sure you don't want to go with us?" she asked. "Moral support."

"Nah. That dog and pony show is Ray's thing."

"Maybe he'll need a friend in the audience. He isn't used to public speaking."

"Maybe he shouldn't go." James appeared, unannounced, having approached with uncanny silence.

"Why not?"

"I doubt those at the presentation will have the experience needed to understand what he has to say. And that means he will encounter nothing but doubt. Which can only be bad for him."

Chase, in ways she hadn't acknowledged, agreed with James. But she wasn't about to construct a road block in the middle of Ray's chosen path.

"They'll not accept what little he knows for what it is," James continued. "They'll demand he explain everything. The entire story of creation in great and exacting detail. If he fails, if there's the tiniest detail he can't explain, they'll claim he's a fraud. Better he remains silent."

"Sounds like you speak from experience," she said.

James nodded, but did not elaborate.

"That doesn't bode well for the retreat," she said. "Everyone keeping secrets."

Hal smiled to himself, amused with Chase's offensive probe, and swung the axe, notching another log.

"The difference," James replied, after a moment, "is those

who come to the retreat make a commitment to discovery. They'll not be expecting tidy little answers tied up with ribbons and bows. They'll expect hard work. They'll eschew the quick-fix."

"I sure as hell hope so. If not, they'll be terribly disappointed," she kidded. "Ray feels Les Crane's work is important. We need scientists to recognize life is about more than random lumps of clay. If we don't, they just might blow us lumps of clay off the face of the planet."

"Les tilts at windmills. The scientific community is not ready to understand. They have other goals, and they will remain true to those goals. Anyone who thinks such minds, mired in prejudice and fear, will be open to discovery is dreaming. Les is a latter-day Quixote who will mount his donkey—or was it Pancho who rode the donkey? Anyway, he'll lead the charge against the windmill with Ray at his side. We can only hope Ray's injuries will be slight."

Chase flustered. She caught Hal smirking and tossed a wood chip at him. James gave her a hug, expressing his undiminished affinity. "Hey, don't worry. It'll be fine. I'm just cranky today."

"Yeah, okay, you cowards stay here. Mystery mongers. Keep your little secrets. Ray will return with the enemy's blood on his sword."

She tossed air kisses and jogged toward the cabin, chuckling at her rebuttal. She knew that if either Hal or James thought Ray was in any real danger they would stand in the way of his departure. They were having fun at her expense, creating faux drama where real drama did not exist—*weren't they?*

Later, as Chase navigated the steep road that wound down the hill toward the city, with Ray in the passenger seat, tying his shoes and tie, she cast covert glances his way, enjoying the opportunity to observe her new husband unnoticed. The work on the retreat was good medicine, he was healed and healthy, and yes, vibrant. The near-death experience had changed him. He now sprinted through life, apparently without extra baggage. She hoped it wasn't a temporary high—a prelude to a tragic plummet into depression. She banished the thought. There was nothing transient about the changes he had undergone. She had watched him closely and saw him approach life with a new set of skills. When he was faced with destructive emotions, when others tried to get in his face, he became detached. It was not apathy he showed, but rather the detachment of a neutral, dispassionate observer. If anything, when he was confronted with opposition and negative emotions, he was more there, more of a presence, than ever before.

He had tried to explain detachment to her, but it didn't totally sink in. He had used an analogy to make it more clear. She imagined a large vat of boiling water filled with Jell-O mix, as he requested. He explained that if a knife was passed through the hot water with the mix in it, clumps of gelatin would stick to it, no matter how clean and sharp and shiny its blade. The spirit, however, being immaterial, could pass through cleanly, nothing would stick—with the spirit there was nothing to which the gelatin could stick. Continuing the analogy, he told her that if the spirit surrounded itself with its thoughts, if the spirit was clinging to its mental energy, the metaphorical gelatin would stick to that energy.

He explained that as the Jell-O cooled, it would gel into shapes patterned around that mental energy. Falling in love with those forms, spirits would continue to collect more and more mass. The forms they created in unison would stick together and make even larger forms, and pretty soon the entire vat would gel into a wiggly solid. After that, when one spirit moved a form, the vibrations would shake other forms. That, he explained, was called holism. As the universe had become more solid and forms had taken shape, spirits had become surrounded by the mass shaped and formed by their thoughts. They no longer moved about freely and cleanly. She didn't follow completely, but she did appreciate the metaphor of the spirit moving through the mix with nothing sticking. That was exactly what he now appeared to do when faced with destructive emotions.

When she popped out of her reverie, she found him eyeing her with an expression that was one big question mark.

"A penny for your thoughts," he said.

"Jell-O. Trying to make sure the Jell-O doesn't stick."

He leaned over and kissed her on the cheek.

They arrived a half-hour early and cruised past the lecture hall whose marquee announced: "The Afterlife: Is It Real?"

"Sure you're ready for this circus?" Chase asked.

"Not really," he replied, at the same time gesturing for her to pull into the lot at the end of the block. He was attending the event, ready or not.

On the way to the front door of the auditorium, they zig–zagged through a sparse crowd carrying signs: "Fraud." "Welcome to La La Land." "God is dead. Leave him alone." "Delusions for Sale." "You live, you die, get over it."

Ray suppressed a sarcastic smirk and fought off the urge to engage the protestors. "If these are his closest friends, I'd hate to meet his enemies," he said. He tossed the protestors noncommital smiles as he and Chase threaded their way toward the entrance.

Chase wondered if James had been more prophetic than she anticipated. Were these surly protestors capable of inflicting harm? Were they bent on destruction? She pushed the thought aside, looked closer at the demonstrators, then chided herself for being overly paranoid. Many looked as though they had spent way too much time staring at computer screens; their raster-weary eyes had been rendered permanently out-of-focus. One older gen-tleman with an ample girth looked like he had probably spent the last twenty years in the dark and dank basement of a library pouring over mildewed back issues of Popular Science. Two women, their faces pinched into sour pouts, protested on the general principle "life sucks." No doubt all the demonstrators had once been vic-tims; no doubt they had suffered bruised knuckles and derrieres, standard injuries inflicted by ruler-wielding nuns, and now *they* were ready to smack some knuckles and kick some ass. She could not blame them.

A different sign caught her eye. A fellow with close-cropped blonde hair toted a poster board on which was scrawled: "Jesus died for your sins. Show some respect." Maybe the protestors would end up brawling, she mused. Science fundamentalists, or fundies, versus religious fundies. It was bound to happen one day.

Ray had been right, she realized. She could actually feel a tangible presence, a cloud of some sort, surrounding the fundamentalists—whether they lobbied and protested on the side of science or on the side of religion. With either group, it seemed as though dogmatic commands were being shouted at them from some invisible realm—commands that demanded their strict obedience. Rigidly-held beliefs had become puppet masters pulling hidden strings. How could mere ideas possess such power?

Ray had tried once to explain Idealism to her, but she had not grasped the concept. Now she wondered if she was glimpsing an upside-down version of the philosophy. Was this a case of inverted Idealism, a weird twist wherein thoughts themselves and programmed minds had become masters dictating the actions of their flesh–puppet slaves? They pushed through the entrance before her nightmare musings gained any more life.

Inside the lobby, the protestor's chants faded. The mood turned warm and convivial. Moments after they entered, Les greeted them and presented Ray with a gift: a pink unicorn pin. As Ray fastened the pin to his lapel, he was temporarily blinded by the flash of a still camera. Even before his vision cleared, giggles revealed the identity of his tormentor. It was Bren. She was wearing her maid of honor dress, having rarely taken it off since the wedding. Feigning jealousy that Ray, and not her, had received a pink unicorn, she pouted. Les gestured for an assistant to fetch another pin. Ray tousled Bren's hair. She pulled away and clicked off another candid snapshot. Ray flashed a whataya–gonna–do smile to her mother. Before he could say hi or chat with Eva, Les took him by the arm and led him away.

"How's your mother?" he asked.

"Fine. She flew back to the coast. She sends her best."

"She's a lovely woman," Les said, meaning it. During the weeks she had stayed on for the wedding, Les had developed a fondness for Randi.

Ray, hearing the longing in Les' voice, recalled the wedding reception and, for the first time, it registered that Les and his mother had danced frequently and late into the night. He nudged himself mentally, he must pay closer attention to others. Life was teeming with events and, if you paid too much attention to your own thoughts and concerns, you missed too much.

"I'll look her up during my upcoming lecture tour. What's wrong?" he asked, noticing Ray's fleeting concern. Or was it regret?

"Mom called this morning. You know how, in my NDE, I saw my father in the woods. How I said he was different from the others?"

"Yes."

"When Mom returned home, she did some checking. My father died, six months ago. No one contacted us. Probably no one knew we existed. He'd been out of touch for so long. Anyway, I'm sure my mother would love to hear from you."

Les put his arm around Ray's shoulder and slipped him his paper titled "The Spirit Hypotheses."

Ray had seen the work before, had critiqued a rough draft, making numerous suggestions Les incorporated into the final edition. Tonight, for the first time, Les was presenting the paper to the public, which was why he had asked Ray to give a short talk about his experience. It was a way, perhaps, for Les to underscore the fact there *was* evidence. There were normal people, people like your next-door neighbor or your family dentist, who had stumbled into experiences that demonstrated the existence of the spirit. Ray didn't mind being used to support the research, if it helped other people with similar experiences understand what they had gone through.

Les, glancing at the protestors outside, warned Ray that, at the last minute, he had invited a more diverse audience than usual. Some might be critical, he said. But they were mostly harmless, silent critics. However, one could never be certain. Hecklers were known to make an appearance at such events.

Ray didn't mind, he felt he could withstand heckling. After all, hadn't he heckled Alice through much of their encounter? He understood how challenging it was to grasp spiritual concepts without firsthand experience. Perhaps it was impossible. Besides, he planned to keep his comments light-hearted and entertaining, encouraging rather than challenging. Thinking back to the unwavering patience Alice had shown in the face of his disbelief, he smiled to himself. Then he noticed Chase staring at his grin, mouthing "what's up?"

He responded with a quick kiss, led her and Bren to front row seats, then climbed the steps to the speakers' dais where he found Kyle, the physicist, puffing on a home-rolled cigarette, scanning his handwritten notes.

"Coming out of the closet tonight?" Ray kidded.

"I'm here to critique your presentation. Hope that's okay with you, chap."

Ray's features darkened. He had no idea he was being critiqued. A second later, he realized Kyle was putting him on. He recovered with a quip, "No longer afraid of the shunning?"

"Their indifference will be severe, but I can live with it."

"Tenure, right?"

"Say," Kyle said, "I've been giving our discussion more thought and I have a question for you. I'm having a problem with the idealistic model, particularly the concept that our thought has something to do with the physical world. Obviously, our thought is so weak it can have little affect on the solid—"

"My guide, who I called Alice, explained how we started out, very early in the universe, an extremely long time ago, able to create and control thought forms, but then, as we made the forms more and more solid and became more and more entangled in our creation, the relationship became inverted. The world of forms we had created soon dwarfed our ability to create new forms. New creations, new thoughts, had little effect. They primarily added to existing forms, making them more solid. Our attention, fixed on the forms, merely added energy to old patterns, making them more and more solid. Now we conceive the physical world of forms to be real and solid and we consider our thoughts to be nothing."

"You've given me an idea. In quantum mechanics, there's the concept of quantum decoherence," Kyle said, racing off on a tangent. "The quantum state of our thoughts interacts with macroscopic forms and decoheres."

Les, stepping up to the podium to kick off the evening's events, interrupted Kyle's train of thought. As Les introduced "The Spirit Hypotheses," Ray scanned the copy folded in his lap.

The first hypothesis postulated a human being was a composite of body, mind, and spirit. Les argued passionately that it was possible to separate the parts of the composite whole. He asserted that such separation had already been reported, numerous times, in the volumes of NDE reports. What was needed, he argued, was research to explore and identify the nature of each part: body, mind, spirit. Based upon preliminary empirical data, experiments could be designed to intentionally bring about separation of one part from another in a controlled setting.

Ray studied Les, admiring his dedication and passion. Though Les had not lived through an experience like Ray's, there was an inner certainty, an inner drive, that informed his work and kept him doggedly pursuing the goal of bringing awareness of spirit to the scientific community. It was the same drive that had inspired all great scientists to make the lonely trek into the frontiers of discovery.

Les added to his first hypothesis the idea that science would be wise to become familiar with spiritual practices that focused on the separation of spirit from the body. These practices, he noted, had been in existence since the beginning of civilization.

A few isolated coughs in the audience expressed skepticism.

His second hypothesis postulated spirit was the seat of consciousness. Spirit was that part of the body-mind-spirit triad in which researchers would locate consciousness. The body would be found to be strictly a stimulus-response machine, he argued, whereas the spirit was the seat of consciousness and free will. The mind, which was the glue, the interface, between spirit and the physical, would be found to be multi-faceted, with stimulus-response characteristics, as well as properties more closely aligned with the nature of spirit.

The rhetorical fireworks started early, although, initially, the audience's challenges remained good-natured and playful.

A bearded, bespectacled gentleman rose and stated his firm conviction that consciousness emerged out of the aggregate neuronal activity of the brain and claimed the hypothesis Les advanced had already been proven false.

Les thanked the professorial guest for his contribution, then rebutted the assertion, arguing there was no evidence that consciousness emerged from brain cells, only conjecture, whereas we had ample evidence of consciousness existing separate from the body in NDE accounts.

Les glanced in Ray's direction and, for a moment, Ray thought it was his cue. But it wasn't. Les continued, stating the purpose of his hypotheses was to provide theoretical statements that could be tested by science. He segued to his third hypothesis which stated the mind separates from the body along with the spirit. The further separation of spirit from its mind, covered in the fourth hypothesis, was yet another step. In other words, the spirit, when released from the body, retained its memories. Separation from such mental content led to a state of pure consciousness, to what the eastern mystics called the Void.

Ray caught on to Les' plan of attack. He was creating a set of interwoven hypotheses which could be subjected to definitive, although difficult, testing. He was setting the bar higher for those who summarily dismissed spirit. He was undermining their ability to launch ad hoc attacks based on false assertions by offering hypotheses that could either be proven false or left standing as valid alternatives to the brain-only model which had been put forth by what Les called the "brain boys." He was pulling the rug out from under unreasoned attacks by clearly stating the existence of spirit in scientific terms. This approach was something new. In the past, paranormal and spiritual research had been helter-skelter, scattered, poorly organized, lacking in overall guiding principles.

As Les wrapped up his presentation, Ray, along with the audience, applauded his efforts.

Les introduced Kyle, the next speaker, and, as the physicist took center stage, Ray's attention wandered. He scanned the sea of faces before him. In spite of personal prejudices, in spite of spiritual insights, or a lack of insights, they were all here with a common purpose—to tackle the age-old question of *why* we exist, *why* we were alive and aware, in this particular universe. This quest to know that fueled both scientific and religious pursuits was not what one would expect to emanate from a bio-organism rising up out of the mud with its total existence the result of chance and accident. No, the passionate struggle to know was exactly what one could expect from a spirit who had lost its way. It was a quest that haunted all of us—a fact Ray could see clearly written on the faces before him. The search for self-knowledge was not a quirk of human behavior, nor a query that surfaced from random neuronal firings. The quest went deeper than flesh and blood, it was a spiritual quest. Even those who denied their own spiritual nature were drawn to the search, heeding the call from a deeply-buried past that refused to be suppressed, a past that refused to totally disappear from sight behind the dark clouds of amnesia.

Fragments of Kyle's presentation drifted in and out of Ray's awareness: "Special Relativity teaches us the nature of reality depends on where we stand to observe it. .... Our aspirations and beliefs do not seem to be states brought about by neurochemicals, so perhaps that hypothesis is false. .... Consciousness exists distinct from objects, energy, and processes. .... Dualism is a model that should never have been abandoned."

In the audience, a young curly-haired man, college age, stood abruptly and staged a noisy exit, tossing his program in the air in a display of defiant disgust.

Ray experienced a raging case of stage fright. He wondered if it made sense for him to speak before an audience that did not welcome his message. He felt himself slipping, mentally, and realized he was suffering from much more than stage fright. The fear went deeper and was more profound; the fear had its roots in a past he could no longer remember; the fear commanded him to be still and mute. An inner voice shamed and ridiculed—*who was he to speak about the great mysteries?* Pain, fear's enforcer, darted about his skull like a ninja assassin attacking in the dark of night, stabbing randomly and viciously. He rubbed his temples, trying to ease the tension. He empathized with the heretic bound to the stake who smells the first wispy tendrils of smoke rising from the slow-burning kindling at his feet. This was not going to be pleasant. He knew that, if he disobeyed the primal command buried in his subconscious that ordered him to remain silent, he would suffer for his defiance.

It was during that moment, while he was trapped in the midst of a full-blown panic attack that rendered him deaf and mute, that Les made the introduction. "A long, long time ago," Les started, "the philosopher Plato wrote that we lived, chained, inside a cave, and only observed the shadows that were cast on the wall by the light from outside. Our reality was but a shadow of true reality. Tonight we are blessed to have with us someone who hiked outside the cave into the light. Plato also wrote that when the brave explorer returns to the cave, after his journey, he will be greeted with distrust and hatred. Tonight, I ask you, if you should experience distrust or hatred, as Plato warned, if those base feelings come alive, I ask you to set them aside and simply give our guest a warm welcome and a patient ear. Please welcome Ray Carte."

Immobilized—pinned down by his panic attack—Ray missed his cue and sat paralyzed. Fear had him by the throat and was not about to let go.

Bren, alone, intuited the unfolding crisis. She jumped to her feet, aimed her camera, and shouted, "Uncle Ray, smile."

Ray, upon seeing her smiling, playful face, was jolted into the present. Purpose overcame fear as he shuffled to the podium with an embarrassed shrug. Bren clicked away like a veteran paparazzi.

Ray faced the audience, sheepishly, "Sorry, I was in the middle of an out-of-body experience."

His joke was greeted with warm laughter and appreciative applause. The welcoming response broke the choke hold stage fright had on him and encouraged him to continue, though his body was shaken and his mind rattled.

"I guess I'm what researchers might call raw evidence," he said. "One who has experienced separation from the body during the NDE, one who spent time on the other side. My journey was not something I planned. I didn't drug myself into a stupor to see what would happen. I'll leave that to others. In my case, unfortunately, I was in a car wreck."

Chase encouraged him to continue with a smile.

"Before my close encounter with a tree..." He looked up to find scattered smiles. So far, at least, the audience was with him. "I considered myself a diehard skeptic. Though I didn't attend meetings and I didn't demonstrate with the folks who have gathered outside tonight, I did adhere to a skeptical viewpoint. The wacky idea that we're more than a meat body was not only inconceivable, it was, I was certain, the rantings of madmen. As far as I was concerned, this body was it."

He paused and sipped water from a glass stowed on a shelf inside the podium. Fear nibbled at the edges of his mind, but he had gained the upper hand. It was one thing to be different, to have seen and experienced that which most men do not consider to be reality; it was quite another to stand before them in an attempt to alter their reality. As Alice had taught, we create our reality, but, in the case of the physical universe, it was not an individual affair. We were entangled with one another's thoughts; we shaped reality through agreement. And Ray was trying to shift that agreement, if ever so slightly. That was not something one accomplished with the stroke of a wand, or with a well-chosen phrase. It was a difficult and emotional process, one which required and rewarded tiny, persistent steps. The steps he was now willing to take.

"I assumed, like most of us, that when I died, not only was there no more Ray, there was no more "me" or "I." After death there could be no awareness. Death was dust to dust, ashes to ashes. The long sleep."

He was taking it slow and cautious, no giant leaps that might appear to be wild-eyed fantasy. Most who had gathered before him could accept the opinions he was sharing. For a moment, he imagined himself, as he used to be, before his NDE, sitting in the audience, listening to the presentation. He wondered how long it would take his imaginary self to stand up and walk out on his lecture. How could he blame others for turning their backs, if who he used to be would turn his back on who he was now?

"After the impact, after my car slammed into the tree, I found myself outside." He paused, shrugged. "Yeah, outside my body. Strange? Very strange. Not something I had even considered could happen. Yet, there I was."

For a fleeting moment, he considered he had discovered a perfect time to end his presentation, a perfect time to bring it to a close. He had delivered the essence of what he had to say: he had found himself unexpectedly outside his body, conscious and still alive. And that was that. An inner censor counseled he should play it safe and say no more. But another impulse rose to the surface as well, an impulse wedded to freedom, an impulse lined up against silence and servitude and slavery, an impulse which lifted him and encouraged him to press on with his story.

"When I was outside, I had no desire to discover what had happened to the body. No desire to experience its pain and suffering. You could say the moment I gained my freedom, I lost my courage. Very soon thereafter, I found myself in a strange world that seemed as real as the auditorium in which we sit tonight."

Scattered coughs signaled the presence of balking skeptics. Ray had crossed into dangerous territory and some were refusing to accompany him on his story-telling journey. He continued anyway.

"Then I met someone who many would call a guide. She showed me a world I never imagined could exist. A world that's a part of this world, although it's a world whose existence we reject. In short, I discovered we survive the death of the body. For many, no, for most of us, the greatest challenge we face when we find ourselves in that awkward state, is our own confusion. For so long we've been certain we're only the body and that makes it hard for us to let go. Extremely difficult. I did not find the transition easy."

In the audience, a man cleared his throat loudly and stood, obviously wanting, in fact, demanding, the floor.

Ray shielded his eyes, blocking the stage spotlights, trying to make out the silhouetted figure who rudely interrupted. Such a figure, rising incognito from the dark to assault him with a hostile question, threatened to resurrect the stage fright he had defeated. Ray, making the decision to face the challenge straight on, asked, "Did you want to say something, sir?"

The man addressed the audience, not Ray. "The incredible story this gentleman has told is the product of an overly-active imagination, the work of a brain suffering from trauma and fighting to protect itself."

It was Seidman!

Ray, shocked at the psychologist's presence, responded with flat-footed silence.

"This speaker was my patient," Seidman continued, "and I informed him, in great detail, of the reasons behind his illusory visions. He chose not to listen to my professional opinion. That choice is his prerogative, but he's not free to pretend his delusions are real science. In response to that hubris, I object. I strongly object."

Ray felt his bubble of bliss shatter. He may have been out, and may have gained a new viewpoint, but here he was, once again, very much among the living, seemingly being shadowed by a very persistent and dark force. The opposition that had, a few minutes ago, lived only in his mind was now manifest—out there—in the world. Through its agent, Seidman, the universe was ordering him to shut up, commanding him to keep his thoughts to himself. The universe was invoking its make-no-waves policy.

Les grabbed the microphone, "Sir, you're welcome to submit a paper rebutting the contents of my paper. You're free to engage in scientific debate. But you're not free to harass my subjects. When he was in the hospital, you were free to insult and badger him, but you're not free to do so here."

A smattering of applause arose.

But Seidman wasn't done. "Sir, wherever there's fraud, I'm free to point it out. I'll not let you present false evidence and play to the public's false hopes. I'll not let you con them with your slick game. You do us all a disservice here tonight and I intend to point out your transgression. It is my duty to warn this audience."

Onlookers stirred, would the shouting match evolve into something darker—perhaps violence? Would the heckler be tossed from the auditorium? Or would his protest bring the show to a close?

Seidman remained standing, apparently intent upon disrupting the meeting and discrediting Ray.

Ray felt a hopeless anger swell, his body became saturated with adrenaline, primed to mount an attack. He became aware of how incredibly easy it would be to lunge at his tormentor's throat and silence him forever. The social veneer that smoothed over our ancient violent impulses was razor thin, a protective film that could be rent on the smallest of pretexts. If Ray exploded with rage, his reaction would be completely justified: Seidman had tried to drug him in the hospital, he had ruined his business and destroyed his future plans, and he was now publicly assailing his credibility. The man was insane, vindictive, relentless.

Ray found himself entangled in fear and worry and anger; he became caught up in destructive emotions. He was letting the Jell-O stick. He realized he was battling more than Seidman; he could destroy Seidman and little would change. There would be someone else, and then someone else. There always had been. This universe was rigged to silence any who would dare pry into its secrets. The prohibition against uncovering its hidden truths was exactly what was wrong with this universe: too little light illuminated too many dark corners. Wherever the voice of light and clear reason arose, a darkness would appear to oppose it. Seidman was simply an agent of these ancient dynamics. But now, unlike before, Ray knew the universe was something we create together and there was no longer any reason for him to stop, no reason he should *not* tell his story. The negative emotions grew thin, then vanished. He summoned the courage to be there, simple and naked and compassionate.

Les, seeing the change in Ray, handed him the microphone.

"Doctor Seidman," Ray said, in a calm voice. "With all due respect, it must be pointed out that, in the hospital, you provided me with no evidence supporting your point of view. You offered opinion and prejudice, as you do this evening."

"Scientific opinion. That's right. Scientific opinion which this audience prefers to the unprofessional speculation which has been presented."

"But opinion nonetheless," Ray countered, his voice steady. He no longer held any animosity toward the man, he refused to accept Seidman's invitation to hate. Such invitations were extended regularly, the trick was to avoid them, as they only led to a spider's web of emotional entrapment. He continued, in a soft tone, "I'm unwilling to toss aside firsthand experience and replace it with your conjecture. The guests gathered here tonight have the right to form their own opinions. They can listen to my account of what I experienced and come to know what I observed. I'm confident they're competent and can make up their own minds."

Once again, a smattering of applause.

And yet, Seidman was not about to relinquish the floor. "I'm sure the scientists in the audience, should there be any, are in total agreement with *my* opinion," he said. "Science is not about what the man on the street thinks, it's about experts making judgements that adhere to the facts."

"The facts here are my observations," Ray said. "The facts are what I experienced, not suppositions or wild conjecture about what might have occurred, unobserved, in my brain. That which I observed was not in my brain. As I was in a coma, my body's senses were dormant."

"If we let you decide what it is you experienced, then we might as well let everyone decide. That's not science. The mind's perceptions are notoriously flawed and unreliable. We are deluded by our perceptions. Only the scientist observing the brain itself can tell us accurately what happened."

"When you go home at night does a neurosurgeon inspect your brain and inform you what it was you observed during the day? Is that how you know what took place?"

In the audience, there was a smattering of chuckles.

"Some, like myself, are professionally trained to evaluate our experience, others are not," Seidman replied.

Seidman might have a point, he might not, but his attitude made the audience uneasy. This was not the cool, calm, collected voice of science speaking, this was someone who seemed daunted, even threatened, by a former patient who refused to be told what he experienced.

"And you are trained?" Ray countered, the edge in his voice playful, not malicious. "There are traditions thousands of years old in which people are trained to observe consciousness, to under-stand consciousness, to reach spiritual awareness. That is the train-ing that matters in this case, and sir, you lack training in that discipline." Ray paused to consider his words, then spoke, "Sir, you are an untrained observer who fantasizes that he receives commands, like a robot, from four pounds of gray matter acting on its own volition."

A few appreciative snickers in the audience should have served as warning to Seidman that his time was up, but he paid them no heed.

"The spiritual is not science," Seidman replied dryly. "Science and superstition do not mix."

"I wouldn't be so sure, Doc. When it comes to understanding consciousness and the observer, science trails far behind the spiritual tradition. Unfortunately, there are those, like yourself, armed with prejudice, who choose to attack, rather than investigate, this rich tradition."

Seidman scoffed. It was apparent he was getting nowhere.

"Sir, please sit down," Ray commanded, without anger, in a soft voice that nonetheless conveyed unyielding intention. "While I was laid up in a hospital bed, unable to walk away, I listened patiently to your lectures. Now I want you to listen. Tonight, the audience, perhaps, wants to hear a different point of view."

Seidman searched the faces in the audience for support and found none. He plopped down in his seat, his eyes narrowed with anger.

Ray had turned a corner, no longer would he give in to the unspoken commands that dictated silence, no longer would he give in to those, like Seidman, who demanded he be mute and obedient. He knew it was time we shared that which had been hidden for so long. There was a new awareness, a new willingness to explore, a new inspiration that lifted men up.

Ray found a handle on what he was experiencing and shared it with the audience. "We are like children who wander into a dark cave and lose their way. Some among us will search for a way out. They will attempt to discover where we entered, so that we might exit. They will toil to discover our true nature in order to recapture the memory of who we are and where we have been. Some, however, will not make the effort and will stumble further into the darkness. Slipping further into unconsciousness, they will claim we are robots with no past and no future, with only a transient mechanical existence devoid of meaning and purpose. They will do their best to impede the progress of those who search for the way home."

Ray paused, catching his breath, assessing his progress. He

felt the audience shift; they were going with him, they wanted to know where he had been, what treasures he had discovered.

"I can't tell you which way to go, or who to follow. If you want to believe you're a machine, a robot, I will not try to dissuade you—though I might point out we have no evidence that such is the case. I can only share with you that which happened to me; I can tell you what I observed. You can compare my account with reports you gather from others and together we can map the way out. Some will call me delusional and tell me they know my mind better than I do. There are those willing to evaluate and tell you who you are, what you experience, what you should do. If you believe you're a robot, there's no harm in following their commands. But I, for one, would rather not. Unfortunately, I've only been given a glimpse of what lies ahead and what lies behind. I have only meager insights to share. I do know, however, there are worlds beyond this one."

He paused for a moment to collect his thoughts. He felt a new strength welling up. "I've never been afraid of death. I've never had the need to invent a myth to deny death—I've no idea what good that would do—but I've also never needed to create a myth to dismiss the existence of that which lies beyond death. As my critic asks you to do."

Ray scanned the faces in the audience. There were those who looked up, expectant, receptive, listening; there were those who looked down or looked away, unsettled, unwilling, unable to listen. At that moment he recognized harsh reality. They *were* children in a dark cave and they all responded differently to their dilemma, though their fates were intertwined. He realized he was connected to them and they were connected to him. He realized the knots that entangled his awareness, entangled theirs as well. He realized he was not going to walk out of the cave alone; they were tied together and would have to leave together.

At the rear of the auditorium, a figure moved: *it was the monk*, who had once been Alice, dressed in his robes.

Ray was certain he must be hallucinating; surely this was an apparition. He twisted around abruptly to see if anyone on the dais saw what he saw. Les' stare, a look of puzzlement, was locked on the departing figure. Ray looked to Chase. She had turned in her seat and was watching the robed figure who departed with a kindly wink. She spun around, the color drained from her face, looking to Ray for an explanation. All he could offer was a playful wink, an imitation of the monk's wink. It worked. Her color returned and a spontaneous smile lit up her features.

Ray felt his past surge into the present. He *had* been a monk, and he *had* vowed to find a way out of the dark cave. That intention still burned, a flame passing from life to life, as the wheel of birth and death turned. He recognized the emotion he had felt for the audience, a few minutes earlier, when he understood clearly how their fates were bound to one another. He recognized the feeling was compassion; a feeling, an emotion, unlike any other. The more one exuded compassion, the more compassion one received in return. It was paradoxical: one filled the reservoir by emptying it. He renewed a silent vow to keep that compassion alive, in spite of all invitations to hatred and division and strife. He scanned the faces in the audience one more time and knew, *really knew*, it was time they departed the dark cave. Their departure was long overdue. He knew, with certainty, that the monk who walked with him on the Other Side also walked among us, ready to show the way. He sensed the path that led to disentanglement, to a release from suffering and attachment, was within reach— if only men and women would reach.

For a long moment, he stood there smiling, lost in an intensity of bliss he had rarely, if ever, experienced. The audience didn't seem to mind. Intuitively, they understood something profound was taking place.

"Thank you for being here with me tonight," Ray said. "Thank you for being here with me, for such a long, long time."

Some in the audience caught his meaning, and nodded.

"I appreciate your kindness, your caring, your compassion and consideration. We have a lot of work to do, so that's enough of my chatter. Let's get busy."

Les took the microphone. "Thank you for attending the program. That'll be all for tonight."

Ray walked off the stage and mingled with the crowd, shaking hands and peering into eyes, each time discovering a universe. For the first time in a long time, he recognized his purpose. And it wasn't to remain silent. It was time for the old lessons to reappear. It was time for our spiritual heritage to resurface. Across the planet, people were experiencing a spiritual rebirth, and he recognized it for what it was—the search for a way out of the cave, a way back home. He vowed he would no longer be silent, nor forgetful. He would search and he would share the fruits of his searching. Then he became aware of the contagious giggle.

On the other side of the auditorium, Bren had cornered Dr. Seidman and was offering him her pink unicorn pin. He was doing his best to refuse the pin. Bren, however, was not to be denied. She grabbed his lapel. Though he flushed with embarrassment, he did not shove her away; he bent his knees and lowered himself to her level. She pinned him with the unicorn.

Though Seidman had been unable to accept Ray's intellectual argument, though the entanglements he suffered as a result of his tenure in this universe would not allow him to be free, he still could not deny the love and enthusiasm of a child.

Ray chuckled, the deep, rich chuckle of a compassionate old monk. He experienced a new and profound awareness: there was hope; we would find our way home.